honest*

a novel

JB Burgess

"Books that start with quotes or lyrics are dumb.
Books should start with either a map or just nothing.
Like just get on with it already."

~Bob

2

ONE

I say You look really nice tonight.

And I'm lying.

The reason it's a lie is not because she doesn't look nice tonight. She does. She looks really nice. She looks nice and cute and sexy and beautiful just like she always does. She's wearing this sea-green dress that has kind of tiny little squares of texture on it and coarse stitching which I would like to rub with my thumb and finger to feel it. And the sea-green of her dress makes her blue eyes look a little bit green but it also makes them look even more blue somehow. And there are no straps on this dress so it shows off her nice smooth and white shoulders that have no freckles on them at all. She has no freckles anywhere I have ever seen that's for sure. I think a girl with nice shoulders can be really sexy without looking like a slut for showing off a sexy part of her body.

Anyway. I say You look really nice tonight. And I'm lying. But the reason it's a lie is not because she doesn't look nice. She looks great OK I said that already. The reason it's a lie is because I already decided I was going to tell her she looked nice like fifteen minutes before she arrived no matter if she looked nice or if she looked like shit. I mean chances were good that she was going to look nice because she always looks nice to me at least I think so. But I just felt myself wanting to give her a compliment about something physical when she arrived because it has been a while since I have complimented her looks it has been eleven days. So I decided I would give her that compliment about looking nice even if she looked like shit and so I did I gave it to her.

And so that makes it count as a lie I think even though

I've told way way bigger lies than that in my life I mean god don't get me started on that subject but anyway this little lie about her looking nice is still a lie because I was ready to be dishonest. I have this theory about lies and here it is this is the lie. I mean this is the theory I mean.

I think that deciding you're willing to tell a lie is really the only bad thing you can ever do. That's where you be bad or be good is when you say OK I could tell a lie right about now or you say Stop no that's not a true thing and so I won't say it. Once you've decided you're OK with telling a lie then the lie will just happen or it won't but it's out of your hands at that point. It's up to the lie to decide. It's like how in the stories vampires can't come into your room unless you give them verbal permission to come in. And so up until you agree to let the vampire in it's still you who's in control and you are still good and the only bad thing you can ever do regarding a vampire or a lie is to say Yes you can come in vampire or Yes lie you might be useful or fun right now so please do come in. Because after you open the window the vampire doesn't have to listen to you any more because he's the one in charge now and he can come and go as he pleases from now on.

And then he will bite you and make you bad like him.

So anyway the person I just lied to is my only friend and her name is Bob even though she's a girl but yeah her name is Bob because I guess she thinks it's like cute to be a girl named Bob and I guess it is pretty cute I guess but I don't think it's as cute as I think she thinks it is that's for sure. Her real first name is Roberta though and that's an awful old frumpy woman name and her parents were dumb for naming her it

4

in nineteen eighty-five because Roberta sounds obese or old or from Florida or something. It's like Ethel and Pearl or Maude there is no one named that who is alive any more. Maude. It makes me feel angry to even hear that name. Mmmmaude. So I guess Bob calling herself Bob is the best she could do with the cards she was dealt in terms of name wise but if I was her I would have just taken my middle name and used that. Unless the middle name was like even worse somehow. Unless the middle name was Maude. Bob's middle name is Emily though which I always thought is a really pretty name. And that name Emily would have suited her personality pretty well too. But that doesn't matter anyway because she goes by Bob. I think she thinks that having a boy's name will make her sound like the girl out of some hipster movie or something.

I think Bob thinks if they ever make a movie out of her life that she should be played by like Zooey Deschanel or something. I think Zooey Deschanel is very cute that's for sure but not as cute as I think Zooey Deschanel thinks she is. And not as cute as I think Bob thinks Zooey Deschanel is. And not as cute as Bob is.

OK so I want to write this movie one day where Zooey Deschanel and Katy Perry would play sisters who have to trade places. And Zooey Deschanel is the nice little indie one who believes in true love and like she would work in a book shop or like a quirky store that only sells one too-specific thing like spoons or socks or doormats or something and she would keep a weird pet like a sugar glider or a fennec fox who would have a ridiculous name like Bernard or Mister Bojangles or Bartleby-the-Sugar-Glider or —the-Fox and it would cause mischief. And then Katy Perry would be the slutty punk rocker one who does not believe in true love and she drinks Whiskey all the time and works in like a bar or a Guitar Center or no job. She would keep a bulldog. Or no pet.

And so then Zooey Deschanel and Katy Perry in my movie they would have to switch places or bodies or something for a while and that is what the movie would be about. I will make up the how they switched bodies later. Probably magic or science or something. Probably magic. Or maybe they would just make out with each other but then I think no wait that's just something I think would be hot and that's not an idea for an actual movie but the other thing is a good idea for an actual movie and so I want to write that movie. And one day I will. I will write it.

That was kind of a lie actually. I don't think straight girls making out is all that hot honestly. It's more like really LOOK AT ME and it's like a just barely scandalous thing for girls to write like OMG I DID A CRAZY THING TONIGHT in their little like journals. Although then that might be perfect for this movie because Katy Perry kissed a girl and she liked it right. She's the biggest LOOK AT ME of all I think. But no that is still not a real idea for a movie.

But anyway in the real movie like the characters would learn stuff from walking a mile in each others shoes and stuff and everyone loves a good body swap movie right and it's been a while since a good one of those came out. I can't even remember the last one. I think the last one was that Michael Cera one where he plays Michael Cera and then also like Michael Cera with a mustache who is like supposed to be his alter ego or something. I don't know the deal really I never saw it because by now I am so sick of Michael Cera. So is everyone honestly. Like I'm sorry even if you're one of those people who goes through life just waiting for the opportunity to yell at strangers about how Arrested Development is the best show of all time. Even if you're that guy still deep down you think Fuck Michael Cera.

Once I saw Michael Cera go into the movie theater with this girl he was on a date with and guess what. They were going to see his own movie. It was actually this mustache movie I just talked about. And on that day I thought to myself Michael Cera you suck. That is a really true story that is not one of my lies by the way. I would also have a rule about my movie idea about Zooey Deschanel and Katy Perry that Michael Cera and Wes Anderson and Jason Schwartzman and Ellen Page and Jessie Eisenberg and Jonah Hill and every Wilson and Culkin are not allowed anything to do with it. Bill Murray would be allowed to be in it though because I think new sad Bill Murray is great and maybe he is their dad. Sad dad.

But then I think that it's dumb of me that I want to write something just because two famous people look a lot alike because I mean you should want to write something because you have a really good idea or you realize something important about the world and not just because two people who are famous and hot at the same time look a lot alike. There's already enough fake things in the world that aren't real things but that people are trying to convince you are real things. And fake things pretending to be real things is a form of lying too I think. I mean it's not lying like saying Oh yeah I fucked her. When you didn't. But it's still dishonest and like a different kind of dishonest. It's not saying something untrue but it's saying that something matters when it totally doesn't.

Like it's dishonest and cowardly and irresponsible to

keep insisting that a dumb movie like this Katy Perry and Zooey Deschanel movie is a real thing when it's not it's just bullshit. And bullshit can mean two things it can mean a lie and it can mean just something of no value. But I think it's not an accident that the same word is for both. And so anyway I don't need to make the world worse with another dumb movie about Zooey Deschanel and Katy Perry looking alike but I bet the Zooey Deschanel and Katy Perry movie would do better than like some really original script that is all smart and good and challenging and stuff.

Wait. That was a lie too just now. It was a lie of me to say that the dumb movie with famous lookalikes would do better than something really good and smart and it was also a very lazy and cheap lie because I was really just being bitter about Hollywood which is such a lazy easy lie for anyone who's creative and living in LA to tell because it's like you're saying that Hollywood is the one who sucks and not you and your dumb writing and shitty ideas. So like shut up. Honestly being bitter about Hollywood is the same thing as quickly breaking up with someone you know is about to dump you.

I think I was also lying and pretending I'm like smarter than people who go to the movies just for fun. And that's dumb because not every movie you see has to be like Ingmar Bergman or like Tree of fucking Life or whatever. When I saw Tree of Life halfway through the movie a man stood up and screamed REFUND over and over for like seventy three seconds before he was taken away by security and I was very afraid of that man. That is a true story too and not a lie.

OK no sorry that never happened I made it up.

I'm mad at myself now for telling that easy boo-

Hollywood lie because it was lazy and impulsive and I am trying not to be those things so much when I lie.

I guess I only want to write that movie about Zooey Deschanel and Katy Perry because someone else is going to write it one day so it might as well be me. But that's no reason to do something either. Just so someone else doesn't beat you to the punch and cash in on an idea that's only barely halfway to being a good idea in the first place. And besides I don't even really write movies anyway because I write poems and short stories and two novels and I only wrote one screenplay by on accident kind of.

But yeah anyway back to my friend Bob. I think being cute is what Bob really wants the most out of life. More than like having a job or accomplishing something important or just basically being a real person I think her main deal is just wanting to be this really cute like manic pixie dream girl Zooey Deschanel girl all the time. Emma Stone is becoming kind of that girl now too and I think she is pretty cool and I bet she is nice and chill in real life and I really hope she is not a total Hollywood whorebrat disguised as a funny kind of girl next door. It would make me sad to learn that if she is. Emma is also a nice name I think and would be a fine name for Bob but no her name is not Emma is it. It's Bob.

But so Bob only wants to be cute and Bob is definitely very cute that's for sure she's so beautiful and great. So she's basically got everything she wants in life already. And that makes me feel sad and a little bit angry because everything I want in life feels so very far away and impossible for me to ever deserve to get it and then Bob is just like basically already happy just like that. She wakes up and she just goes like Oh it's a new day huh well let's see am I cute yes I am well then guess what I am happy already for today. And that is Bob's morning.

All the hipster guys fall in love with Bob obviously and she dates some of them to pass the time and a couple of times she even has called them This is my boyfriend named blahbeddy blah but she never really falls in love with any of them. I'm glad Bob doesn't fall in love with any of those hipster guys because I am in love with Bob.

That was a lie. Actually it was sort of two lies. Maybe. I don't know.

The first maybe lie was that I'm glad she doesn't fall in love with any of those hipster guys. At first I definitely am glad that she doesn't fall in love with any of those hipster guys because they're lame stupid hipster guys. I mean they're all just big fucking pussies about life and they hide themselves behind irony and fashionable nihilism and they act all cynical and shit on people who are enthusiastic or who are trying the best they can to make it all a little bit better. And they use that cynicism as an excuse to do fucking nothing with their lives and they have gross straggly mustaches like Michael Cera's alter ego in that movie and they wear stupid tight purple pants that show off their weird butts and tiny dicks and so yeah Boo them basically. Except it's not Boo them because everyone loves those guys at the moment. They are the fashionable thing. But I still say fuck 'em.

And Bob is so cool and beautiful and really smart and brave and awesome and so she shouldn't need to fall in love with those kinds of guys she could fall in love with much more awesome guys than them that's for sure. But then I think about it even more and I realize maybe I actually feel angry and not happy about the fact that she doesn't fall in love with those guys because then I think of her letting these guys who she isn't even in love with fuck her with their tiny dicks and I feel jealous and angry because I haven't fucked Bob even though we're best friends and she says she loves me all the time and I'm like the greatest most smart and deep person she'll ever know in her whole life and she doesn't know what she would do without me and one time she told me I am really handsome and I will never forget the time she said that I am handsome it was a Tuesday. Sometimes she says mean things like How is it possible you're still single and all kinds of that kind of thing but she still doesn't let me fuck her or will be my girlfriend. So that's the first maybe lie is I don't know if I'm glad or sad about Bob not loving the hipster guys.

The second lie I told just now is that I am in love with Bob. And I don't even know if that is a lie or not because actually it's a complicated question so let me think about it OK. I feel a lot of feelings towards Bob that sound like Yes I am in love with Bob. But then sometimes I realize that I also make a point of always talking about how I'm so in love with her because if you're in love with someone it's not your fault if you really want to fuck them but if you're not in love with them then you're just a bad selfish and like sexist person or something if you really really want to fuck them. If you are a guy. Girls just do whatever the fuck all the time and everyone says That's cool and like progressive or something.

So I don't know if I love Bob is a lie or not but she is my best friend that's for sure and I definitely think she's really amazing and so beautiful and brave and interesting and so funny. Like she's not just you know pretty-funny-for-a-girl but she's like actually funny and we have the exact same sense of humor like we're totally two sides of the same coin is how she called it once and I agreed Yes we are we're basically the same person with different privates. Which could make it tricky to date each other I see that but I still think it would be great or at least worth a try. And she is very interesting and smart and I never am not in the mood to hang out with Bob I always like being with her and talking to her and just looking at her and even though I've known Bob now forever I still get a little bit nervous in my stomach when we're about to meet up because she's a little bit scary to me but scary in a nice way just because I like her and I am looking forward to talking to her. And so I think that if I am both excited by Bob and she is also my best friend in the world I mean alright she's my only friend shut up I get it. But yeah so that really does sound like I am in love with Bob so never mind. That was not a lie and yes I am in love with Bob.

Bob is different from most girls though and maybe that's the reason I'm in love with Bob is because she's so different and unique. But then again that sounds like it might be a lie too because it sounds so much like exactly the perfect thing to say. So chances are it can't possibly be true and maybe I am lying about that. I don't even.

It's hard sometimes to tell if something is a lie or not in the particular situation that something happens exactly like how I was just about to lie about it. Like I'll say the sentence Oh you look nice and it used to be a lie because it was based on no evidence of how she looks but it's become a true story but it's still the same lie I was going to tell or.

So am I even lying about Bob looking nice or about being in love with Bob I don't know.

You can see why I drink so much this is all very stressful for me.

But whatever. I don't care about that gray area stuff because it's better to tell a lie and be deliberate about it than to just say whatever the fuck random thing happens to be technically true. I mean because what if the thing that is true is not the thing that is best.

The only fight I ever got in with Bob was once when she said she wished she was creatively gifted like me and she would trade her content boredom for some passion and the bug for writing. And I got so very mad about that because first of all I hate that expression The Bug For Writing. It is dumb and like it's something that fat middle aged women who pretend to be writers on the internet would say. They use that phrase I Got THE BUG FOR WRITING! And they go on websites like www.mommaswithstoriestotell.com or something. That is not a real website by the way. Or it might be but if it is a real website then that's just a coincidence and it's one of those things I made up but it happens to also be true just by coincidence but it's maybe still a lie. But anyway these lame fat women they buy brand new two thousand dollar Mac laptops that have nothing on them but MS Word and like Sudoku and they play with their newfound BUGFORWRITING! and they sit down and balance their brand new laptops on their FUPAs and they go online and talk about writing before they've even done any writing to talk about. And they say things like Oh yeah after my last daughter FINALLY went off to college I just got the bug for writing yeah the bug to tell MY STORY! And then they all

circle jerk sympathy and self-congratulation on the internet
and participate in National Novel Writing Month which I
completely and utterly and always will refuse to call NaNoWriMo
YUCK and these stupid landwhales write these heinous wish-
fulfillment stories which on the one hand they're intended to
be like feminist or something and yet on the other hand the
stories always end with like Richard Gere or Fabio or the
sparklefairy from Twilight coming to rescue these obese middle
aged women from being alone. Or even worse than being alone
they get saved from being stuck with their awful lame husbands
who are always the villains of their stories and do you know
why. Because they're boring. And all they do is work very hard
to bring home a paycheck every week to support the family and
they're not Richard Gere or rock stars or Hot Topic vampires
who fart glitter. They're just real normal guys trying their
fucking best every day and so obviously they're beneath
contempt and they are the big bad guy in these women's stories
and I think that's fucked up.

So that's what I think about the phrase The Bug For
Writing. And second of all I tore Bob a new one for what she
said because

Don't you ever wish you have this thing I have Bob this
darkness I carry around which yeah OK it makes me be creative
sometimes that is true but only because I'm so afraid of it and
it calls me names when I don't work and it won't let me sleep
or rest or ever be at peace and don't ever wish that Bob take
it back. You look very peaceful when you're sleeping Bob but I
never sleep so don't wish that. I told her Look Bob obviously
the best possible way that a person can be is to be just
exactly like you. You are really happy most of the time but are

smart enough and deep enough to enjoy and appreciate the good writing that some other poor wretch spent his whole miserable life creating. And then when you're done being moved by the good book or music or painting or whatever art you come across then you just go back to being happy enough being cute and you are now a little smarter and deeper or better from having seen the art but you can just go back to being happy again. Meanwhile I'm up at five AM every night staring at my computer wondering if I should try to write another thing now or just fall in front of a train. And Bob said

    Wow OK touched a nerve or something never mind. But she said it with this tone of like suggesting I was the asshole in this scene and not her. And I said Sorry I am drunk perhaps fourteen Whiskey Diets might be too many for all in a row and she said

    Let's drop it OK and I said OK lets drop it and we did we dropped it. But so yeah I probably do love Bob I mean come on have you been listening. But Bob is also really annoying a lot of the time. Actually more lame than annoying really. Her lameness is annoying to me. There we go. It makes me feel angry that she doesn't really do much with herself other than be cute. Like she's funny a lot and she's really super smart and smarter than me even which I am actually very surprised that I enjoy having a smarter than me person who is my best friend and my person who I'm in love with because OK this is not a good quality in me but I'm trying to be more honest right. And so here is a bad truth about me OK.

    I like knowing I'm smarter than most other people I'm around because it makes me feel safe. OK is that so bad honestly. Like there's worse things. But Bob is way smarter than me and I spend most of my time with just Bob so it's very weird to me that I choose to spend most of my time being the stupidest person in the room. At least right now at the bar there is this bartender here for me to be smarter than him so I am the middle smartest person in the bar but obviously like a billion times smarter than the fucking bartender I mean come on.

But so Bob is smart and insightful and stuff but she doesn't really do anything with any of that. Like she doesn't want to achieve anything real or even really engage with the world on any real level and so she just sits around being cute and beautiful and amazing and receiving adoration from all but not having a job or accomplishing anything important. And I feel angry that that's enough for her because I get so much accomplished and it's really hard stuff and scary stuff and brave stuff and I worry about it all so very much but still I never feel like I have worried enough or done enough meanwhile Bob just sits there being cute and content and that's enough of a dumb happy life for dumb happy Bob.

I would be happy all of the time if I was with Bob though that's for sure. Maybe what I really want the most in life is to earn my happiness on my own terms. To get the kind of happiness that I am working hard for and worrying about every day. But obviously I'd have to actually GET my kind of happiness for me to want that more than Bob's easy just-decide-to-be-happy happiness.

So I guess I'd rank the kinds of happiness like this: last place is where I am now which is wanting my kind of hard earned happiness but not getting it even though I work so hard and worry so much and so I think I should have earned it by now so where is it. Second place is Bob's kind of happiness where she just wakes up and as long as she looks cute she has all she needs and all the boys fall in love with her and so she gets sex and happiness and everyone saying she is great. Great job Bob. And then first place best case kind of happiness would be that all my worrying finally pays off and then I would happy because I'd finally have the one thing that has made me sad for so long because I haven't had it. Whatever that thing is. Maybe it's Bob. Or maybe it's like some award for my writing or something. Maybe it's just nothingness. Silence. Peace. Oh and then that would be even more the best situation because it will mean that I have been right to have been worrying so much all this time and it will not have been a complete waste of my time and my energy and my basically life.

So anyway. Jesus. We're at our bar. Bob and I.

And I say You look really cute. Or nice yeah I say You look really nice tonight and Bob says

Aw thanks! And she sounds fake-surprised just how I knew she would sound that way and she kisses me a peck on the cheek because I'm sitting on the bar stool kind of weird and hugging me would be awkward because she'd have to like climb my leg to get at me. I don't know why I sit on bar stools so weird but I'm always kind of half on them half off them with one foot on the ground so that if I lose my balance I could put my right leg down like the kickstand on a bike and not fall over on my face.

It's very uncomfortable.

And I spend a lot of time on bar stools. So I guess I spend a lot of time being very uncomfortable. That's something about me. But when I sit all the way on top of the stool like

17

you're supposed to with your both feet up and resting on the things I feel like I'm in a high chair a million miles up and I feel like I could fall over at any moment and everyone would laugh at me. And that would be terrible because Bob would never be the girlfriend of some dumb guy who falls.

So Bob sits down next to me and there is already a Rusty Nail waiting for her to drink because I ordered it for her as soon as I got into the bar because I was early on purpose. I am always early for Bob because it is better for a guy to be sitting alone at a bar waiting for someone than for a girl to wait at a bar alone and so I always make sure I am there first. Anyway when I sat down the bartender asked me just like he always asks

Whiskey Diet and a Rusty Nail?

And I said You got it my man and he told me it was coming up.

A Rusty Nail is Bob's Drink because that is a grumpy old man's Drink and she thinks it's cute for a pretty little 26 year old girl named Bob to ask for that Drink because like you say Rusty Nail and I think of like Clint Eastwood in Gran Torino or Don Draper or like the old man from the movie Up if they were allowed to drink Alcohol in Pixar or Dreamworks whichever one Up was and I do not think of like cute little Bob when you say Rusty Nail. I mean I do now because I have known Bob but I wouldn't normally think of a young girl.

Whiskey Diet is the Drink I drink the most often even though it is not my favorite Drink to drink. My favorite Drink is just Maker's Mark On The Rocks but I do not order that ever for some reason probably because it's more expensive. Whiskey Diet is three dollars and fifty cents here on happy hour which is insane like seriously how are they making any money with prices like that. I sounded like a commercial just then.

So I guess the sum up of my life is that I spend a lot of time being uncomfortable and the Drink I drink the most often is not the Drink that I like the best. I realize that is a pretty dumb situation to be in. Bob is always saying how life is so short and just get what you want and she's right. The Drink you like the best should be the drink you have the most often especially if you can afford it which I can now so I should order Maker's Mark On The Rocks but I never do I stick with the Whiskey Diet. I don't even remember the last time I had a Maker's Mark On The Rocks and I wonder why now.

There's this one kind of old shriveled guy at the other end of the bar which is weird because no one usually comes in here at all before like ten o clock at night and it's not even three o clock in the afternoon now. I give this man a look of HA-HA now because when I first arrived he was already here drinking all by himself at like two forty five in the afternoon. And the man gave me this friendly sort of look as if he was saying Hey buddy we're both sad lonely men getting drunk at two forty five in the afternoon so maybe we are both hopelessly alone in the world but at least for this little moment you and I are alone together right now. Or something gay like that. And I nodded at him like I understood.

But just now Bob came in and she's a beautiful girl who kissed me so I'm sort of pretending to this other guy kind of like Bob's my beautiful girlfriend and I'm not a sad lonely drunk guy like he is and so now I'm like HA-HA to him. With my face. But the joke's really on me though because now I'm imagining Bob really is my girlfriend and that later today we

will leave this bar and go to Bob's apartment that has almost
no furniture in it and I will fuck Bob in her sea-green dress
and then we will take a long hot shower together followed by a
naked nap spooning in the sunlight while we are still wet from
the shower. But of course then I remember Bob is not my
girlfriend and never ever will be and I won't get to actually
do any of that. Ever. And so now I feel very sad about that and
a little bit angry.

I feel sort of ashamed that I made the face of HA-HA at
that guy just so I could feel good about myself for one-upping
a stranger. I feel like maybe doing that makes me a bad person.
But I don't care.

And anyway do you know what.

I actually think that I am a bad person actually.

TWO

So Bob and I we're at this bar we always go to in Downtown LA because it's like the only bar in Downtown LA that's open all day. It even opens at eight in the morning I think. Yes that's right because we came here one time at eight in the morning just to see if it was really open that early like it said on yelp and it was it was really open that early. But that was only once that we ever came here that early even though I have wanted to do it again ever since because on that day we drank all day and basically never saw any sunlight or other people all day it was just me and Bob. And we just drank and talked about sad things so it was basically like a perfect day I would say. But I feel embarrassed about just flat out asking Bob if she would like to drink in the dark and talk about sad things all day again because that does not sound like much of a date and I'm trying to do more date-like things with Bob and hopefully one day she will say

Hey this is a fun date. Maybe I should date him after all.

So we don't come here and stay all day like we did that one time. We just come here pretty early in the afternoon a lot of the time and get really really drunk and that's pleasant enough so I can not complain. And no I do not count that as a date when we do it it is just a hang out session with Bob.

Bob doesn't do anything for work because her dad is rich in New York and so she just sits being cute in her nice apartment that has nothing on its walls except a few of Bob's own painted self-portraits and like there is no furniture hardly and in this apartment there also lives a cat I am good friends with which is Bob's cat who Bob has not named because she says

It doesn't matter he's just The Cat and who is any person to give a creature a name.

But I think it does matter and so I told Bob about how in Breakfast at Tiffany's Audrey Hepburn's cat is just named Cat and that made Bob feel angry that her idea of not naming a cat had been taken already and also she was mad because she did not know that reference to a very famous movie. Bob paints self-portraits sometimes in oil but not very often and just for fun not for work although some of them are definitely good and look just like Bob and that means that they are also beautiful.

As for me and work I wrote this one book which was a novel that did pretty OK even though now I hate it and I feel angry when I think about how stupid it is in hindsight but it did pretty OK and then the men paid me a lot of money to write a screenplay of it and I did that in like a week and made more money than I'd ever made in my life. And then I wrote a second book which was a lot better than that first one that's for sure. And then THE RIGHT PEOPLE said this second book was like really good and important LITERATURE! But if that second book is so great then why has no one asked me to make a movie about that book huh. But whatever the first one made me a lot of money so that is nice and I don't much care about money anyway as long as I have enough to get through the week. Like money is one of the few things that I don't automatically worry about even though it is a reasonable thing to worry about.

I worry about a lot of other things that I should not worry about though. Like I worry do the people at Netflix think I keep my movies too long and that I rent stupid movies only.

22

And I worry about any unread emails in my inbox I might not have gotten to yet or that might not even exist yet. And I worry will my lies catch up to me one day. And I worry about the scary time between getting Thai food delivery at the door and getting it into my apartment because it would be so embarrassing to be caught by one of the other people in my building getting Thai Food delivery for just myself. And I worry about is it too soon to order from the same Thai place because do they then think I am lame for ordering from them almost once a week but what can I say their food is good and spicy and not very expensive and lasts me for days and I can order online and not have to talk to anyone except for the delivery guy at the end. But yeah I guess all that is lame of me and I guess I am hopelessly lame. So yeah apparently I worry about the Thai Food delivery man's opinion of me but I don't worry about running out of money. I didn't even worry about money back when I had no money and I was poor.

I think I'm technically rich now. I mean like globally obviously I'm rich you know compared to the average person on the planet in like a mud hut I'm very rich but not like compared to you know real rich people like I couldn't even retire forever now. But I'm definitely all set for some time. I don't want to talk about money really I don't care about money but my only point is that that's how Bob and I can go to a bar at three o clock in the afternoon on a Monday is because Bob and I don't have jobs. That is my only point here.

We like to go to this one bar because it's quiet and usually empty so we can talk about things like taking hallucinogenic drugs or stuff about sex or just very very sad things or we can not talk at all and just drink. And at this

empty bar no one tells us to stop talking about those things
and no one tells us to talk about something and not nothing and
certainly no one tells us not to drink so much that's for sure.
This bar is close to Bob's house in Downtown LA and so she
walks here and I take the subway from where I live in Hollywood
which I like to do that because there are really weird people
to look at on the LA subway. I wrote some poems just about the
people on the subway but I haven't shown them to anyone yet
because I suspect they are shit,

In New York legit people take the subway all the time
but no one legit takes the subway in LA that's for sure just
poor people and crazy people and me. And Bob when she comes to
Hollywood to visit me at my house. We take the subway and we
say it is because we do not want to drink and drive but really
neither of us likes to drive period. I am not lying about us
having houses by the way I am just saying my house and Bob's
house meaning the places that we live even though we both just
live in apartments but I like to say my house or Bob's house
because that is kind of fun and sounds is like we are kids who
are friends with each other so I would say like Oh I'm going
over to Bob's house and it does feel like Bob and I are just
kids and friends sometimes and that is fun and nice. So I'm not
really lying to say my house or Bob's house. It's just a little
make believe that hurts no one it is just fun.

They don't call it The Metro or The Subway here in LA
though they call it The Train and that makes me feel angry to
hear that because a train is something different than a subway
or a metro because a train does not normally go underground in
between every station like a metro or subway does and so I wish
they would stop calling it The Train that is a lie and a dumb

not important lie. And so LA people just call it The Train so
that when you call it The Subway or The Metro which is what it
really is then they can be like Oh you're not from LA then if
you just called it The Subway or The Metro because we call it
THE TRAIN HA-HA!

As if anyone who lives in LA is actually from LA in the
first place so why are they so proud of being LA people. Wait
stop sorry that was a lie too. I hate that one lie a lot
actually. Lots of people here in LA are from LA originally.
Loads of people are. It's just this stupid thing people say
whenever someone says they're actually from LA then the other
person goes like Oh wow you don't see that very often an actual
LA native HA-HA! That's what they always call it An actual LA
native. And it's like some stupid joke everyone in LA is in on
and whenever it happens everyone has a big old fake laugh even
though it's dumb and they are dumb and lying. And no one ever
says to themselves like Wait when I think about it I've
actually met like a thousand people in LA who are actually from
LA so I should stop making that joke about LA Native now. No
one says that they just keep on saying about LA Native and
laughing because it's this joke but also it's just this easy
safe thing you can say when you want to talk without having to
actually say anything that someone could possibly disagree
with. But I disagree with it so like what do you say now huh.

I'm trying to say the word LIKE less often because
saying LIKE all the time makes me sound like I'm from here or
stupid or both and I'm not from here or stupid or both. Like
when you were a teenager you'd just be like

Wait goddammit I said the word LIKE already twice.

But when you were a teenager you would say Oh I'm so tired. You'd say that whenever it was Awkward Silence and there was nothing to say and everyone else would agree and say they were tired too because it was safe and no one would tell you you were wrong or disagree with you. So it would feel good to have people be like OMG yes I am tired too because then you felt less alone for just a minute. But it's still a stupid lie that I hate and the LA native lie is the same exact kind of lie I think I hate it when people use their words not deliberately especially when they're lying. That really is the worst kind of lie. The kind of lie where you just spout generic phrases which you don't even think about whether or not you believe it or not but you just say it anyway because you know you heard it somewhere.

It's OK to tell a casual meaningless lie if it's a phrase that has already been validated by being in a movie or a TV show or something. That's the rule I guess. And everyone just nods and accepts the lie even though deep down and not even really all that deep down they all know what it really is which is a lie. It's like you're not listening and answering the question you hear. You're just waiting for chances to plug in little catchphrases and ideas and lines from TV because lines from TV have been vouched for by someone else. So if you say it and it happens to be total bullshit you're off the hook. Or if everyone calls you out you can say LOL I was just referencing Parks and Recreation didn't you see that episode yet and why not. And so you have no responsibility for it and no one wants any responsibility for anything they say or do nowadays.

I'm glad I don't work in an office because I am so sick of hearing about Ugh it is Monday or Yes it is Thursday almost the weekend woo hoo. If I worked in an office I would be in a youtube office meltdown video within like the first week. The ALMOST THE WEEKEND thing is another dumb lie that is just meaningless air because what are you going to do on the weekend that is any different from what you're doing now. You're just gonna do nothing that makes anything better.

And that is the sort of dumb weak lie that messes with the climate for the real good deliberate lies I tell like the good big deliberate planned out ones that get things done in my world for me.

When I lie all I'm doing is I figure out what would be best for the people around me and I just tell them that's how it is. I have it all planned out and on purpose while everyone else just mouthshits out half-truths and say that it's OK. But if I ever got caught lying at the same time as everyone else in the world did I would obviously be the big villain here and everyone else would all be forgiven.

So anyway Bob and I go to this bar all the time because it's close to Bob's house and the subway for me and also it's really cheap like three dollars and fifty cents a Drink which is insane for LA in 2011 I mean come on. Yeah you have to get Well Drinks like just Whiskey Diet which is what I get even though it is not my favorite Drink. Maker's Mark On The Rocks is my favorite Drink but it is not the Drink I order the most. And the Whiskey Diets are so strong you have to drink the first one really fast and try to not to taste it and usually the same for the second one as well. I have no idea how this place stays in business honestly.

Sometimes Bob jokes that this place is secretly a front for like a dog fighting ring or a brothel or something and they expect no one to ever come in here and actually sit for a Drink because it is so shady looking and not clean or comfy really. And so Bob and I are ruining their crime racket by always being here drinking their too-cheap Liquor and so we are actually not just being drunken do-nothings because we are actually taking a bite out of crime. I loved Bob when she said that phrase Take A Bite Out Of Crime because she didn't like make a scene over the fact that she said a cute thing. She just said it and moved on. Like it would be a huge joke moment in like a Diablo Cody movie or something but Bob just said it and moved on she did not wait for me to say Wow Bob that was cute of you to say. So it was actually much cuter that way and so I loved Bob extra for that.

I could pay a little more for better Drinks but I just like being frugal and not wasting money and a three dollar and fifty cent Drink that is strong is a good deal I don't care who you are and so I drink Whiskey Diets even though it is not my favorite Drink to drink. And then on top of the Drinks being cheap already since Bob and I come here so often they give us Free Drinks sometimes and packs of cigarettes sometimes too which again seriously how are they in business. I think we get free stuff partly because this one bartender has overheard Bob and I talk for so long that he knows I'm not fucking Bob and he wants to fuck Bob so he gives us both free stuff to act like he's this big awesome stuff-providing alpha muscley man and I'm just some little wimpy bitch receiving his gifts exactly like a girl would so that I look weak and emasculated in front of Bob and he looks like a boss so he can fuck her one day. I think that's what he really is doing but I don't worry about him because I know Bob wouldn't want to fuck that bartender because I know she doesn't like big muscles or Asian guys. Sexually I mean she's not an actual racist no way I just mean attraction. Like I don't think Asian women are very sexy usually either but I'm not a racist against them OK it's just attraction and I should stop talking about this now I think because I am making it all much worse. Maybe Bob thinks I'm Asian and that's why she won't date or fuck me. I'm just white but I do look kind of something. So anyway I just take the Free Drinks from the bartender all the time and the cigarettes and I don't mind and I think the joke's on him and he thinks the joke's on me so everyone's happy and I am actually right so I win and that makes me double happy.

I love that Bob and I like to get really really drunk during the day and neither of us says anything dumb or judgy about it. That is one thing I definitely love about Bob that makes me want her to be my girlfriend right away is we get really really drunk really often and with no like occasion because we understand we just have to get drunk if we're going to be able to deal. But we have never said that out loud we just understand it and that's really important to me. It's just like Bob not making a joke moment out of saying Take A Bite Out Of Crime.

Bob is the best because she does the great thing but then she doesn't be like How great was that thing I just did wasn't it great of me! Because then that would not be great any more it would be needy and whorish. It is also good that Bob believes I am an Alcoholic which I am not. I mean I prefer being drunk to being sober but like if I don't drink for a week I'm not like tweaking out and pulling my arm hair out. I'm just very afraid. Anyway it's good Bob thinks that we are kind of Alcoholics together because OK here's why.

So my giant constant lying is obviously my main terrible secret but then my excessive drinking is the second darkness. The difference is that the drinking is a darkness that I let people know about because if people think they know a big secret about you and they think you don't know that they know about it then they don't go searching for another worse secret. Most people only have room inside them for one big bad secret so most people think all other people can only have one big bad secret too. And so Bob thinks she knows my only secret darkness and it is that I drink a lot and she doesn't mind that because she drinks a lot too.

But the truth is that there is a worse darkness and it isn't even the lying exactly. I think the lying is a symptom of the real bad thing. The thing that is most awful in my life is that there is another very bad person who lives inside me and lives with me and he knows the whole truth and he tells me that I am worthless and cursed and doomed and fat and then all of that makes me lie or something. I hate that guy very much and I do not want to think about him now.

But anyway so I let Bob know I drink too much and so my main darkness of lying is safe from Bob for now. And just as importantly I think she is safe from it. But it really impresses me or something that Bob understands that our drinking is a darkness. You know it's not like she justifies it by saying like Oh we're just drinking to celebrate life! Or some lie like that which lots of people who drink too much tell that one lie and it is dumb because it's obviously a lot more fun to celebrate sadness than happiness and besides who can even look at the world and be like Yeah that's a basically awesome place and not a scary and empty place full of nobodies and liars all clutching at nothings that might one day possibly become a half of a something but probably won't.

Sometimes I think as much as I lie I am the only honest one around. That thing about drinking and Bob would make a good first sentence of a book about emptiness. Something like

That Thursday afternoon, Protagonist realized he was doomed to love what was left of his alleged life, as long as he could share it with Her. Not because they were complicit in a desperate dependence on drink, but because they silently shared the knowledge that drinking is best when it is not a celebration, but a mourning. Not a fond farewell to a day that had been kind, but a grieving for a dead expanse of time that would never return, would never give them a second chance to do it better knowing what they know now. He found sad peace in the realization that, save for this wretched understanding between them, the world, and the two of them, were crushingly, incurably, and aggressively empty.

Or something like that. But something should be made of that idea that's for sure and that's an OK first paragraph I think and I will write it in a note in my iPhone quickly right now. I hate when people are like You don't need to take every little interesting thing that happens to you or that you think of and make something out of it or put it into a story! Because I think Of course you do or what the hell else are you going to write about. I know I know all this talk is coming from a guy who hasn't completed a single project since that one book and then its screenplay and then the other book which was like a year ago or more. But whatever.

I've been telling stories.

THREE

Although it's weird to talk about Bob drinking out of sadness
because like I said I know that Bob is happy enough with her
life of just being cute and not really doing anything of much
but at the same time she definitely drinks because she's sad. I
know that's true because she's really good at talking about
very sad things with me and you can't get away with lying about
knowing about very sad things unless you have been very sad for
a very long time. Maybe she's content every day but long term
very sad and that's what it is. Like Bob is sad but there isn't
a deep hole in Bob like there is in me and there isn't a scary
other person who is inhabiting her like there is one in me but
she still is just sad anyway. Like I'm sad because something
actively bad is happening in me that I am afraid of every day
and she's sad because not enough actively good or satisfying is
happening to her. Maybe. *Malaise* I think it's called. Or *ennui*.
Of course the French have two different and really sexy words
for it but all the American words for it are like medical words
like Depression and Anxiety and Asperger's Syndrome and Chronic
Fatigue Syndrome. Artistic *malaise* is highly fuckable but who
wants to go to bed with a syndrome. You're not supposed to
write about sad things I know I know I know. Or at least you
have to disguise them or call them something it's not or put
them in metaphor because no one wants to hear about real sad
things because if they wanted to do that they'd just look at
their lives and allow themselves to be honest and therefore
sad. And if they wanted to read about other people's sadness
then they'd go on like a random livejournal and just read some
fat emo girl's vampire poems. Wait I've talked about a vampire
already. Shit but oh well.

So Jesus fucking seriously anyway Christ enough sidetrack and now back to Bob at the bar. Bob sits down next to me and by now she has her Rusty Nail in her cute little hand and I already saw that the bartender put more Drambuie than Bob likes and she will not be very happy about that in about ten seconds that's for sure but she cheerses her Rusty Nail against my Whiskey Diet and she says as if it is a surprise she is just realizing now she says

I missed you

And that makes me feel really nice because we saw each other only the night before last night so it is very generous of her to say that I was missed in just that little time. Bob is really really great at being a girl. Like she can really just know when I'm feeling especially sad without my having to admit it to her out loud and then she says the exact right thing that both makes me feel much better and much sadder at the same time and then that is completely perfect and I love Bob. But not all the time because sometimes she doesn't say the exact right thing but then that is even more perfect because when she does say the perfect thing it feels even better because it's just a little bit of a surprise. It's not like Yeah yeah yeah that's just Bob being perfect like always no big deal. Instead it is Oh wow I am really moved by that perfect thing Bob did but you know what I shouldn't have been surprised she was perfect because do you know what Bob is pretty great and beautiful and wow I love Bob. I think the feeling of finding out you are in love with someone is the best and saddest feeling you can ever feel and I have realized that I am in love with Bob like hundreds of times and so that is very

great and very sad and very perfect. Seriously why will Bob not
be my girlfriend.

OK so for example this one time a long time ago which
was one of the first times I realized that I love Bob OK it was
way before I was published. At that time we were new friends
and I asked her to read some of my poems and she said she would
and she did she read them and she said they were all really
good and that was all she had to say about that. There was
nothing bad for her to say. And then I said Hey Bob one day I
am going to purposely write a really shit poem and give it to
you among a pile of normal good poems just to see if you are
just telling me that all of my poems are good just to be nice
to me or if you could figure out that I deliberately wrote a
piece of shit poem and slipped it in the pile like to trick
you. Or if you COULD tell that one of them was shit would you
be honest enough to tell me that. And then Bob took a sip of
whatever I forget if it was a Rusty Nail but it probably was
and then she held my hand for the first time and Bob said

Do you know what. One day you really will write
something shit and you will be trying to write something good
but it will turn out shit anyway. And I will still like you.

That was really the perfect thing of Bob to say because
it made me both happier and sadder at the same time and because
I expected her just to say

No no no you will never write anything shit.

But it was so much better of her to say that it will be
OK if I do write something shit and that she will still be my
dear friend Bob. When she said that thing it made me want to
say Bob I love you and kiss her and have both of us get naked
and all tangled up and stuff and have me say I love you Bob

right while I was coming and I probably could have made that happen if I'd had the balls because I think she maybe wanted me to kiss her then or at least she was so drunk she wouldn't have minded if I did.

But of course I didn't kiss her because I am lame and so guess what womp womp friend zone forever. Girls' dating windows are too small or I am too slow or it's both. I also sort of wanted to cry at that time that I just described but I didn't because I am not sad. I haven't been able to cry for years even though I've only gotten sadder and sadder as time goes on but still I can't cry and I haven't cried since I had to leave home. I guess that was the last time I cried was when I was thrown out by my family for lying.

But now back to Bob. She asks how long I've been here at the bar and I say Two Drinks. That's sort of a lie that I just told to Bob but it is also not a lie because yes I have been here for Two Drinks but what she was really asking me was how drunk am I. And about an hour ago I had breakfast at the good breakfast place by my house and I had an Irish Coffee and four Bloody Maries along with my poached eggs with turkey sausage and spinach and that was all really really good for my breakfast even though apparently no one in LA can poach an egg worth a god damn but it was still very good and I took a quick Shot of Tequila on my way out on impulse but anyway yeah I am much drunker than the Two Drinks like I told Bob and the reason I lied to her about that is because she likes it better when I only drink with her and not alone. And I like that better too actually because when I am with Bob I feel a lot less alone.

But it was mean of me to lie to Bob about how drunk I am though I realize now because if I said I had an Irish Coffee

and four Bloody Maries already with my shittily poached eggs
then that would give her an excuse to drink like four actually
what seven I guess Drinks really fast to catch up with me and
she would have liked to do that and so that would have been a
little kindness if I had let her do that. But instead she just
says OK and asks for Another Rusty Nail with less Drambuie this
time OK. And then Bob drinks her first Rusty Nail through the
wide red straw very fast. She drinks it all while holding her
hand up to me like as if to say

Just wait one second we will talk in one second but I am
attending to this business first.

The bartender has learned to give Bob the wide straws
not the little thin ones because she likes to drink fast but
she wants to look cute and still like a girl too so she uses a
straw instead of sipping straight from the glass but a big
straw not the thin little kind of one which she calls bitch
straws and she says they are not good for anything but stirring
and I agree with that for sure they are too thin and sometimes
when you drink through them they make that squeaky sound and I
am afraid of that sound that they make that squeaky sound.

I look Bob over as she drinks her whole Rusty Nail in
one long sip with four gulps and she does look really nice in
her sea-green dress but then she is done with her Drink and she
scrunches up her face and does a little bouncy dance from how
strong her Drink is and the tops of her pale breasts bounce and
all of the sudden Bob is way sexier than I was expecting and I
wasn't ready for that and I start to get horny over Bob and I
think Oh No. Bob's breasts are a 34C and I know that because
one time we were drunk at my house because we had been playing
the The Big Lebowski Drinking Game which gets you very fucking

drunk very fucking quickly by the way and so we got surprise
wasted and she wanted to have a nap and cuddle with me but not
fuck me of course and her new bra was making her breasts
uncomfortable and so she borrowed one of my t-shirts and put it
on on top of everything and then took her bra off underneath it
and when she was asleep I looked at the tag of the bra on my
floor and it said 34C. I think a 34C is the best size of
breasts and now that I realize I'm thinking about Bob's breasts
as specifically and I am looking at the tops of them bouncing
now and I realize I'm feeling really horny today and I should
have gone out and had sex with someone last night and then had
sex with that person again this morning so that I wouldn't be
feeling horny over Bob now because that is going to go nowhere
and it will just make me feel sad later and maybe even angry. I
mean I just imagine myself five or six hours from now saying
good night to Bob while really wanting to fuck her and knowing
I will not.

So I decide that lots more Whiskey will take care of
that problem and all the rest of them to boot. Just so long as
I make sure to get really really fucking drunk. If I just get
kind of drunk that will make it all a lot worse because I will
want to fuck Bob a lot more so I have to get really drunk so I
know I couldn't even fuck Bob if I wanted to and all I want is
to go to bed for sleep. Or I could just go home early like soon
and make up some excuse so I don't end up back at Bob's house
just to hang out and not to fuck her and then have to walk home
on my own all miserable and horny.

Bob told me once that the problems I have are the best
problems to have and I should complain less and this problem of
being horny over Bob's breasts feels like one of those not so

bad problems. It feels like #whitepeopleproblems. Like globally speaking? Bob's stupid tits are really not a big problem. There's Famine Genocide AIDS Recession War Global Warming and Poverty. And then there's rich white me getting ten tons of butthurt over a set of stupid fucking tits.

People get angry when I say things like I should have had sex with someone last night because not everyone can just have sex with someone whenever they want so I shouldn't complain. I know I shouldn't say things like that because I couldn't have sex whenever I wanted for the longest time and that was a very bad thing to be the case.

Actually that's a lie. Not having much sex didn't even really bother me that much at the time. Like pretending to be dumber than I am and more fun than I am and less serious than I am just so I could have sex with hot girls wasn't really worth it to me and it did not make me satisfied in any real way and I felt like a whore. Not for having sex but for selling out in order to have sex I didn't really want anyway. I just felt like I should be going after it all the time so I did but it sucked.

So yeah I was pretty much take it or leave it on the subject of casual sex with hot morons whether or not I could have lots of it. So that was sort of merciful I suppose. Lots of guys my age get very upset over the amount of sex they are not having.

But don't get me wrong OK it's not like now I can have sex with any woman because I'm suddenly good looking or I've learned to be good at seducing or being fun or whatever. It's just that the book-world people I meet out and about think my second book was really like

OK this is uncomfortable for me to even talk about but it's true OK some people say it's like important and genius all because that's what THE RIGHT CRITIC says. And so I get introduced by my agent John sometimes to like super-sexy and not-so-smart women and he says I'm a big important writer who wrote Catcher in the Rye for the Twitter Generation. That is what he says about me even though I am not even on Twitter at all and I hate Twitter actually it is so dumb. It is an example of one of those things that is not a thing but is pretending to be a thing I think. And besides my book was just a weird little book about not much in particular but THE RIGHT PEOPLE liked it a lot but anyway that means I get to have sex with women who are way sexier than I should be allowed to have sex with them and so sometimes I do. Even though I really just want to have sex with Bob and no one else forever and ever.

Also I am very good at lying and playing other parts or characters to get different kinds of women to have sex with me. Like there's this one fancy bar I go to only when I am dressed up in a suit and just got a haircut and a straight razor shave and I have like this one particular suit that really makes me look like a million bucks in a very Mad Men way and when I am there I pretend I am a big entertainment lawyer and I say I represent somebody pretty big but I can't say who for privacy reasons but I hint around whoever is very famous that week. And that whole character along with tons and tons of super douchey cockiness and gross aggressiveness works on especially like late thirties semi professional women really well.

I only take those women to a hotel though and not my place. My place is nice but it's simple and no one would ever mistake it for a mega lawyer's place and there is something nice about a hotel when you want to be anonymous. The women like the hotel idea because often they are married or something. I like it because you can be anyone in a hotel or you can be no one. I always choose to be no one. In a way it feels like it is only then that I am finally being my honest self is when I admit that I am no one.

I sometimes feel like I am a hotel for all my characters. Like I exist for sure and I have a certain amount of objective physical features and a name and a location but at the same time a lot of very different people come and go inside me at their leisure.

I've always been better for a visit than a stay.

But anyway yeah I can lie my way into bed with some pretty hot women because my characters are good at seducing and being confident whereas I am good at neither of those things and Bob is the only one who I am really just myself around. I mean minus the enormous lying obviously because I do not tell Bob about that very dark secret. But anyway Bob is the person I am the most like myself around and she appears to think I am completely not even worth considering fucking or dating or loving and she doesn't even know I have a darkness. But I want to be with Bob that's for sure and I want to be good for her.

Bob isn't like Hollywood ten out of ten magazine cover sexy so much as she is indie movie cute but then actually really really beautiful when you get to know her expressions and face a little better and also her little body is really great but not like so skinny that it can only be evidence of body issues and obsession. It's just normal and great.

Actually I think that Bob is way more sexy than like Megan Fox or Paris Hilton or Angelina Jolie or whoever it is

I'm supposed to think is sexy. And also I want to fuck Bob the most because I love her. And so I fantasize about fucking Bob a lot while I'm fucking other women who maybe are technically sexier than Bob. I know it's supposed to be the other way around you're supposed to think about hotter women than the ones you're fucking but either way I think about fucking Bob almost every time I have sex.

Also like I said Bob has the best size of breasts I think and her butt is like a little bit too big for her body. It isn't a fat butt it's just a big butt which I don't really care either way about a butt personally I like breasts way more than a butt but the fact that she is generally normal awesome proportions and then there's just this big dumb butt just kind of sitting there is kind of funny to me and then that is all kind of cute and adorable to me also and then that becomes sexy to me because adorable is sexy to me and it all adds up to Yes I basically love Bob top to bottom.

Ha-ha top to bottom. I'm retarded.

OK I mean I know you're REALLY supposed to just think about the person you're fucking right now and not think about someone else at all. I know that OK. But I think Bob in my imagination is way hotter than any real life girl and so I imagine Bob because it's a waste of my good imagination to just think about the person who is right in front of me I think. And at the end of the day imagination is all I've got.

It would be funny if I said Bob's name out loud while I was in bed with someone else though wouldn't it. But at the same time I have said the phrase Oh Bob yes In my head a lot whether it's while I'm fucking someone else or just masturbating. I don't like to talk a lot when I have sex though which I guess is sort of weird for a writer I guess or maybe it isn't who knows. But it is true I don't like to and so I don't dirty talk unless the woman starts doing it first and then I play along with it but in my head I'm really making fun of her because it's so inauthentic and so not hot and it just feels staged and phony like in a porno and it's not really genuine or sexy at all to me. And besides that's not what words are for. And there is no good word for a vagina and there's no good word for doing oral sex for a woman that isn't totally gross and so I always end up just laughing a little inside and stopping feeling truly sexy I am just playing along until I come or I decide I'm over thinking about if I'm going to come or not and I just decide that I'm going to fake

What do you want for Our Birthday?

Bob says interrupting my thoughts about all of that. That is how she always says it Our Birthday because we have the same birthday but different years but the same birthday and it is coming up in a couple of days. I say I don't want anything in particular just some good books she would recommend maybe or an album and let's have a really epic dinner somewhere. She says

OK but I want to get you something as well. I say I don't want anything. And that is a lie because I do want something. I want Bob. Even though we share the same birthday and we always do something nice together to celebrate it I suspect that Bob also has a second birthday party with all of her friends who are not as much my friends as just her friends and I actually think that is very kind of her not to bring me to those parties because she knows I am sensitive about birthdays and feeling alone on them because she knows that I

once dated a girl who is dead now and that is not a sympathy
lie that is just really really true.

OK I guess we're talking about this now huh. OK my first
girlfriend ever is dead now and I really cried a lot when she
died that's for sure I was like sixteen and she was the first
person I fell in love with and she died she killed herself. I
cried a ton back then but that was way before I got thrown out
of home for lying which was the last time I cried and I have
not been able to cry about anything since then even though
things have just gotten sadder and sadder all the time.

But anyway this girl who was my first girlfriend once
told me that the people who show up to your birthday are the
only people in the world who give a shit that you didn't die
that year. And then that girl did die that year she killed
herself and then a few months later I had my birthday party
that year and not many people came to it at all and I was
embarrassed and I thought about death a lot on my seventeenth
birthday. Not like actual suicide for myself because I know how
bad that is but just about death like as an interesting subject
and I was very very sad around that time and so I am now
officially weird about birthdays.

So it is nice of Bob to not invite me to her second
birthday party and I do not ask about it because I do not want
to know. You see sometimes a lie is kinder.

Bob would probably have a split birthday party with me
if I asked but I would feel uncomfortable like it was a huge
act of charity and I would not want that. And anyway Bob's
friends really are not my friends. Like I would never just hang
out with them without Bob because I don't love them that much
they are OK but not that great. Actually they kind of suck I

don't know why Bob is so great and hangs out with those stupid lumps. But then I also realize the reason I don't have any friends other than Bob is because I only want to be friends with people that are as great as Bob which no one is as great as her and so maybe I should make more of an effort or kind of lower my standards for friends. But anyway nothing to be done about it this year because it is Monday and our birthday is on Friday. If Bob was my girlfriend it would be OK to have a split party and it would not be weird if we were living together to share a party. Oh God I wish we were living together and throwing parties together as Me and Bob the Couple.

Anyway I tell Bob I don't want anything really what about you Bob. Bob says

I don't know I don't want anything either except how about a decent boyfriend ha-ha.

Which I think is super ridiculously fucking mean of her to say that to my face. Then she says

Dinner sounds like a good idea though what about seafood. And I say Sure as long as it is like French or American seafood not like Korean Live Sushi. We went to Korean Live Sushi for our last birthday or maybe it was the time before. I forget. But it was fun you eat like crawling octopus tentacles and twitching shrimps and like live baby sea cucumbers that squirt their guts out in your mouth and it's obviously totally foul but it's fun and then when you're bored of all that crazy stuff you have as many soft shell crabs as you can eat. And you have really fresh but normal sushi too and we like had a Maine Lobster apiece too because I think I had just gotten some award for my second book so it was like double celebration. And obviously we had Soju which is like the Korean

version of Sake except somehow they make it taste totally
appalling even though it is the same thing basically. Oh no
wait we had Scotch that night that's right. But Soju is a
thing.

One thing I do like about Korean restaurants and clubs
though is they let you smoke inside the building after like ten
or eleven at night even though it's totally illegal and so they
must have a deal with the cops or something. And then also they
often have Bottle Service and they don't give a shit if you
order a bottle of like Johnny Walker Blue Label for the table
which is what we did that year because why the hell not life is
short. I mean yeah it's supposed to be for like ten people and
not just for me and one hundred and ten pounds of little Bob
but the Koreans they act impressed and cheer you on and
congratulate you if we finish it all which we did not finish
all the Johnny Walker Blue Label that night but honestly that
was because the live seafood made us sick first and not the
Johnny Walker Blue Label but who would believe that story. Not
the fucking Koreans. Lying to Koreans is actually very hard
because they are all very suspicious people. But anyway I do
not want to go to that restaurant again this year. Bob says

Sure like what about somewhere with really good lobster
that maybe also has even steak and mussels and oh what about
calamari and I say Yes definitely that sounds good but grilled
not fried right and Bob says

Sure but I like fried too. And we should make a deal
with each other to not have any like bread or pasta or salad or
soup or any of that filler but just total amazing sea food and
booze all night long. And I say You have a god damned deal Bob.

I like it when I get to call her by her name because it is cute and like a little bit formal and sexy and I say Yeah and oh how about like two dozen oysters apiece and Bob says

No way gross!

Because we both hate oysters because they are totally gross and they're like little slimy vaginas so that was like a little bit funny of me just now and she's actually kind of dry heaving a little bit like not jokingly but actually dry heaving thinking about eating two dozen oysters because she hates them so much but she is also laughing at the joke I just told.

And she touches me on the leg while she is laughing and I think to myself that if I wrote a character in a book that was just exactly exactly like Bob with no changes at all then no one would believe that she could be real because she is so great.

FOUR

Bob is my best friend for a few legit reasons like I have
described how great she is and how well we get along but one
very bad reason I keep her as a friend is because she is very
very trusting of me and not a suspicious person at all by
nature. And so I have to be careful about it but sometimes I
can revise details of some of my stories if I really need them
to be something different later. The one thing Bob is
suspicious of though is money. That is because she is rich and
normally kind hearted so she has to be on the lookout for
people who want to mooch from her but I have never wanted to
mooch and I prefer to treat her to things even dumb little
things even when I was poor and she was mega rich I would
rather treat her to dinner at In N Out than have her treat me
to a nice restaurant. And not because I was trying to be the
man or make her owe me but just because it makes me happy to
treat. And she liked that gesture and soon enough we were close
enough friends that she was treating me to things sometimes but
only because she wanted to do it and she knew I was poor but
working on it and she was rich and not doing a damned thing
with it.

Actually Bob is doing this sort of thing where basically
she is trying to spend herself broke and see if that is even
possible in a lifetime because she is so rich but she earned
none of it. She says it is a sort of modern art statement like
she is deliberately squandering her life to try and make
something beautiful out of total self-destruction. I said Maybe
me too I think. She said

Right?

Then it got too heavy for a second so we changed the topic and we talked about dinosaurs instead. And anyway so we became close friends even though I did not make a move on her fast enough so I got in the friend zone and I still am here years later.

But yeah I can kind of revise my stories to Bob because I tell her very personal things and she mistakes that for me only telling her honest things. But I try not to revise stories too much. Not just because the more I do it the more likely I am to make a mistake and fuck the whole thing up although that is also a true concern. But mainly because there's this weird kind of code of honor to it like on Dexter but instead of killing people it's lying and I have rules too that I follow.

I know you're not supposed to talk about pop culture so much because it dates what you're writing and it is a really cheap way of making a connection with your reader because it's just stupid fads and trends but still someone would read it and be like Yeah I just watched Dexter too ha-ha wow this writer is like totally talking about my life!

Whatever. And I've already talked about Zooey Deschanel and Dexter and Michael Cera and so it's kind of too late to worry about that any more. And Katy Perry.

I don't have hard rules about when it's OK to give in to the dark thing the way Dexter does. It's more of a gut feeling thing that I just know when it's wrong or I am going too far. I know funny to talk about right and wrong when I'm deciding about little details within something that's so obviously just enormously evil from the get go and so obviously just the worst and most fucked up thing you can do to someone which is tell a lie. But there it is and besides he kills people on Dexter and

I just lie. And killing is worse than lying so. But maybe it is not worse because Dexter harms only bad men and he kills them pretty fast then it is over and I harm good people like Bob and the other people in my life I have harmed by lying and they have to live with it.

Also Dexter is you know. Made up and not real.

Oh wow I just figured out that Dexter is named Dexter on the show because in Latin the word dexter means right and sinister means left so like he is split in half between the good side which is just the Dexter everyone thinks they know and who they talk to and work with and then the Sinister is his secret dark identity of killing people. I feel really stupid now that I only just figured that out and that is pretty clever and cool I think. It's gross though that Dexter is dating his sister on the show in real life and her mouth looks like a Muppet's mouth I think it looks like Bert's mouth and she has no breasts at all.

One other thing that I never figured out for the longest time even though it's obvious is that there is this music venue here in LA called the Wiltern Theater and it is at the intersection of Wilshire Boulevard and Western Avenue so it takes the Wil from Wilshire and the tern from Western and then puts Wiltern. That took me like three years to figure out and that was another thing I felt dumb for not knowing and I do not like it when I am feeling dumb.

But yeah I can kind of tweak stories I tell Bob if I need to. Like last month we were talking about what actors and actresses we think are hot and she asked me if I think the dragon girl on Game of Thrones is hot and I said definitely she has an amazing body but her face is kind of weird and I did not say this part but I think her breasts are really incredible and look like a 34C if you ask me which is the best size but anyway I did not say that last part about breasts obviously. To Bob. All I said was that the dragon girl on Game of Thrones has a great body but her face is kind of weird. And I saw Bob get a little bit sad inside and then I remembered Oops because one time ago Bob said that she thinks that she looks a lot like the dragon girl on Game of Thrones and I agreed she does actually and that was not a lie Bob does look like her because Bob is really that beautiful and so then I accidentally made Bob feel sad because I accidentally sort of said her face is weird. Bob's face isn't weird it's just normal and great but I do think that the dragon girl's mouth is kind of weird when she yells or says big speeches but of course Bob thought I was saying that Bob's face is weird and I don't blame her for thinking that because that is basically what I said to her it was just an accident but still. And so then Bob was sad because I was honest and that turned out badly.

So I decided I would revise what I said in order to make it right so what I did was a few days later we were at Bob's house to watch Game of Thrones together even though we usually don't watch it together because usually she watches it at her house and I watch it pirated streaming on the internet at my house and make jokes with my internet friends who are also watching the show with me at the same time and typing in a chat room to make jokes and enjoy the show. I really like to be a nerd online about Game of Thrones because it reminds me of playing Dungeons and Dragons with my friends when I was a kid because yes we would earnestly enjoy playing the Dungeons and Dragons but then we would also make wise cracks about it to each other while we were playing. But it was like fun and not mean spirited wise cracks because we loved the game so much actually and honestly but we also knew we were total nerds for loving it so much and so we were both having our fun and also kind of laughing at ourselves a little bit but safely and not meanly. And that meant that we did not feel like losers for doing the lame little things that made us happy and so all in all that was a very nice time in my life. It was not like me drinking Whiskey Diets now. I didn't feel bad about having and enjoying the little pleasures that I wanted in my life back then. But now I do I guess.

When I would play Dungeons and Dragons I would be the Dungeon Master. OK so that means like I would not pretend to be like a knight or a wizard or one of the adventurers who had to explore and defeat the dungeon and monsters OK. It means that within our friends I would basically be the one person who was a bad guy who also thought up and wrote all the challenges. And so like days before everyone met up to play the game I would sit down on my own and invent a complicated story for my friends to play through and I would draw out a whole brand new dungeon every time with very unique tricks and traps and riddles for my friends to solve and monsters to defeat and then my friends would be the adventurers and they'd have to figure their way through the tricks and traps and the story that I wrote for them.

I would have all of my notes written down about what I had written but I would get this big cardboard kind of shield to separate me and my notes from the players so they do not cheat and read the notes. I liked being there behind my magic screen where no one could know the extent of the stories I had

52

worked up for them. And yes sometimes I would change the story
I had written on the spot if I had an Idea I liked better. I
never got caught and besides if it makes for a better story for
my friends then what is the harm. Although doing that taught me
a sloppy habit for lying because now I know it is much better
just to invent a whole story top to bottom beforehand and stick
with it. It's an awful lot of stuff to remember if you are
changing the story up all the time.

Whenever a game was all finished though my friends would
not be mad at me for setting up the hard traps and monsters and
challenges because it was just my job to do that and they would
say that they enjoyed the challenges and being frustrated when
they died and having to go back and try again and figure it all
out. And once they had eventually beaten the dungeon which
would usually take about six or seven hours we would just go do
something else where we were all equal and normal friends again
and I would be very proud of the fun story world I had created
for my friends to play in. And because I was the Dungeon Master
I always would get the first and hottest slice of Pepperoni
Pizza with the gooey stringy kind of waxy cheese that looked
and tasted exactly like the pizza that the Ninja Turtles ate in
the cartoon. That is if we got pizza.

We got pizza most Saturday nights that we played
Dungeons and Dragons but except when we were at Dean's house
because Dean's mom was the kind of mom who hated junk food and
video games and burps and basically who hated all fun and so we
did not get pizza from her we just got like just grilled
vegetables and rice and fish every single time and we were
always so very hungry when we got home. And so one day Dean
said to his mom Hey mom I love you but you are embarrassing me

in front of all my friends because we are eleven and this healthy dinner is fine for you but it's bullshit for us. That was the first time I ever heard the word bullshit and I didn't really know what it meant but then when Dean got grounded we all knew he had been brave.

Obviously all of that is now significant in hindsight and I realize now that I am still acting like the Dungeon Master inventing stories and a whole fantasy world that I am building as I go along and that Bob is working her way through my maze and story I have written and that I am re-writing for her every day and I wonder right now how it will end for Bob. Then I wonder if I really want Bob to figure her way out through my maze of tricks and traps and escape at the end or if I want her to be defeated by my stories and lose her way in the dungeon forever. With my friends I wanted them to make it through the dungeon safe and sound by the end but to have been challenged by me and my evil genius and to have died a few times.

Even though I had to be the outcast and the bad guy while we were playing still all my friends would become closer to each other because of the adventure and trials I put them through and so I thought that overall that was a worthy trade. For me to sacrifice myself and be a little bit hated just for a while if it meant I could put my friends through a struggle that brought them together after it was done then that was OK. But now I think it is weird though because in my real life now as a person who is twenty nine years old I feel like even though I am the one doing all the work and inventing the whole big dungeon piece by piece still everyone else I know acts like

they are so free and I am the only person I know who lives his
life trapped in a dungeon all the time.

And it is a tricky unfair lose-lose dungeon that I live
in with no way out for me I think sometimes. I realize that
there are definitely rules to the game of being a happy grownup
but I also feel like the game is rigged and there is no way I
can win it without cheating. Like my attribute rolls were so
weak when we made my character that I can either just be made
of failure for my whole life or I can cheat. So I do I cheat.

So anyway back to Bob and the dragon girl on Game of
Thrones I told Bob I wanted to watch an episode with her
because I had this plan and so I told her that because I've
read the books and she hasn't that I knew what was going to
happen in the next episode this Sunday and I wanted to see her
reaction to it in person so could I come over and watch it with
her and I would make and bring Hot Spiced Wine like they drink
on the show and we could watch it together and drink the Hot
Spiced Wine together and she said Yes we could and that made me
feel happy. So I made sure we both got pretty drunk on a few
goblets of the Hot Spiced Wine that I made and yes Bob owns
goblets. And the Wine I made had cloves and orange peel and
honey and nutmeg and cardamom and plenty of Brandy in it but
Bob did not necessarily need to know that last detail about the
Brandy. And then we settled down together to watch the show and
we were both pretty loaded by then and it was just nice to
settle together on the couch shoulder to shoulder with dear
Bob. I mean I would have liked better to put my arm around her
but it was just nice to be excited together that the big show
was just about to come on. It was also nice to not feel totally

55

responsible for making up the whole story for once and just be told one by someone else.

The HBO logo came on and said KRSHHH-ahhhhhh and I wanted so much to put my arm around Bob and hold her bare white shoulder and give her a peck on her cheek but I didn't because she is not my girlfriend and I would be basically a rapist if I kissed her on the cheek just because I liked her a little extra just then and then I got very angry because why do I feel like such a rapist for thinking Bob is amazing and wanting to just kiss her and tell her that I love her.

But anyway before I could get to the bottom of that the dragon girl came on on TV and she even had clothes on for once which was perfect for this and so then I said Wow I think that dragon girl is so very beautiful what do you think about her Bob. And Bob said

Yeah she is.

And so Bob was happy about that because she figured she must be mistaken in thinking that I said the dragon girl had a weird face and she also figured she must not have told me she thinks she looks like the dragon girl herself. So overall she thought it was like a nice little secret she could have with herself that I had accidentally just called her beautiful and only she knew that that was what I had done.

So yes it was a lie but it was actually a nicer thing to do for Bob than if I had just flat out said Hey Bob you are so beautiful. Because if I had just said Bob I think you're very beautiful then she would think

Oh no he's going to try to ask me to be his girlfriend again or try to fuck me.

And so then Bob would not have been able to just enjoy being called beautiful because being my girlfriend or fucking me must be like the worst thing she can imagine apparently but this way she can just enjoy being called beautiful and not have to worry about those so awful things like letting me try to make her happy. And so it was a lie but it was still more kind of me to lie I think. You see everyone takes pleasure in having their little secrets. It's not always awful and bad. And this lie just made Bob feel beautiful like the dragon girl and she is beautiful and doesn't get told it often enough even no matter how often she gets told it and so what is the harm honestly.

She knows I want her to be my girlfriend though but she says I'm too serious and she just wants to date fun guys who aren't serious and that she is not even sure she wants a relationship that is serious ever and she says we couldn't start dating because we know each other so well and so deeply that it would be a full on relationship right away and I'm like Yeah sounds basically great to me let's give it a shot but I guess Bob says no to that.

But I keep trying to get her to be my girlfriend anyway because I am in love with Bob probably or yes we decided definitely and since when was being in love with someone something to be so afraid and ashamed of but I am ashamed of it I guess and afraid. But I can't just keep telling her things I love about her to her face because she's tired of hearing about how I think she's beautiful and smart and amazing at least when I just come right out and say it and even if I come up with a really beautiful or well written way to say it she is still

tired of hearing it. So I have to kind of disguise it with
things like the dragon girl lie.

I think Bob is dumb for that. If a girl that I thought
was not hot but who I thought was still basically cool kept
telling me that she thinks I am handsome and smart and amazing
even if I did not want to date her I would not get tired of
hearing those things from her it would please me I think but it
annoys Bob. But I guess Bob is just not perfect like that and
then I don't know if I am a bad person for having there be one
or two little things about Bob that I do not much care for.
Because on the one hand I am supposed to love her for her flaws
right. I mean that's the phrase is Love her FOR her flaws not
Love her DESPITE her flaws. But that's dumb why would I love
flaws. So yeah why is it so bad to just say Yes I like Bob very
much AND there are a couple of things she does that make me
feel annoyed at her but overall yes I love her so much that I
don't mind the annoying things when they come along because
they happen rarely and they are not super serious when you
compare it to how much I like her for the other things.

Like that sounds healthy and honest to me but I guess it
is bad and not romantic and not the right thing to say and so I
am bad I guess. Besides who the hell am I to talk about healthy
and honest. But still I just feel like the whole unconditional
love thing is another big lie loads of people tell or pretend
to believe in. But like why is unconditional love so great of a
thing anyway I mean loving someone no matter what they do like
literally no matter what even if they went on a murderous
rampage or one day woke up and started kicking your dog and
calling him names no way would you still love them. You would
have to be psychotic to still love them through all of that.

Like I love Bob very much but if she suddenly started being too mean or lame of a person I would be like See you later Bob good luck with all of that and I would get over her and why does that make me such a bad person. But it does I guess and I am a bad person. Or I don't know.

I still hope we'll come back from the bar one night and I'll kiss her and she'll kiss me back and then she'll let me fuck her and it will be very good and then we will take a long hot shower together followed by a naked nap spooning in the sunlight while we are still wet from the shower and then when we wake up she will now be my girlfriend. Of course I will have to work on the whole being more fun thing. That will be a lot harder for me than fixing or tweaking my stories for Bob.

Or we could be like one of those stories you hear about where two best friends reach like thirty five or something and just say Oh the hell with it dating is stupid and being best friends with your husband or wife is a whole lot better than what a lot of couples have going on so let's just go ahead and be married. But I don't want to have to wait that long and I admit I want to have sex with Bob right now because even though I will probably like her more and more over time I mean it's not bad to admit that she probably has the best body right now that she will ever have and I would like to enjoy it right now.

I say that's not bad to admit but obviously I feel like the worst person on earth for having just thought about fucking Bob at all and even worse on top of that for wanting to fuck Bob while her body is at its best.

Bob and I have kissed each other before a few times and kind of rolled around touching each other over the clothes but that's all we've done before she said

Stop it is better if we should be friends only I think.

FIVE

I think a lot about what Bob would be like in bed and if she's
loud or quiet and what positions she likes and stuff. I just
think a lot about Bob in general and I think about sex a lot
too in general and so there is naturally going to be overlap on
that Venn diagram but Bob also makes me think about sex even
more than usual so.

So here we are still at the bar and I order another
Whiskey Diet and I do not order Maker's Mark On The Rocks even
though that is my favorite Drink. Bob is always saying how life
is so short and I should say Yes to more things than I say No
to and that I say No to too many Maybes. And she says I am an
old stick in the mud and if there is a question in my mind
about whether or not to go for something I want which maybe I
could get it and maybe I couldn't that I should try to say Yes
more often instead of No and just see what happens. Of course
she says that while I'm the one who's written things and gotten
them published and Bob has done nothing ever but be cute.

And also it's all well and good for her to tell me that
but the only thing I want that maybe I could or couldn't get is
Bob but she gets all weird when I make a move or like ask her
out like that is the one exception to her rule is when it comes
to her. So she is either a hypocrite or dating me is like a
hands down nightmare scenario for Bob to be avoided at all
costs.

Either way I am feeling angry about this whole situation
now and so I decide to do just like always and I settle for
what is easy and old habit. And so I get a Whiskey Diet and not
a Maker's Mark on the Rocks like I really want. Holy shit

apparently I am all kinds of bitter right now I had better
change the subject. Of my mind.

Bob asks me what I did last night and this morning and I
lie and I say I did some reading and some writing and I did
some exercise. I did read but I only read the internet just
like random blogs and stuff and especially this one girl's
tumblr I found that has a lot of sad pictures and stuff about
Satanism and witches and black metal which it's not like I'm
actually into any of that stuff seriously it was just
interesting. Although I do like black metal because it is the
loneliest music I think that ever has been made is black metal
music from Norway but anyway it was still addicting to read
this tumblr and interesting to think that like this very bleak
and sad tumblr is a window into this girl's whole world and she
might be sad and have a real darkness like me. So last night I
read her whole tumblr in one night and it was like three
hundred pages of these pictures and animated gifs and poems. So
yeah I tell Bob that I did some reading which is not untrue but
it's misleading so it's a lie. It's not like I read a good book
or even the news or anything but that is what I want her to
think I mean when I say I did some reading.

I didn't really write at all either. I wrote the sad
Satan tumblr girl a message because oh and she lives here in LA
too and so I was thinking it might be fun to be sad together
with her and maybe have sex if we feel like doing that but I
didn't say the part about sex obviously and my message was
pretty well written but you still can't really call that
writing because it doesn't get anything important done or
achieved and I know that I meant for Bob to think I was saying
I wrote stuff for my new book when I said I did some writing.

I do have a new book I am writing though. The protagonist of my new book is also a writer we will call him whatever name how about Dan then OK so are you with me the protagonist in the book is named Dan. And Dan is a writer too and he writes a book about a guy who meets a girl and she is just the perfect girl OK so Dan makes up and writes this imaginary perfect girl. I made up Dan and Dan made up the girl. Sorry it's confusing and a little too Inception here but bear with me. Yo dawg I heard you like writers LOL.

And in Dan's book the main character and the perfect girl they meet on the subway and they fall in love but then she dies tragically at the end of the book and this book that Dan wrote is like the best and saddest book ever written. So it is about to be published and be the best book ever but then Dan is on the subway on his way to deliver the final manuscript to the publisher but then he meets the girl from his book. Like not someone very similar to her like 100% actually her like the perfect girl he invented. So now Dan has to choose between having the best story ever but his perfect girlfriend dies at the end or he can sell out and change the ending so she doesn't die and he will get to be with her forever but he will have a book with a cheated and dishonest happy ending. I think it's an OK idea really. But yeah I didn't work on that last night either I just messaged this girl about being sad.

And I didn't do any exercising like I told Bob. But I'm on this new pill that is called an ECA Stack that's basically just legal speed but it's supposed to be for dieting which I don't care about it just makes you focus crazy hard which I do need because I have trouble concentrating but the extra weight loss part of it is as good as exercising so I say I exercised.

I have no objections to a little weight loss because you can't
drink as much as I do and not get some belly going on even
though I am generally average body but one stereotype about LA
that is true is that you have to be skinny to be valid so. This
medicine also has good effects on my orgasms but I really feel
like I am talking like way way way too much about sex stuff so
I am sorry about that it is bad to talk about it. I meant to
use the extra concentration from the pills to work on the new
book but instead I just focused on that one girl's sad tumblr
all night and I had red Wine to take the edge off the speed
pill that is called an ECA Stack because red Wine seems like
the most brooding thing to drink and I was surprised I could
not think of a more Brooding Drink than that other than like
Absinthe but that stuff is needlessly expensive and doesn't
make you trip at all I'm sorry.

So before Bob asks me specific questions about that
stream of lies I just told I change the subject and I ask Bob
what she did today and she read two entire books already just
today one non-fiction about like politics or something and one
fiction and she says I should read the fiction one. Something
Japanese she says it is good and that a character reminds her
of me but she won't tell me which one I have to read it and
figure it out or guess. I know this is supposed to be cute and
fun and it would be cute and fun except now I am afraid what if
the character that reminds Bob of me is a total jerk or even
worse a liar and this is her elaborate way of telling me she
knows about my lying and Oh No. And also what if I make a
mistake and say Oh is the character that reminds you of me this
character X and he is not me at all but then Bob reacts badly
to that and what if I get the wrong answer so now I am afraid

of this entire scenario. Bob didn't bring the book to lend it to me though because Bob read it in actual Japanese and I don't read or speak any Japanese. Bob is totally the kind of person who teaches herself Japanese just as an intellectual like trophy. I called her out on that once and she got so mad and defensive I knew I was right. And that was just a little bit nice to just for once have a one up on Bob rather than the usual of me being prepared to roll over if she ever asked me to. Bob reads lots of books like six or eight a week if they're short or medium. I like that she does that because then she recommends the best ones to me and sometimes lends them to me and she also tells me the names of books she reads that were not good and that way I don't have to read bad books. I have lots of books on my shelves at my house but I'm afraid one of them will be bad if I read it so I don't read them and I only read the ones Bob tells me I will like and I always do love them or at least like them. I shouldn't be so afraid of books being bad I guess. I think to myself that Bob recommending me a terrible book on purpose would hurt my feelings a lot more than Bob finding out about me and lying. That's a lie there's no way that's true the whole lying coming out thing would be awful.

Bob asks me if I want to go outside the bar and smoke a cigarette and I say I do even though that's a lie too. I just had one. But I want to be with Bob all the time so I say I do. Bob puts white cardboard coasters over the tops of our Drinks to protect them from being taken away but just now the guy in the corner just gave me a very weird look. So I am thinking about roofies because this guy looks totally rapey and I say Hey Bob let's just finish our Drinks right now and she says

You're right good call.

And I can tell she saw him look at me really weirdly too. So I know Bob is thinking roofies as well and so we do that we finish our Drinks now and make for the door. The bartender nods down at the Drinks and looks at me as if to ask Do we want another one waiting for us and I shake my head and I say In a minute. And I make a smoking sign with my hands. I feel stupid for this because both the bartender and I are making hand signals as if the bar is too loud to talk but it is not loud at all and we are like five feet away from each other so we could totally hear each other. There is a little music but it is pretty quiet overall and it is the piano part at the end of Layla which everyone forgets is there and then it's always like Oh no it's the ten minute long piano part I only put this on the jukebox because of the beginning awesome part.

For some reason Bob putting the coasters on the tops of our Drinks makes me think of the tops of Bob's breasts in her dress again and as we are walking out I look at them again and they are still great.

We get outside and she goes into her bag which is this sort of giant brown satchel that I call the alchemist's bag because it has loads of little pouches on the inside which to me look like they should be for reagents and potions and herbs and things. In a way it is an alchemist's bag because one pouch is for cigarettes and she keeps pot and papers in another one if she's smoking pot these days and always a flask of Whiskey in another one because you never know. But she just takes out the cigarettes this time and they are Marlboro 27's which are our favorite cigarettes. We like it that the description on the box says they are Smooth Rich and Mellow because we joke that smooth rich and mellow are good things to be. And they taste good and they smoke pretty fast and they don't make your mouth taste horrible afterwards or your fingers smell bad. I mean they're still cigarettes but they are not as bad as other kinds.

So Bob puts one in her mouth and gives me her lighter to light her cigarette for her because she knows I like to do little things like that for her. I like to do those little chivalrous things like lighting her cigarettes and holding her doors and chairs and take her out to dinner sometimes. She doesn't let me take her out too often though because then she thinks I might think we're dating or that she's even open to that idea and again that is a fate worse than death obviously. It's nice of her to let me do these little nice boy girl things with her and that makes me love her a lot now realizing how nice it is of her because it's basically a little bit dumb of me to be old fashioned and stuff so it's nice that she lets me be that way even if it sort of is agony too because I wish it was for real and we were dating. So I light her cigarette and then she lights mine because then that is part of her cute thing of being a kind of tomboy named Bob like sometimes she bes the guy and I be the girl which it is kind of fun to play around with that stuff.

We hear this noise like a bunch of drunk people who don't know they're as drunk as they are and so they're shouting without realizing it and we look behind me and a big crowd is coming. They're all hipsters and old people and so Bob and I realize it must be Art Walk. Art Walk is this thing that happens downtown where lots of shops and galleries open their doors and have special exhibitions and people all walk from place to place looking at all the art and there is sometimes

music or like local artisanal craft organic something or other
food that obviously tastes awful but it has no carbon footprint
and one time Bob said

That's fine but it tastes like carbon toejam. And I
loved her for saying that. And people drink a whole lot too at
Art Walk because some bars have special deals but I know that
Bob and I are safe today because our awesome bar would never do
something special for stupid Art Walk.

It maybe sounds like Art Walk is OK but the art is
always really bad like literally always completely pretentious
trend chasing and not good at all and everyone lies and says it
is good because they don't want to admit they wasted their day
looking at awful art. And then they find themselves going again
and again to Art Walk every single month all just because they
don't want to admit it sucked the first time. And that lie
makes me feel angry and Bob agrees Art Walk is dumb and so we
don't go to Art Walk any more.

I saw one painting that I liked though one time on Art
Walk and it was done in charcoal and it was of a guy kneeling
and leaning all the way backwards so he was holding his ankles
and he was naked and he was hard and like he was in the middle
of the picture and on the left side there was a sad looking
Asian girl who was also naked and she was on all fours in front
of him like she was about to go down on him and she was looking
up at his face like hopefully but sadly or something but he was
looking over his shoulder behind him at a doorway that had a
silhouette in it and the silhouette was of another woman
walking away. I know it's weird and gay of me to say I liked a
picture of a guy who is naked and has an erection but I liked
how the painting reminded me of myself kind of because I think

68

maybe there are nice women right in front of me who maybe want to be nice to me but all I want is Bob who's walking away. Like I'm not even talking about women who want to be sexual with me but just be genuinely nice to me as a person and give something of themselves to me and accept something real of me into their lives. But it's no use because all I can be hard for and think about is Bob who will never love me or go down on me or let me love her and so I keep looking over my shoulder hoping for Bob but Bob is going out the door and leaving me so. And I decided that painting was both kind of sad and also kind of sexy which is my favorite kind of sexy is when it's also kind of sad.

Later that night I saw the guy the painting was of. He was walking around the gallery with the Asian girl who was on all fours in the painting and she was very happy she was with him now in the gallery but he didn't look happy to be with her and I looked at his eyes and he saw me and we knew we were both sad about something and I smiled just a little but I realize he probably thought I was gay and wanted to fuck him which makes sense because the first thing you look at in the painting could only be the penis because I mean it was right there it was like the main thing in the painting and so why would someone look at this guy smiling now other than to be like Hey dude nice penis I would like to touch it or something.

He looked away from me and then that was a different kind of sad to me because when he looked at me Bob was with me and I think he then maybe thought Bob was my beautiful girlfriend and he felt like he was the only lonely person in the whole world when the truth is Bob was not my girlfriend but I am aching for her to be that but she is walking away just like the girl in the painting who I guess is his version of

69

Bob. I hoped like maybe us knowing that we both had a Bob that was walking away would make us both feel a little bit less sad and lonely about that but we never said anything and he went away with the Asian girl feeling like the loneliest person there ever was. When I brought Bob over to look at the painting she just laughed at it because of the penis.

Back outside the bar now the crowd of drunk people walk past us and they are very drunk and loud and laughing and saying things like I hope it is better than last time and What time is Jacob's band playing and Do you have any pot and Where are we even going. Bob and I are quiet and still and we lean up against the wall of the bar trying not to be noticed and we just watch them go by and I drag on my cigarette a little extra hard and breathe the smoke out my nose which I hardly ever do because then I'll be stuffed up in my nose all day tomorrow but it feels really good now and it just felt like maybe a fun thing to do just now and so I did it.

We watch them leave and we try not to attract attention or look like we are outside of a great cheap dive bar because we don't want them all to come into our bar now and then have discovered it and start coming here again later and being loud and drunk or start talking to Bob and me and trying to fuck Bob and telling us not to talk about taking hallucinogenic drugs or not to talk about stuff about sex or not to talk about very very sad things or not to talk about nothing at all or not to drink so much.

Bob and I are successful at looking how we wanted to look and now they are gone and Bob rummages in the alchemist's bag for another cigarette which makes me feel happy because then that means we are going to smoke one more cigarette and

then go back inside and probably start really drinking more
heavily. It also probably means that we will play a drinking
game or a word game that involves drinking as well or we will
tell riddles and Bob has really good riddles and word games to
play and I think she even invents some of the games herself
which I think is really amazing of her and again I remember
Dungeons and Dragons and for some reason I wish I played
Dungeons and Dragons with Bob way back then. I feel myself
loving Bob even a little bit extra once the people have gone
past us and we are smoking the second cigarettes because I look
at Bob and she smiles.

I look at her and smile back and I know we are both
thinking the same thing that the bunch of drunk hipsters looked
like a shamble of zombies. We decided one day that there had
to be a word for a group of zombies that is not as big as a
horde because a horde has to be like a hundred zombies or at
least fifty but you have to have a word for under fifty
zombies. And so we came up with that it should be called a
shamble of zombies because you only ever really say that drunk
people and zombies are the only things that shamble really and
that is a good collective noun for zombies is a shamble of
zombies.

And so I feel myself loving Bob a little extra right now
because I look at her and we look at the people shambling away
and I know we both think

zombies.

SIX

It is evening now and I am going into the subway alone because
I was at the bar and I got up to use the bathroom and suddenly
I was completely wasted and needed to go home. Like honestly
right now I feel twice as drunk as I should be for the amount
of Drinks I ordered and yet amazingly I am still wide awake and
really horny over Bob and the tops of her breasts and so I
decided to go home and not be around her any more and so I lied
to Bob at the bar and told her I feel like I want to write and
that I had good ideas while we were drinking and being quiet
together so thank you Bob but now I have to write them on my
own. Bob said I could write at her home if I like and she likes
watching me write and being with me while I do that and she
just reads or paints or naps while I write and it is nice for
her. I do not like to do that with Bob because I really do want
to do that with Bob but with her as my lover or girlfriend or
partner or whatever.

OK so this one time Bob had people over and we all got
drunk and played Truth or Dare. You'd think the Truth part of
that game would make me afraid or at least that I would always
do the Dare but I like doing the Truth. It's freeing.

Anyway this guy named Clay got the question What is your
ultimate sex fantasy. And he said some stuff about a
cheerleader lesbian threesome or something and I think it was
actually a lie for him to say that and that he was just saying
that because it is not a risky thing to say as your fantasy. No
one would hear that fantasy and be like Dude your fantasy is
weird and gay. But then again what do I know that might have
been his honest fantasy. I mean after all a threesome with
cheerleaders must only be a clichéd fantasy because lots of

people have had that fantasy I guess. Maybe I am as usual being
a snob and hating on someone with a pedestrian sex fantasy
Jesus I'm a piece of work.

But anyway it got me thinking what my ultimate sex
fantasy would be and it is such a lame fantasy but it is my
real fantasy and it is that Bob and I spend the morning and
afternoon working on our own projects in the same big room
which would be Bob's huge empty living room and we would be
drinking something nice together like Champagne or Mint Juleps
or even just espresso and smoking cigarettes and we would smile
at each other every once in a while but not really interrupt
each other just work on our projects and be together sharing
our energy but leaving each other mostly alone. And then once
it was like lunch time we would check in and see if we had
gotten enough done and we would say Yes! And then we would have
sex all afternoon right there on the floor in the middle of the
empty apartment in between our project stations like three or
four times in a row while we're still high off our creative
energy and then we would take a long hot shower together
followed by a naked nap spooning in the sunlight while we are
still wet from the shower.

But I did not get that question for Truth or Dare I got
something about having to pick a celebrity to sleep with and
where would I come on them. I thought that question was pretty
seedy but I guess that's the point of why other people enjoy
Truth or Dare I have no idea. I think I went with Alison Brie
and on her breasts which I think look like a 34C to me. I am
glad I did not get the ultimate fantasy question though because
my fantasy is really gay I guess or not gay obviously but it's
like sentimental and weird and personal and intimate and so it

is a bad fantasy to have for two reasons. One because it's not like super macho and two it sounds really dumb to have my honest ultimate sex fantasy be something that's so totally possible for me to have. Like it doesn't involve like four gymnasts in zero gravity dressed up as Disney princesses or anything. And also like the point of the Truth or Dare is not actually honesty but fun. Like I sometimes feel like when I answer a Truth question I am missing the point because I actually take the term Truth or Dare at face value and I answer honestly. Like if I got the ultimate fantasy question I would tell people about my honest real fantasy even though I think I'm just supposed to invent something weird.

Like OK everyone in the room would be asked the same question: what is your sex fantasy. And I would answer the question I was asked but everyone else would answer another question instead: Invent a porn you would whack it to. And that is the question they answer. UHH duh huh huh I'd do all Charlie's Angels at once. And someone would make a HILARIOUS joke about Bosley watching from the corner. Shut the fuck up. Again how is it that I'm the one being more honest than everyone else.

Although I guess in a way some ludicrous porno fantasy is probably more likely to happen than my ever having Bob. But anyway that is not a lie the art thing is my favorite thing possible to think of in terms of sex.

Anyway I don't want to write with Bob today because I am already horny over her and I don't want to set myself up for more aching and so I told her I kind of want to be alone now to write and that I will probably be up all night long writing too and Bob says

74

OK. Because Bob needs a lot of sleep at night whereas I sleep more in the morning and can't usually sleep soundly at night. It's especially bad if I have been drinking because the other bad person who is inside me who I should really get a name for him but the mean person who calls me names and reminds me I'm lame and bad well he comes out way more strongly at night and also when I have been drinking so I cannot usually sleep at night because he is there being awful to me. So overall I just don't sleep a lot like probably ten hours a week or so. But it's OK because that way I get a lot done even if it is just reading or watching movies or the internet.

So anyway I told Bob And besides I would only be distracted by a having a pretty girl around me. I had thought that would be a nice little no big deal kind of throwaway compliment to give to Bob which also would be true and not a lie. But it looked like she didn't even notice it so whatever. So she said OK and we hugged goodbye and then when we pulled away she kind of held on for a second extra too long and then she looked up at me with her blue eyes in this one particular sad way that she does sometimes and I know that that look means that I need to either kiss her or walk away and of course I walk away but I wish I had kissed her.

SEVEN

So now it is later and it is evening and I am going down into
the subway and I think wait is my metro month pass still good
and I look at my iPhone and it is the twenty seventh of this
month and so it is it is still good. I wait for my train to
come and put my headphones in even though I don't want to
listen to music I just don't want to be bothered by crazies. I
don't mind waiting for the train and I think it is a lie how in
movies whenever someone is going to get on the subway they
always just barely catch the train as the doors are closing.
You never see people just wait by themselves.

The train comes after like eight minutes and I get into
the train and I sit down and I don't feel tired at all which
surprises me because I drank like eight or ten Whiskey Diets
with Bob and we took one Shot of Jose Cuervo Silver to
celebrate that Bob had a good date with some musician last
night so we took the Shot and I immediately felt sick to my
stomach and not from the shot of Jose Cuervo Silver but from
Bob's news and so I had all those Drinks plus what did I say
four or five Bloody Maries or was it Mimosas with my eggs and
bacon and hash browns for breakfast and I have not eaten since
then so I should be sleepy as hell but I'm not. I am very drunk
but very awake also.

I think this must be because of this weight loss
medicine I'm on to lose some weight mostly but also to focus on
my writing that is called an ECA Stack because it's basically
just caffeine and speed and allergy medicine put together but
it's totally legal because I even got it off Amazon and you're
not supposed to drink any Alcohol with it but obviously I do
and I read on the internet that when you do that it adds up to

bad news and feels a little bit like ecstasy and that would explain why I could not stop being horny over and in love with Bob today and also full of awakeness and also full of feeling OK about myself. Relatively.

So I sit down on the seat in the metro and I smell some cheap cleaning solution that must have been used recently and at first it is actually a pleasant smell because it is the same cheap cleaner smell they used at my school when I was a kid — during the Dungeons and Dragons time and then I am sad remembering that I will never be as simply happy as I was then. I still am not tired and I look around to see if there are interesting or crazy people I should watch or be afraid of and there's really not. There's a skinny couple who are cute and they are dressed like hipsters but they don't look like total assholes so I think they are probably from France and they're kissing but not exactly making out so it's actually kind of cute and not needy and gross. There is a very fat man who is Mexican or something and he is sweating and there is a mom with a baby who are both Mexican too and the baby is in a stroller with groceries piled up on top of the baby and I nearly didn't see the baby under all those groceries until it moved and I thought it was just a stroller full of groceries at first but there is a baby under there. A celery falls out of the bag onto the baby and it says Bah.

None of this is interesting and I wish there were more interesting things to watch but I realize it's OK because I'm going back to Hollywood and there are always interesting things to watch there like punk rockers and people in costumes for no reason and trannies and tourists who are scared by the punk rockers and people in costumes and trannies and that is why I

live there is for the peoplewatching probably and also because
there are bars and restaurants I like to go to there and a good
movie theater. And I can walk places I do not have to drive
just to go get like toilet paper and a soda or whatever.

I do like my one movie theater there because it is
assigned seating so I get the seats I want ahead of time. I do
not mind going to the movies alone like a lot of people do I
like it because I can just be quiet and zone out in the dark
and it's not weird and it is anywhere I will not be called
weird for just sitting and not talking for two hours or more.
One time I went there and OK so before the movie starts a
person always comes out who is always like a high school
student or who knows these days even a film student but it's
usually young nerdy people and they work at the theater and
they introduce the movie and tell you how long it is and to
turn off your noisy devices and stuff right. Well one time I
went to the movies alone and it was a matinee of a movie that
had been out forever but I hadn't seen it and so I was the only
one in the movie theater at like noon and this girl comes out
she's not really cute but kind of nerdy cute I guess like I
would want her as my friend more than I am thinking about
fucking her right now but anyway she's like nineteen so off
limits anyway. Or is she because it's half your age plus seven
is the youngest you can date which I am twenty eight so
fourteen OK twenty one is the youngest so yes she is off
limits.

But anyway there's this weird moment where it's just me
and her and so it's this awkward moment where I imagine that
she's thinking like Do I really have to do my welcome speech
for just one dumb lonely dude right now fuck my life. And so I

am trying to think up a joke to say to her basically saying she doesn't have to do the speech for just stupid little me but before I can think of what to say she just looks at me and bursts into tears crying full on bawling and I am not sure what to say to this and so for some reason what comes out of my mouth is to say

Me too.

And she nodded and she came up to me and hugged me and then she ran away and the movie started and I never saw her again I assume she quit her job or at least was hiding in the bathroom or something until I left. I know that sounds like the beginning scene of like a sad hipster movie but it's not it really happened. But I still might make that the first scene of something. Then I was afraid during the movie though because I felt like the projectionist might have seen that interaction and is now sitting up in the booth looking at the back of my head thinking bad things about me. So I left halfway through and so I have still never seen No Country For Old Men even though obviously I told everyone I did see it because for some reason I was very embarrassed by this story about the girl. I felt like for some reason it was evidence of my badness.

But anyway I like this theater because it is assigned seating so I can stay in the seat I wanted no matter what. Like at other theaters I will get there early so I can get the seat I want and then some like Jappy high school girls come in a group of like ten and want me to move to a bullshit seat because they are late and there are ten of them and they still want to sit together. But at my theater that I like I can just be like No sorry it's assigned seating it's the rules. And that way I'm not as huge a dick for saying No to these girls as I would be if it was not assigned seating. So I like my neighborhood I guess.

I get out of the metro into Hollywood at Hollywood and Vine and a song comes into my head about Hollywood and Vine and I think it's a Kid Rock song and I don't like that song at all but I still think of it and sing it in my head whenever I see Hollywood and Vine and then that makes me feel angry and a little bit afraid and right now yeah it does it makes me feel angry and a little bit afraid to remember that song. And then I realize that I will remember that scary song every time I see my own metro stop so that is pretty bad.

OK sorry that thing about the girl crying in the movies never happened I made it up. I really left No Country For Old Men halfway through because that movie fucking sucks I'm sorry it's 100% Emperor's New Clothes and Javier Bardem didn't even act let alone Best Actor level act because he just had a dumb haircut and everyone was like Wow over that. But that means it's OK to use that story about the crying girl in a movie or book so.

It is night time now which I am happy about because the sun and heat were bothering me when we were standing outside the bar smoking and now it is cooler. There is no breeze which is a shame but at least it is cooler. I think that the bars I go to will be quieter tonight because a lot of people will be going to Art Walk tonight and not going to my bars here and so I wonder what bar do I most want to go to since I will fit at any bar tonight.

The Druid is walking down the street towards me and OK so The Druid is my name for this homeless guy who lives here who is this awesome old black guy who wears like gypsy robes and a cowl and has loads of trinkets and bones and stuff and he has this big wooden staff that has like beads and gourds and stuff hanging off of it and he often is smoking a joint right there on the street and not even giving a single fuck who knows it and when he asks for money he is always super polite and friendly and not scary or rude and so basically he is awesome. Sometimes I do give him money which normally I never give homeless people any money and I do not have a concrete reason for not giving them money other than that I just don't. I tell people that at Christmas I give a big sum to the local homeless shelter and that is my contribution to the problem of homeless but that's a lie. I don't give shit. But today I get up next to The Druid and he makes like he is about to say something to me which I assume is he is going to ask for money so I start reaching for my wallet because I feel like randomly giving him five bucks but instead he says to me

Any good dreams have you lately, boss?

And I kind of start to say

What?

To him because I'm wasted and what the hell does that mean but he just laughs and keeps walking and then a few seconds later I hear him laughing still but it is a friendly kind of laugh not a mean laugh. Then he says or I think this is what he says anyway because he is far away and I am wasted but I think he says

Coyotes comin'.

I look behind me as he goes and I stumble a little bit over a star that is on the ground you know how in Hollywood they have stars in the cement with famous people's names in it and this one is James Cagney's and it is chipped so I trip over it. Now I have to admit to myself that I am really very drunk and so I should be more careful and so I decide to go somewhere that has good beers and carby food where I can drink slower and chill out a little bit and have a bite and then probably I will pretend to be happy so I can try to have sex with someone much later since it is early still and I'm not really tired so I should try to have sex.

I am supposed to go to a thing in Santa Monica tonight for my agent Lawrence he wants me to meet with this TV guy who thinks I'm a good writer and wants to talk to me tonight because if I am good at talking to him one on one tonight he will put me on his talk show in a week or two where I can talk about whatever I want. Obviously that means I can plug my books which I hate doing and besides going on those shows is not really talking on the spot because the guy would insist that we write the things we would talk about beforehand. Which I know making up lies and then making them sound authentic and spontaneous that sounds right up my alley right. But it's not up my alley I am terrified of this idea. And my agent says that this whole dog and pony show would be good for me because lots of smart young people watch this one guy's talk show and they would then buy my books and anticipate my next one but I know I don't watch this guy's show that's for sure except I watched a clip on Hulu just to see what the deal was and it was really stupid and phony and blatantly scripted and to be totally honest the guy is kind of not smart but pretends to be and I think it might be some kind of trap like I am being brought on as a trick to embarrass me or maybe he knows my secret about lying and he secretly plans to expose me on live TV to watch me die of shame and so I am not going to go. And also Santa Monica is always too far to go for anything. And also also like hell I'm getting behind the wheel of a car right now I am way too drunk and if I take the bus that will take forever and I will have to pee before I get there and I'm not taking two separate buses or one fifty dollar cab to that nonsense and then again later to come home so yeah totally forget it I'm staying in my neighborhood tonight.

I think I should maybe go home and not go out tonight because I stumble a little again over nothing this time just my own feet. And lighting a cigarette is like impossible right now and so I am afraid because I might make a scene somewhere or fall off of a bar stool or fuck up a lie to someone important and get in real trouble so I decide no I should go home and I have some Netflix at home. I do not remember what movies they are so that could be OK. So I do I make the decision to go home wondering what The Druid meant.

This medicine is interesting I think and I definitely feel kind of like I am on speed or at least like what I imagine speed is like because I have never even taken speed and I don't actually even know for sure what drug people mean when they say speed. I think speed means meth but yeah I would never do meth because I mean Jesus are you fucking serious meth what is this Hicksville or Breaking Bad. But anyway whatever speed means I do know that I am not really feeling tired even though I'm wasted. And my body does not hurt like it usually does like usually I have a sore back and my legs would be a little tired from walking around today and I always have a headache which I still do but it's not as bad as usual and so I feel pretty good about all that.

I try to repeat out loud what The Druid said which was Any good dreams have you lately? And I am trying to like understand that sentence. Like is he trying to talk in like Olde English or something like you know like What have you for sale today merchant. Then I'm like Oh wait no it's like some hippie shit. Meaning like am I actually the imaginary thing that is being imagined by my dream and my dream is the real thing. Like when I think I'm dreaming the truth is that there is a sort of interdimensional convergence like the Real Person I dream about is dreaming of me and he lives in Real Life all the time and I am the illusion and I live in this photo-negative shadow world but we see each other and each other's worlds when we both dream.

I try to say this sentence out loud: I am the real person. But when I try to say it what comes out is not even real words it's just sounds and so I decide yeah no it is time to go home.

I get home and log on and there is an email from the sad tumblr girl through last.fm which is what I messaged her through because we were at the same black metal concert last week and although I did not actually see her there last.fm says we were both there so I used that as an intro to my message to her. But the message back from her is her saying she thinks I'm full of shit and I am pretending to be very sad and like dark and brooding just to try to meet up with her and probably try to fuck her so I should fuck off and if I come up to her at a show she'll kick me in the nuts. I can't decide if this is her honestly saying fuck off or if this is like a test to see if I'm really interested or not. I kind of like that she is not interested in fakers but then I mean that's exactly what I am so I don't really know how to proceed. I get this reaction a lot because I actually have a lot in common emotion wise with like goth people and black metal chicks so I try to talk to them but they think I am just a tourist into their world because I do not have tattoos or dress like I am from Marilyn Manson or The Nightmare Before Christmas and so they think I am a phony and react badly. But I'm sure I could tell them a thing or two about what being sad is all about.

So I write a message back to this girl and I lie to her and say I'm not trying to fuck her she just seems interesting and deep. And actually it's true that she seems interesting and deep and I do like sad things and I would like to talk to her about those things and about black metal especially about the bands Wolves in the Throne Room and Agalloch I would like to talk about. Bob does not like any heavy metal let alone black metal so it would be nice to talk to someone about them.

But then I think to myself also that this sad tumblr girl is also really very pretty even if she has very small breasts I would guess they are like a 30B. And she is really gorgeous in a Russian looking way and so maybe I was sort of trying to at least meet her and see if we might hit it off and maybe one day have sex and honestly is that really all that bad of me to send a message to someone who I think is very pretty and who we have similar interests. But I guess that Yes it must be very bad of me because I feel like the worst person in the world for this. And besides it would never work. I mean come on Bob knows about all the things that are truly the best about me and none the less dating me is like a fate worse than death for her so why should this sad tumblr girl want to date me. Only stupid girls I don't even love want to go to bed with me and

then I think that this kind of bitterness about girls only
comes out when I am drunk and oh yeah I am drunk as all hell so
oh yeah that explains that. But I should not be online while I
am this drunk because who knows what could happen. Waking up to
the internet after a night of being really drunk is so scary
because what mistakes did I make. One time I woke up and went
to the computer and there was a full confession email all typed
out to Bob with even her email address in it and I have no
memory of writing it and all I would have had to is hit send
and it would be all over.

But anyway I say some things back to this girl that are
not a lie about how meaningless and alien I think existence
feels most of the time and I say to her some of the things Bob
and I talked about about sadness and I tell her about this book
to read called The Outsider and I don't mean the Camus novel
but it's a non-fiction book by Colin Wilson about the role of
like tortured outsiders in literature and I haven't read it yet
because it looks like a little too close to home for me
personally and it looks like a hard book but Bob gave it to me
and told me to read it because it reminded her of me so I have
it on my shelf where it sits there for me to be afraid of it.
So I tell this sad tumblr girl she should read it and I will
lend it to her and I lie and I say I've read it and it's good
and my line is

Let's meet up for coffee or a Drink and if she still
thinks I'm full of shit after a half hour she can leave and
I'll never talk to her again and she can keep this book as well
so what do you say.

But then I don't like how she's already talking to me
about lying and being a fake though and that is just too soon

and too dangerous frankly and there are other sad girls to meet
in the world and so I don't send the email and just delete her
email and then I go into my regular email which is kind of a
scary place to me because it's only ever full of more stuff I
have to take care of like it's never some nice surprise.

I am also always afraid that my email will have someone
from my past catching up to me to punish me or it is Bob saying
she figured me out and she's telling everyone and never talk to
her again or maybe she is telling me she is getting married or
something. But there is nothing like that tonight there is just
waste of time bullshit which sometimes trivial stuff makes me
feel way angrier than like dread or this dark other person who
lives inside me. I go through and delete spam emails from the
people I sort of keep around even though I am only kind of
friends with them and I delete those emails because they're
stupid links to things like internet memes from like months ago
and evites to parties that sound like my worst nightmare and
like celebrity gossip news and I think who even cares about any
of that but I do click on one link from Bob that's about the
girl from Paramore because I think the girl from Paramore is
really cute and she sort of reminds me a little bit of like a
Warped Tour version of Bob with smaller breasts like 30A
breasts probably but they both have a kind of toothy grin that
I like and think is cute and so I click on the link and the
girl from Paramore is very hot in it. It is also hot to me that
Bob sends me links to pictures of the girls she knows I think
are hot because it's just cute and I like thinking that Bob is
helping me get off but then I also realize it's sad because I
don't want Bob's role in my sex life consisting of her sending

me pictures of the Paramore girl. I want Bob's role in my sex life to consist of having sex with me.

I realize that I'm still horny over Bob and so I decide to take care of myself but not to the Paramore girl just to the imagination of Bob in her sea green dress with her 34C breasts coming out over the top of her dress and I think it's not evil of me to think about this because in the dream she's my wife actually and we're in love and we really really love each other and so it's OK for me to be made happy by thinking about having sex with my beautiful wife Bob who loves me right back. I said dream but I just mean fantasy because I am awake although only barely.

I mean please let's not take seriously that thing about dreams that The Druid said. I mean it's 2011 and the man's job description is Druid. So we do not need to pay him much heed. Just respect for being an awesome homeless man.

I realize I've never thought about Bob as my wife before but I would marry Bob in a second flat except she has said lots of times that she doesn't think she wants to get married to anyone ever at all but I think I am still allowed to at least think about marring whoever I want and besides it's just a fantasy and it is my fantasy so let me do what I want to whom and shut up.

I was married one time already in real truth like honestly I was. I guess I'm still married technically. It was pretty nice to be married and I really liked my wife a bunch because she was smart and really mellow most of the time but also took no shit if you messed with her and she had incredible breasts and I realize now that I am talking way too much about breasts but whatever I know what I like and anyway my wife was

very very smart but she was like not super sharp if that makes
any sense. Or like she was not skeptical is the right word for
it and anyway so we were married for about a year when I was 22
to 24 I think and it was great but then she found out about my
lying because she stuck her nose in somewhere I never thought
she would and then she split up with me and then I had to move.
It sucks because I loved my wife. I mean like she never drove
me crazy with passion and aching and longing like Bob does but
she was a very dear friend to me and we never really fought
about anything other than circumstantial stuff that we got over
pretty quickly and we agreed on lots of like life issues and
child raising ideas and I thought she was really very sexy and
we had really excellent sex at a bare minimum of once a day and
so overall I think we could have made a very comfortable life
together I think. But no of course not because I'm awful.

I have moved around the country a lot since then because
I have had to start over in new places a lot of times but that
time I had to run away from my wife was the only time I
actually had to leave a place because I was exposed and it was
all so terrible that I just had to run away. And it is too bad
that that was the one place I had to leave forever because it
was also my home town and so I can't go home ever again. And
that's hard because I find myself feeling homesick a lot out
here even though I never really liked home in the first place
but I still would like to go back to somewhere safe. Now I
start feeling kind of sad and hopeless for being homesick for
somewhere that doesn't exist. I wanted to build a new home here
I guess or at least in theory but I don't see that happening
with Bob because she does not love me like that and I do not
want to be with anyone else so. I cried when I had to leave

home and that was the last time I cried ever. Like I have had to leave other towns and I have had people I know really die and like I said my life is just getting harder and sadder and less likely that it will ever get better but I can't cry even though I sit myself down and try to cry sometimes because the catharsis would feel really nice I think but no I cannot cry any more.

After I had to leave home for good and never come back I traveled around just me in my car driving in the desert for about a month or maybe six or seven months I don't know I was drinking an enormous volume of Whiskey but not Maker's Mark which is my favorite but Knob Creek which I like a lot but not quite as much. And then I kind of settled in this one nice small town I found myself in in Wisconsin for about a year where my story was that I was a stock broker who had gotten sick of the rat race in New York and just was looking for somewhere to start over and live an honest to goodness wholesome life. The details of that story were obviously lies but in a way the part about starting over was very honest.

While I was there I sobered up without even really trying to. Like no drugs at all and like just normal amount of Drinks like a Beer or Wine or two with dinner and then sometimes at barbecues we would all have several Beers and I found myself pretty good at pretending to be One Of The Guys with the guys there who were the age I was pretending to be and so we also had Scotch at poker night sometimes but anyway it was the most sober I've ever been like I was never really wasted for days and days. And I have to say it was pretty nice and I met this really sweet girl who was a soft redhead with deep sad black eyes and she really was a little sad for no real identifiable reason. She was just born a little bit sad just like me and just like Bob.

But she was also very hopeful and wanted very much to meet someone worth investing her trust and love in. And so here I come I am the stranger who made it big in terms of money but didn't want that because all he wanted was a straightforward life and some real affection. And of course I understood her sadness better than her family who were very very nice people but they just don't understand about darkness and so this girl and I we dated very very slowly which was OK by me I could use some slowness for once after a lifetime of running. After six months of dating this girl I was the first person she ever had sex with but don't worry it wasn't like a gross age gap like statutory situation I was twenty five and she was twenty one she just hadn't had sex yet and it was OK and legal OK.

She was probably the nicest person I'll ever meet before I die like just so sweet and nice and open to building a good life with a good partner. But then because of facebook and stuff my old wife and stuff caught up with me. And the new girl I was thinking about asking to be my new wife got really heart broken over that because she had never been in love with anyone before. But she had fallen in love with who she thought I was which of course she did because I made up my story to be exactly perfect for her and the character I created really did make her happy and the fact that I had crafted a whole life just to make this girl deliriously happy also made me happy too. Just like being a good Dungeon Master and just like Bob letting me light her cigarettes and so what was the harm because honestly I could have easily played the role of her husband for her and then eventually I would not be playing the role any more I would just be her real husband. Sure it would have been playing house a little bit but is that so bad. And we both could have been very happy and I liked her family and they liked me especially her older brother liked me and he is a super nice guy and I could have helped their cheese making business for a little while. Like I am not making this up they actually make cheese and if I was making this up I would pick a business that was not so totally clichéd and on the nose for a Wisconsin family to have. But I could have helped with that business and then done some writing on the side and had some kids with her and all of that whole thing but of course no something had to go wrong.

I just said Something had to go wrong like as if she got hit by lighting or a truck or something. 'Something' didn't go wrong. I went wrong. Nothing 'happened.' I happened. Like always. I was only caught because I was dumb and didn't think to delete my old facebook. I never went on it any more but of course it still existed and even though I didn't introduce myself to the new Wisconsin girl with my real name which is what my facebook has but I made the mistake of telling her a few details about my life that were true like where I went to college and where I am from and what books I like and I told the Wisconsin girl some of that stuff so she innocently found me on facebook and it still said married to my wife so yeah game over. And then just I guess I left again so I guess I lied and there are two places I had to leave because of this awful dark thing I have and these lies that I tell. But I left Wisconsin as soon as I knew she knew but I guess before I was caught officially.

I am not on facebook now at all I deleted it. I thought about it but I would have to create like three hundred fake profiles to be my friends and make me look real and I don't want a single photo of me on facebook because all it would take is one old acquaintance to see my photo and post on my wall and blow it. That or any other one of the million things that could go wrong and then it would all be over and the whole thing is just too sketchy a proposition and so yeah forget it.

The real reason I don't have facebook right now though is because I am afraid of reading Bob's status updates because it would just be full of things saying how happy she is. Or if she posted things like saying she is sad about being single that would be even worse and I know I have no self control not to look at her status updates all the time. And also the last thing I need is photos of Bob to pine over and so I do not have any photos of Bob. And so I just lie and say I think facebook is for idiots who have nothing better to do with their time than complain about the weather or something that happened on TV. And I think that is a little bit true too.

So anyway now I have learned you have to start all the way over when you want to move somewhere like you can not keep even a little detail from before. It helps to even try to forget what books and movies and music you think you like and you have to start your entire character over and a new wardrobe is important too. You need to arrive at your new town a totally new and complete person.

Little Midwestern and Southern towns are pretty easy to do this in and not because the local people are dumb or overly trusting. That is just a bad stereotype and a big lie. These towns are good to disappear in for a while because lots of people come to those little towns to start over and start a simpler life. And the local people just know that that is something that happens there and they don't necessarily mind unless someone starts messing with them. They're proud of simple but honest working and raising a happy family and it only is people from the coasts who feel like you should be ashamed of that kind of a life.

Yes yes it is like in A History of Violence but obviously most people are not killers like Viggo Mortensen was in that. Lots of people have the urge to start over more simply and for lots of reasons. More people have big darknesses they are running from than you would want to think.

Loads and loads of people come to LA in particular to start over. And so after I had practiced the process a few times in smaller towns I made up this whole new guy for myself to be in LA and I tried that guy out in Portland and he worked fine with no hitches at all and so I took that guy to LA and now here I am being that guy and I even have a few people to vouch for this character from Portland. I thought about what kind of work I should do and while obviously being an actor seemed like something I might be good at I obviously couldn't risk a job where the whole point is putting my face out there even though loads of actors move to LA and change their names but still it just seemed that was not an option. But I always liked to write and I took creative writing classes in college even though I was a pre-med major so I thought why not do that. And I thought who knows maybe doing creative writing out here will be an outlet for my need to tell stories and craft worlds and so maybe I will lie less to real people. That obviously hasn't happened.

So now I realize I've been thinking about all of this wife stuff and Montana girl stuff and moving and lying stuff instead of touching myself while thinking about fucking Bob with the tops of her breasts coming out over the top of her sea-green dress or even thinking about fucking the Paramore girl who by the way her boobs are on the internet if you are interested they are small like a 30A but they're great. But anyway I stop trying to jerk off because I'm probably too drunk to finish anyway.

Then I realize that I do finally feel really tired and it is when I am drunk as hell and also tired that I do some of my best writing because all the voices go away like the mean other person who is inside me who calls me names and calls me weak and coward and liar and pussy he goes away and I can write and find a couple of hours of peaceful thought.

I go to the other table I like to write at and open my laptop. Way in the distance in the Hills I can hear some coyotes howling and I do not like that sound and so I think I should have a Drink and close the windows and turn on the air conditioning so I do not have to hear those coyotes because I am afraid of them coming and invading my apartment and eating me while I am still alive. So I go to the kitchen and pour a big glass of Wild Turkey with ice because I think I might be able to write something belligerent now and Wild Turkey is what a lot of my favorite belligerent writers drink like Hunter S. Thompson. But once I have drunk most of that Wild Turkey now I just get lazy and lie down on the couch watching something on TV and I turn it to Turner Classic Movies because those old movies are soothing to fall asleep to. The movie is on I don't recognize it but oh there is Jimmy Stewart I like him I think he is cool.

But just in time before I pass out I do remember to set my alarm on my iPhone because I have to meet with my agent tomorrow morning so I do set the alarm on my iPhone and I double check I did not set it wrong like say maybe I put the right time but for weekends not weekdays or say PM instead of AM. But no it is right. And I lie there for a while and then go to sleep on my couch that I like better than my bed because no matter what position I fall asleep on my bed I always wake up on the edge of the left side of the bed which was my side of the bed I shared with my wife and then I feel sad when I wake up and that is no way to start every day off and so I am a little bit afraid of my bed.

I'm fading off on the couch hoping I dream about something happy to be happy about or something sad to write about.

Jimmy Stewart is like walking through a gate or something and he says

Well thank you Harvey I prefer you too.

I don't understand why he says that because no one is there it's only

EIGHT

I wake up feeling like major major shit and the sun is in my
face and I have a headache and I'm in someone's bed that's not
mine or Bob's and my mouth tastes like cigarettes that are not
Marlboro 27s and I would guess they are maybe Parliaments yes
that is what they are but where did they come from and I hear a
shower running and a woman's voice bouncing off of the water
and porcelain and she says Coffee is on the stove and I wonder
how she knew I woke up just then but even more than that I also
wonder why her blinds are open because it is way too bright and
what is this licking dog all up in my face right now.

   I basically wonder where am I.

   There is writing on the bedroom walls in sharpie like
author quotes and stuff which I think is cool and I will steal
that idea and write on my walls and pretend I invented it
later. I don't remember who the girl is but I don't want to be
here to find out because what if she is gross which she might
easily be gross if I can't remember what she looked like and I
can sort of smell a condom so I definitely had sex with whoever
this girl is and I have no idea what lies I told her so I
clearly need to fucking bail immediately. I pull my clothes on
in full blown panic mode and I am touching her front door
handle when the alarm on my phone goes off to wake me up and
it's that default ring on the iPhone that Xylophone is what it
is called and I remember I am afraid of the sound of that
ringtone and I tell myself to change it but I know I never will
remember to change it and I will just go on being afraid of it
every morning of my life which I am already afraid enough of my
iPhone and of waking up and so basically just kill me now.

I swipe the little shut up thing on the phone fast after the first time through its terrible Xylophone ring hoping it does not have a chance to do the ring again at me but I miss and do not drag the little arrow thing all the way across the screen enough and so it does the ring again and now everything is ruined forever but I stop it before a third time thank God but still today is ruined.

I leave her house and I know the way out of her building so I think maybe I've been here before as is this one of my book world bootie calls maybe but I'm not sure. Maybe I just remember the way out because it is the way I came in and then I remember meeting her last night and she was not gross she was very pretty actually but I don't know where this was maybe it was a bar I think.

No it was a poetry reading because now through the cigarette taste I am also aftertasting that one really cheap red Wine that they always have at gallery shows and poetry readings and things and it is fucking foul that's for sure but the real reason I hate it is because it is what I used to drink a lot of it when I was broke when I first got here to LA and so I remember about when I drank it like four bottles at a time for like eight bucks total but of course if you drink enough of anything you forget what it tastes like but it was the first thing I drank at the gallery last night and so tasting it made me remember that time I was poor and lonely so that sucked.

I am actually impressed that I am drinking alone a lot less these days than I did way back then I mean that is only because I am drinking with Bob but still that means I'm not drinking alone and obviously I drank with this girl from last night.

This girl whose house I am freaking fleeing from was like actually a pretty good poet actually I am not even just saying that. She had some really nice images and she used rhymes only when necessary and for good effect and so now I sort of regret bailing on her just now because maybe we could hang out some more because she seemed very neat actually.

I like good poetry because in poetry every single word counts and you have to pick the perfect word all the time like if you pick one word that is only two thirds of the way to the perfect word then your poem is total garbage and that reminds me of my lying because every detail counts and so poets have a respect for perfection in words like I do.

If you perfectly use all the right words no one notices how much effort went into making a good lie work but a bad word stands out like alarm bells. Use one wrong word at the wrong time in a lie and you're fucked.

Now I remember that the lie I told her was that I was an agent and I could be her agent. Ugh I hate that lie I should just delete that character and never use him again he's a douche and it's no fun to be him that's for sure.

That's right because she was that one tall skinny straight black haired girl with really sparkly kind of mischievous green eyes and small high breasts and she had medium amount of freckles and they looked like black freckles which of course is impossible but that's what they looked like last night because the gallery was like dark.

She had this green lace choker on and a black spaghetti strap dress that made me remember the picture from that book of kids' horror stories about the girl whose boyfriend kept telling her to take off her green ribbon off of her neck and

when she finally did take the choker off because she loved him
so much then her head fell off.

The girl last night had black hair and green eyes like
the girl in the book and so I told the poet girl that she
looked like that girl from the kids' horror story and she said
Shut up that is her favorite scary story for kids anyway and
that is why she dresses like that is because of that story. And
I said she was a good poet which really wasn't a lie actually
she was good I think but frankly who knows if she was or not
since I was obviously blackout.

Then we talked about kids' horror and how fucked up a
genre that is to even exist. Like yeah it's easy to scare the
shit out of kids because they're kids and they automatically
just trust you so if you slip your kid a book full of terror
then yeah they're going to get scared no shit. Like how hard is
it to scare a kid and then we talked about how we were both
scarred for life by those Scary Stories to Tell in the Dark
books that had those black and white kind of scratchy weepy
drawings that were nightmare fuel for years and oh my god I
haven't thought about them in years and me either and hey
what's your name anyway mine is

Then I said I could be her agent and I felt like it was
unnecessary to lie now because we were hitting it off really
well just talking about kids' horror and nostalgia and so I
could have just said I'm a writer and that would be easier to
remember because it's true but what can I say the mood struck
me to lie and so I did I lied about that and so I basically
took everything that is my actual agent John and said it was
about me.

It was fun pretending to be a very happy person like my agent John is but I learned that I wouldn't want to be an agent because it sounds boring even the interesting lie version I made up was boring because as an agent you don't do anything real that is progress for yourself or the world you just call people up and make deals for other people and even though you do have to exaggerate a lot and kind of be strategic about the truth there's no real room for straight up lying when you just feel like it or when the mood hits you. And if you get caught even in a small lie then it's game over for your career.

I am remembering having sex with this green eyed girl now and I remember she was bent over and she was a little too skinny for my taste but not like anorexic or unhealthy she was just a very skinny girl which is not my favorite but her back muscles were nice and so was her hair and she was super pretty. Anyway we were having sex and I was closing my eyes and pretending that she was Bob but it was no use because then I leaned forward and reached for her breasts and this girl has very small breasts like 32A and Bob's breasts are a 34C which is like perfect medium-big size I think so I could not pretend this girl was Bob any more and plus this girl was sighing a lot and kind of softly dirty talking to me and she has a very soft and gentle voice but Bob's voice is kind of scratchy and I do not care to imagine Bob dirty talks a whole lot during sex and so then I really could not pretend she was Bob any more and then I felt angry because this girl should have been sexy enough on her own and I should not be pretending she was Bob because that is mean to this girl and this girl seemed pretty cool actually and then this whole situation got me frustrated and I got soft for a few minutes but I got it back later and

got back to it and then afterwards while we were smoking her
Parliament cigarettes she said she came really hard and I think
I believed her but I was pretending to be asleep.

But yeah even though this was a basically a very good
night obviously it still made me sad for some reason and I
think I would not like to be an agent like my agent John even
though John has a nice lifestyle and car and a nice office
though that's for sure.

And that is what I am thinking now as I am walking into
John's nice office even though I am too early for my
appointment with him.

NINE

I'm waiting for John in his waiting room because that poet
girl's house is closer to John's office than my house is so I'm
early and his assistant asks me if I want anything to drink but
then she gives me an 'Are you serious' face when I ask if she
has any decent Ale so I just ask for an orange juice to wash
down one more of these new weird pills I'm taking for weight
loss and concentration that is called an ECA Stack.

They taste a little bit like cherry just at first but
then they taste mostly just like pills and your burps taste
like pills for like forever after you take them.

I'm bugging out pretty hard and pretty fast from these
pills since I have nothing in my stomach but OJ and last
night's Whiskey and Shitty Wine and still no food since
yesterday's badly poached eggs and stuff although frankly who
knows if I ate something late last night or at the poetry
reading frankly anything could have happened but anyway I think
I will get breakfast after this or maybe even just a nice steak
and Martini lunch would be good with like a whole bottle of Red
Wine that is a million times better than that Stupid Dollar
Store Wine from last night.

Or maybe a steak just all for me is too indulgent and I
will just have cheap steak which is to say a burrito. I know
this great place that has good Tequila Cocktails and they have
burritos with carne asada with not sketchy quality meat and
homemade chunky guacamole but then I think No wait if I'm
having Mexican for hangover food it will have to be nachos with
chicken and tons of jalapenos and extra cheese and a Forty Of
King Cobra which means probably two Forties Of It let's be
honest but then I say No wait because Bob and I like to have

that meal together because for some reason one day we just invented that Malt Liquor and chicken nachos with extra jalapenos is a grand old meal for us to have together and it is really great and it's super white trashy we know that but we don't care because we love it together so what is the harm and it costs like ten bucks for all of it for both of us and then epic napping ensues after eating and drinking that and so I will save that meal for a time Bob and I can have it together. The trick though is to have your own pickled jalapenos separate and put those on at the last minute and not let the restaurant use their shriveled up jalapenos they cooked the nachos with. And no olives. Don't forget the extra cheese that is important too.

But all of that makes me feel sad now because seriously if I have found a woman who is my best friend and she is so beautiful and interesting and deep and funny and we can drink Forties Of King Cobra and eat nachos and watch stupid movies or talk about smart books together and I think she is so beautiful and fun and smart and brave and her 34C breasts are just so amazing well at least I know for a fact the tops of them are amazing at least and she is so great and kind then why in gods name am I not with this woman.

But at the same time I know that I am not with this woman because I am too lame and bad of course that's what it is.

So I change my mind really quick and now a really good steak sounds great to me now like seriously just a like sixty dollar Delmonico straight to the dome with no sides or any nonsense like that and either lots of Hendricks Dry Martinis or just one Hendricks Dry Martini and then a bottle of Barolo and

not even while reading a book or playing on my iPhone just
tackling that lunch like a boss and staring down anyone who
looks at me funny yeah that sounds like what is about to happen
to my lunch and I hope my agent John is fast about this meeting
so I can

Oh my god this OJ I am sipping is really offensively
gross like is this even legal food.

It tastes like airplane OJ. I bet there is a tin foil
pull top in John's receptionist's trash can right now Jesus
Christ. I think of a joke that this OJ is not OK like I am
trying to rhyme OJ with OK and I realize that that is the worst
thing I've ever come up with ever and I must be still drunk
because if I am not drunk and I came up with that sober then I
should never write anything ever again. I realize right now
that although my head hurts like hell and I'm angry at the
receptionist for giving me sass over asking for Ale and then
giving me this airline OJ but still I'm kind of being goofy
with myself despite being in pain so maybe today is not
destined to be such a terrible day after all.

When Bob and I ate psychedelic mushrooms one day she
told me to drink OJ with them because that makes it happen
faster and I lied and said I knew that already and then I
panicked because what if she was making that up to test me and
I had just said I knew something that wasn't real but she
wasn't making it up so it was OK but I made a note not to let
myself get in that position again and phew.

John asks me into his office ten minutes before we were
supposed to meet and he kind of jokingly scolds his assistant
for not showing me in right away and which I know that is a lie
because I am his first appointment to see today and I was early

and I know John always needs a cup of coffee before he does any work and so I think it is a silly lie to lie because there is nothing wrong with liking some coffee before you do any work and I was early anyway.

So that makes me mad because it was a needless lie and so it was one of the lies that's just saturating the world with casual lies and making people more aware that little lies are being told all the time and so that makes all my projects harder. Also the assistant was already mad at me about Ale and now this scolding means she totally hates my guts today.

In his office John tells me some things about how I should have met with the talk show person last night and I lie and say I wanted to meet him but I got sick to my stomach and then I stop listening to him and I wonder if Bob is waking up yet and making bacon yet which she makes whenever I crash at her house at least and so I am wondering if she makes bacon every day or just the days I am at her house for the morning and I decide it must be only when I am there because Bob is not obese but then again she always has bacon on hand so who knows.

And she makes pancakes too that she calls hotcakes for some reason and she does a funny voice when she says hotcakes like an accent or something but I do not know what the voice is supposed to be.

I don't know if I've ever had even a single pancake in my life other than Bob's made pancakes and I think Wait isn't there a Bob's House of Pancakes somewhere that is a real thing and then I laugh inside thinking about Bob behind a counter in a diner called Bob's House of Pancakes and she is taking dozens of orders for her great pancakes and then I realize that would be pretty cute actually and maybe a romantic comedy girl I

write about could be like that. Like can't you see someone come
in and see cute little Bob and the guy says Excuse me missy I
wanna talk to Bob the owner. And Bob would be like

Right here homeboy whatcha want.

And it would be super cute. Bob's pancakes would not
have any flavors available at all you would just say how many
you want that is all the choice you get. They would just be
plain pancakes but the best plain pancakes you ever had in your
life because they would be both vanilla and sourdough in one
and oh my god that sounds both delicious and that is what Bob's
pancakes are and they are so great.

You can have syrup though or butter they will be brought
to your table but nothing else no like fruit or chocolate or
whipped cream or any of that white trash nonsense. Not being
racist against white trash but those pancake toppings are
really white trash I'm sorry. Also there would be very good
coffee there at Bob's. And you would just walk in and say to
Bob like

Hey Bob seven. And seven pancakes would be coming up
according to Bob. And Bob would wear a hat.

John is talking still but he is fake laughing about
something so I'm glad he's not really angry about me not
meeting the talk show host person and so I go back to thinking
about Is Bob waking up and stretching the way she does when she
wakes up that looks sexy and a little bit like a cat stretching
and I am wishing I was there to watch her do that and wishing I
could take a shower with her and touch the little tiny tuft of
fuzz she has above her butt that I like and think is cute. I
say

No I'm fine. Because John says something to me which I assume is about my nose being bleeding which is from this weird new medicine I am taking for weight attention but I tell him I have a flu and he says OK because I already told him I was sick last night so that was a good on the spot lie and well done me.

John asks me what I've been working on and his tone of voice lets me know that he knows I haven't written anything since the first book and the screenplay of it and then the second book that all the critics said is genius but that was like a year ago at least. And for a moment I feel sad because I had to change my name to move to LA and I sort of want my family and my wife who I think I am technically still married to but I don't know how that works if the husband runs away but yeah I want her and my family and my wife and the Minnesota girl I want them all to know that I wrote two really famous books and a movie but I can't ever have them know now because I have been too bad in my past and so I had to change my name.

And I didn't put a photo in the back cover of my books because what if I meet someone and feel in the mood to tell them I am a doctor or a drummer or a director or whatever and they say No you're not you are the guy who wrote that book aren't you. And that is also the same reason why I didn't want to go on the talk show is because it is lame but also I could get recognized later from it.

And so I tell John about the book I am writing about the guy Dan or Don or whatever who invents up a dream girl and then she comes into his life and he has to decide between having a story with an honest ending but that kills the girl or he can have the perfect girlfriend but a copout ending.

John tells me that sounds more like a screenplay than a book maybe with Zooey Deschanel starring in it and that makes me laugh inside because even though he says Zooey Deschanel I think of Bob obviously. I tell him Well too bad because I've already started the book and I feel good about where it is headed. That is a lie because I haven't started it and I secretly think it's kind of a shitty idea like not a good idea but like an idea that a bunch of shitty TV writers would come up with in like an expensive seminar or something. All of the sudden I hate movies kind of.

And then I jokingly also tell John that he just wants it to be a screenplay because I could write it faster and make him more money faster but then when I realize that that is true I think to myself maybe that does sound better actually but I've already taken a position so I don't want to back down so I lie again and say it's a quarter of the way done and I have outlines and brainstorm documents and it works better as a book because the voice is good but I can't describe it yet and maybe I will make a screenplay of it another day but the book has to come first and John says OK why not double dip go ahead and write the book first but think about doing a movie later.

I say John can I use the bathroom and he says to use his private bathroom but I don't want to because I forgot that these new pills make everything run right through my stomach which I think is part of how they are for weight loss and so I just go use the one in the hallway.

I'm washing my hands with hot water and scrubbing very hard after that because I am kind of obsessed with cleanliness and the soap smells like Marzipan scented soap which YUCK

And then I say Hi to the actor who played the main character in the movie of my first book because he is at the sink now too and he looks like a handsome and skinny version of me which is weird because I did not write the character in that book to look like me in my mind but it's still weird to talk to this guy now because he looks so much like me but just better in every way and he's there saying he's started on writing a novel too actually about Hollywood and fancy meeting me here and he is being represented by John or so he hopes and isn't that cool.

And I say Yeah that is cool good luck man because writing a book is really hard going. And I honestly meant that nicely and for encouragement so that when he starts writing his novel and he finds that it is very hard then he can just remember Oh no it is supposed to be hard and I will keep pressing on. But no now this guy gets all upset because he thinks I meant Good luck as in Fat chance because actors are stupid people and writers are smart people.

The reason he thinks that is because actors are so insecure and also because let's face it it's basically true actually most actors are pretty dumb and most writers

Well actually no that is a lie too because I know endless stupid writers and they are the worst because they pretend to be tortured or inspirational when they're just hopping on some bullshit half baked trend of an idea like they think OK what can I put Vince Vaughan in where he will be able to look tired and I can sum the entire movie up in one sentence or that it has a pun in the title that lets you know what the whole movie is by the stupid pun in the title.

OK anyway about smartness. The smartest writer is a million times smarter than the smartest actor let's put it that way but well no because Edward Norton is supposed to be really smart and whatever anyway that is not a can of worms I meant to open up when I said good luck with the novel I just meant it nicely but anyway he starts talking about what would I know because I have no idea how hard his role was to play in some movie he was in just now where he played the part of a real person who is like an activist for queer rights or something and the real guy was in the news a lot lately and this actor guy won tons of awards for portraying him. I can't help but think that I am the best actor ever compared to this jackass because he gets advantages like makeup and settings and music and costumes. And most of all his audience basically wants to be fooled by his performance in the first place.

Everyone is so cynical nowadays it's true but everyone wants to be fooled when you go to the movies I think. I do anyway. I go in to the movies wanting to give it a chance to fool me and to tell me a fun story and it is only the fact that most movies are so horribly like unacceptably shittily written that that makes me say Nope sorry movie you suck. And I walk out of them so often because it's a waste of life. Like seriously at some point someone should just say

No wait stop this movie is total fucking garbage we should take the high road and just cut our losses and throw it out. But no they stubborn it out to try and make back a bit of the money and next thing you know a million people across the country find themselves with nothing to do tonight and so they say Hey what should we do oh I know let's go see fucking Marmaduke 3.

But then again I wonder if I am just telling that same old bitter writer lie about being sour at Hollywood blockbusters and maybe it is a lie because I obviously have no integrity at all on a personal level so why should I pretend to have integrity on a creative level. But I think I do. Well I did write that movie of my book but it wasn't a total sellout version it was a good adaptation of something I wrote anyway. I think if someone said Hey want to write the screenplay for Marmaduke for a million bucks! I would tell them to fuck off.

But I am not like this actor guy here who is still talking and yelling even though I'm obviously not even close to listening but actors don't really care about that anyway they just want to talk. We are different him and me. So this guy is like yelling at me sort of now but mostly just yelling to yell and I can only think Shut up dude because your life is so easy compared with mine. OK let's say you do a bad job of acting one day and you get a bad review well it's not the end of the world there is always probably another movie coming up and you could blame other things on it like the script and yes I bet you would blame the script too. I'll put it another way. This guy will never have to leave his home town and his family and have his wife and mom cry and then become better friends with each other than they ever were with him and all just because he did one bad performance one day but that is what happened to me and so just shut up please actor jerk you have it easy as fuck and I am way too hung over to deal with your tantrum about how hard it is to make millions of bucks and be attractive and have everything you want every day like Bob.

Like he's not even ranting because he's like Citizen Kane who has all these possessions but is aching for a meaningful connection or a real relationship with the universe. He's just insecure and taking an opportunity to yell at someone about how hard his fragile little life is. I bet he yells at PAs who bring him coffee that's not hot enough and stuff like that.

He's still talking and I think I will just leave now because I'm bored of all of this and I suddenly am overwhelmed by an angry feeling that life is too short for me to deal with this vapid crying tantrum throwing pantshitting toddler and I want to go home and have a shower and I'm not sure I'm done being sick to my stomach from the medicine and Liquor and no food and so I want to go home to have diarrhea at home in private and also I should eat something and suddenly food sounds like a very good idea to me and might even have to happen before I go home but that might not be my decision to make if you know what I mean so who knows but nothing is getting done here with this chump anyway.

I just nod once and stone cold walk out of the bathroom and once I've left the guy is still yelling but to no one and that makes me feel afraid knowing that he is just yelling all by himself in the bathroom because only psychos have out loud conversations with themselves that's for sure and so I sort of power walk away from him. I guess he was just in a monologue mood or something but still yikes. I go back to John and my stomach feels like I want to be sick to it again and I say John I feel sick and want to go home but I thought about it a little bit and I will write the screenplay too after all but the book has to come first. And he says OK and he asks if I want to go out with him tonight to this art show and I say no not really I don't.

The problem with John is that he is not as good as me at keeping his stories straight when he is drunk and so he is never drunk and so it's hard to have a good time with him because I am always drunk and he never is and we don't know if I am bad or he is lame so I feel bad and he feels lame.

It is good to be able to keep your stories straight when you are drunk because most people can't do that and so everyone thinks anything you say while drunk is true and that is a tool that I use.

Also I don't want to go to this art show because I think it will be a lot like Art Walk or like the poetry reading last night where there will only be shitty red Wine and very strong medical marijuana which I don't even care about potent marijuana and truth be told I kind of like mediocre pot better because getting like super super high can be pretty scary if you happen to have a darkness like I do who is just waiting to come out and be scary. And besides I think tonight it would be better to have a lot of Gin and Tonics and cigarettes or maybe even cocaine yeah when was the last time I had fucking cocaine but John says

This art show is Downtown.

And I say Where Downtown and he tells me where and where it is is near the metro and I ask What will the drinking situation be and he tells me there will be a full bar there at the art show and when I say Is it Open Bar as well as a full one he says Definitely it is but who cares about Free Drinks you have money and I say I will go in that case.

And I do I go to it.

TEN

I immediately am feeling angry when I get to this art show in Downtown because it is not an art show it is a graffiti show that we are seeing which means you have to walk around Downtown looking at different graffiti pictures on the walls of various buildings and I don't want to walk around as much as I would rather just stay inside looking at one picture while drinking and pretending I like the picture very much and then maybe later talking to someone to try to have sex with. However this new medicine I am on makes me really jittery and gross feeling like super overcaffeinated if I do not move my body around and so even just walking around Downtown will make me less jittery and gross than if I was just standing around so that is a plus.

There is a bar at the gallery we start at and it is free as promised but it only is there at the beginning and end of the route obviously and I think to myself This is basically just like Art Walk and Oh No. Also you have to carry your ONE Drink around in like a 7-11 coffee cup because you can't drink publicly on the street which I don't mind about this cup situation ether way except that everyone is making such a big and lying deal about how fun and cute it is that we have Liquor in public in 7-11 coffee cups like OHMYGODSORANDOMRIGHT.

So I feel angry because it's just Alcohol and we are grownups and drinking outside was not even that exciting in college so who cares about any of this just grow up and stop being so easy to please. And so I text Bob that I am at something lame and I want to ditch it and I am close to her house and so what is she up to this evening.

I wish I had stayed home because when I got home from John's nice office in the afternoon I was sick to my stomach

again which was gross but at least I was at home and private.
And I felt way better afterwards and then I did take a shower
and I washed my hair which I realized it had been a few days
since I did that and so I felt really good and clean after all
of that and then I took a nap in the sun but obviously not
naked with Bob which is my fantasy and then I went to the place
that has good Craft Beers On Tap and fancy burgers but not like
bullshitty trendy burgers with like wilted kale and ginger
grass infused Vietnamese aïoli on a toasted artisanal brioche
zero carb bun or any of that food blog bullshit that no one
really wants to actually eat because it's not even food it's
just (technically) edible fashion. But the burgers at the place
I went to they're just really good and simple actually tasty
burgers with good quality meat that has good flavor and like
two or three good toppings per burger and that's it. It's the
place that I wanted to go to there last night but didn't
because I had to sleep and was too drunk but wait I ended up
with the poet girl somehow and wow I seriously hope I didn't
drive last night but I guess I did I guess I must have and that
is like seriously very bad that I did it and even worse that I
don't even remember it one little bit. I should invent some
system of like hiding my keys from myself when I'm that level
of drunk so that doesn't happen again that is really bad of me.

But whatever I went to the burger place today and I had
a rare burger with a runny fried egg on it and arugula and a
lot of horseradish which is my favorite burger they make there
because the egg yolk bursting into the rare beef and then the
beef grease and the sharp horseradish is like fucking are you
kidding me good and I had four pints of Old Rasputin Russian
Imperial Stout which is this black nine percent Alcohol beer

that looks like Guinness but is way more belligerent and sinister and awesome tasting like seriously this beer is hardcore I will get it more often. And the sort of scene-punk girl behind the bar with huge tits and a sleeve tattoo of all of the Muppets said I would like it and I did I liked it a lot that's for sure and so I had four of them.

I made a semi obscure Muppet reference to her and she didn't get it so I decided I hated her for having that tattoo of the Muppets and not even knowing about who Marvin Suggs is. He is the blue one who plays the xylophone made of the fluff ball creatures. So now I think this girl is a lying bitch but I would still like to have sex with her but it's not worth trying because I want to come to this place again in the future and I don't want to not be able to come here because of some dating disaster with this girl and there are other girls in the world with big tits and who know about beer than just her.

So I would have rather stayed there all night tonight and had lots of more beers and who knows maybe another burger even much later in the night because they are so good there and I was starving as soon as I ate some food I realized I hadn't eaten in days and that that might be why I was not feeling so great.

Also lots of sexy punk rock girls go there and I might have wanted to have sex with one of them because it has been a long time since I told this one lie I have that gets good results. This one lie goes that I am in a metal band called Necromunda that I play guitar in and scream in and we are sort of deathgrind but with more punk riffs and hardcore breakdowns so kind of like Black Breath and newer Agoraphobic Nosebleed combined with just a little Social D and that's what I'd call them to show I know all about punk I call them Social D and not Social Distortion the whole name I just say Social D and they influenced our lyrics a lot. Is what I say.

And then that usually gets punk rock girls pretty interested and I have a guitar at home that I can use to play riffs to these girls on if they come home with me but it's just stupid punk so I don't have to be like actually good I just play fast power chords and stuff and I say I can't scream right now like i do in the band because it's late at night and I have neighbors and that usually leads to them saying something like well we're about to make some real noise meaning sex so yeah sex happens. I've got it all figured out and I would rather have done that tonight than go to this dumb One-Drink graffiti walk. It is a little weird though because I have these three riffs I always play when girls are over to hear me play guitar and I always play them in the same order and I know the lyrics that go on top of them and so I think maybe that means I have written a song. I feel like when I tell girls I have written a song I am lying but that is what I have done if you really think about it. That is pretty weird I think.

One time I got a noise complaint from my upstairs neighbor saying to turn my music down or use headphones please. Funny thing is the night he was complaining about I was using headphones. I just listen to music that loud.

Sorry that was a lie that never happened I just made it up it's just something funny I thought of and I will put it in something later.

So that all sounds better than this stupid art show where I don't even want to talk to anyone here enough to lie to them. Besides John is here looking for artists to sign and he

118

is sober and so I can't even talk to him either and so it's all basically terrible and I just end up making up more stories in my head about my imaginary band Necromunda and some more details about us. Being in a band is a great thing to lie about because being like underground and unheard of and a band who never even has played a single show is exactly the ideal thing because then other people feel elite for knowing about bands no one has even seen so that's a very easy lie to tell and so sometimes for fun I add some like really insane details to my story like about how our old singer died from too much cocaine or he got a sex change and is now a Democratic senator but I can't say which one or some ridiculous lie like that that is just ludicrous but I have never gotten called out which is really hilarious.

Honestly though LA is the easiest town to lie in because no one really listens to anyone else so you can flat out say some insane Patrick Bateman shit to people right to their faces and then they'll just go Uh huh and then they'll carry on with whatever they want to talk about.

Bob texts me back in fourteen minutes which is too long not to be shady in my opinion and she is saying she has plans which makes me feel sad because I know Bob is my only friend and I am not her only friend and right now that actually makes me feel sadder than imagining that she is on a date with a lame hipster guy who she will later let him fuck her with his little dick. And so I decide to think about her being my only friend because I decide I would rather feel sad than happy right now tonight.

Our tour group stops and we go into an alley and there is a bum sleeping in a blanket underneath the graffiti we are supposed to look at and the girl who is leading the tour tells him to go somewhere else. The bum says Fuck off I live here and I was sleeping and the woman says No sir you don't understand you are sleeping on and soiling the ground beneath a great work of modern art.

That's what she says SOILING THE GROUND BENEATH like it's the Wailing Wall or something. I suddenly am very afraid that this is all part of the performance like the woman and the bum will get into a big argument that is about to get scary and then the bum will pull off his blanket and will be all clean shaven and in normal hipster clothes and he will have been the graffiti artist the whole time and it's all some big Willy Wonka trick reveal. But he gets up and he has sores on his legs and he reeks of piss and so if this is the artist method acting then that is some deep undercover but then I look at the bum's eyes and he is clearly insane and you can't fake that animal terror that is in the eyes of a crazy person. He looks at me and he recognizes the darkness in me too and he knows I am like him in some way and I know he is right. The bum looks at the leader woman and he says You got Chlamydia for Karma you conceited cunt. He gets his blanket and he goes somewhere else and I slip him a fifty as he walks by me because that is the best sentence I've heard in a long time.

Sorry that was a lie none of that happened with the bum I just made it up. We are at some graffiti now though.

The graffiti is of some people holding up a flag like Iwo Jima but the flag is not American it just has the Hollywood sign on it instead of stars and stripes and then behind the one main guy all the other soldiers are walking away instead of helping him lift it and I think some of the soldiers are supposed to be Will Smith and Ashton Kutcher and Scarlett Johansson and someone I don't recognize who maybe is Tim Robbins and then at the bottom is graffitied the words Celebrity And Justice For All which is really dumb and sounds like it should be the name of a teenager's poem. Or like a Necromunda album title ha-ha YES done and done I am writing that down in my iPhone I will tell people that is our album name and that this graffiti artist stole it from us.

I gulp my Gin With Ice and think I should have put more ice because it's not cold any more and Warm Gin is the worst thing you can drink and I know I did it because I didn't want to run out of Gin over the course of this walk which I didn't know how long it would be but I still should have gotten more ice so at least I could drink what I have.

There's a moment when we're all looking at this graffiti and no one knows if it is good or shit I mean we all have to know it's obviously shit but no one wants to be the first person to say anything especially something bad so I think about yelling It's shit! For a moment because that's what I think but then I realize that this is an opportunity for a lie because people are just waiting to be told what to think like usual so I have an opening to cause some chaos with these dumb fucking lemmings. And so I take a big sip of the Gin which is an enormous mistake it's not even Good Gin I think it is that bad one with the yellow label but then I just clear my throat and put my Gin down on the ground and clear my throat and everyone looks at me because I'm the only one really moving and I walk up to it the graffiti and I close my eyes and nod my head and start kind of shaking like I am about to cry although

of course I am not about to cry because I cannot cry any more
and I just say the word

YES.

And everyone starts clapping and crying and saying
things like Yes and Finally an artist with the vision and
courage to say what we all were thinking and This is the artist
of the year and things like that. It makes me feel good that I
successfully trolled all these people just like that on the
spot and I was better at acting than that actor from the
bathroom who I imagine in my head is still there in the
bathroom screaming at no one. But then I feel sad as well
because now all these people are going to like go home and talk
and blog and say this art was good and that's a really bad kind
of lie really the worst kind actually because it is a lie to do
with mediocrity and not with evil and that is worse in my
opinion that's for sure. The internet makes lies hard to
control in that way because lies are often interesting and
interesting things go viral and then become real even if they
are not real.

This makes me think about that book the guy wrote that
got huge and Oprah found it told all her cult to read it and
they did and loads of people's lives were affected for the
better but then it turned out the guy bullshitted the book even
though he said it was non-fiction. I didn't feel bad for the
guy because I mean he lied so he gets what he gets but I did
think everyone who was so very angry at him was kind of missing
the point and just lying themselves by taking an opportunity to
take a moral high ground and be incensed over something. Like
why can't the book still make your life better even if it's
make believe? Plenty of fiction books make people happier and

better. Also shouldn't the guy get some credit for making the story up and not just transcribing his life. What is so hard about that. Nothing. Anyway not trying to excuse myself but I think people overreacted to that whole thing.

I think the most evil lie I ever told probably was when I was younger and I was still in high school I think or no it had to be college actually and I told my friends at college that over break my best childhood friend from home just died from taking too much cocaine so that people would feel sorry for me and this one girl I was into would maybe fuck me to make me feel better and that was a very evil lie obviously because real people die of things like that in real life and it's really really sad for all the surviving normal people when it really happens so it's really very bad to lie about things like that I know but I was still early in my career of telling lies so I made that mistake but no one figured it out at least until everything happened with my wife and then everything came out and got exposed even including some things that actually were real and really did happen but they were very unlikely and so no one believed that they were true even though they really were. So yeah that cocaine dead guy lie was really evil I know but this one now about the graffiti I almost feel like is worse. Because the cocaine dead guy lie made people say Oh my god that is so sad. And then they felt more alive and had to think to themselves I should be more grateful to be alive and do more with myself and stop wasting my life so much. And I even know this one friend of ours who he stopped doing so much cocaine as he used to because of my story and so you see it was definitely evil to lie for the sympathy but something good came of it like I was a bad person that day but a good Dungeon

Master and labyrinth maker. A Million Little Pieces that is
what the lying guy's book was called. I never read it or even
know what it is about.

But this lie about the graffiti just makes everyone less
alive not more alive and makes everyone expect less out of life
and say that shitty things are good things and I think then
that was bad of me because I already hate hipsters for liking
shitty things and even more for saying there is no such thing
as good things and bad things like everything in equal in
quality and nothing really means anything it's all just ironic
dude and it's meaningless and you have no right to judge
anything. Which of course them saying that to me is actually a
form of them judging me but no they are perfect and I am just
awful so. But anyway I feel like I have made all of that
problem worse just now with that lie about the graffiti being
good. All the sudden I miss my wife very badly but no that's no
good I am not allowed to miss her and so I change my mind and
decide instead to miss Bob yeah I miss Bob.

We're walking under a bridge to the next thing and this
stoner kind of guy with a big red beard comes up and passes me
a blunt which I take a hit off before remembering that I took
one of this new medicine when I was at the bar and so the blunt
hit hits me really hard and gives me a really bad headache
right away and I kind of see visuals a little bit like textures
and patterns wobbling around the streetlights.

I wish I hadn't taken that hit although I usually like
drug visuals because I know it's just the brain lying to me and
for once it's fun to be told a lie that is beautiful rather
than me having to invent beautiful lies and tell them to my
friends and remember all of them all the time because that is a

124

lot of responsibility and upkeep to build better worlds for everyone I know to live in.

Even though it's impossible Downtown I swear I hear a coyote howling and I am afraid of it. I look around at the other people's faces to see if they heard something too but they are all talking out loud even if no one is listening and I doubt they would hear the end of the world and now I am more afraid of them than of the coyotes.

ELEVEN

Now I am back at the gallery that has the bar and I have
changed back to Whiskey Diet which is still not my favorite
Drink to drink but it is the Drink I order the most often.
Maker's Mark On The Rocks is my favorite Drink but they do not
have that here or if they do I do not order it for some reason.
I decide I will not have Gin for a long time after that Warm
Gin I had tonight that's for sure it was bad and I sometimes
think about quitting drinking clear Liquor altogether and
tonight that is a thought I am taking somewhat seriously. John
introduces me to a hot girl I don't think is actually hot at
all but she is very skinny though and has a flawless but
forgettable face and most people would say she is amazingly hot
and John introduces me and says I am this big novelist and the
girl is just like

Oh.

And then John says the name of the movie they made out
of my first book and now she's all excited and I look at my
iPhone again to see if Bob has texted me that her plans fell
through and she wants to get together or something but she
hasn't so I decide to be the novelist John says I am and try at
least a little to have sex with this girl.

I find situations like this the hardest to lie in
convincingly. It's easy to pretend to be a whole new character
from scratch but when I have to just be myself except happy and
fun that is hard. Because even girls who say they like
important serious novelists don't actually want to have sex
with anyone serious or sad and that is just exactly how I feel
right now tonight is serious and sad so I decide not to even
try to be funny and nice and like some big frat boy clown

tonight and so I just be brooding which works on girls like maybe one time in nine and this time is not one of those times so the not-hot hot girl goes away and I think she is a little afraid of me maybe but probably just bored which is worse.

I feel sick to my stomach again and so I just leave without saying goodbye to anyone and I get a taxi back to the beer and burger place but it's way too crowded now that's for sure and I don't want to deal any more so I just go home to maybe watch a Netflix now. I am glad that Netflix did not change its name to that name Quikster it sounds like a Pokemon.

I don't make it through my Netflix movie which is an old French movie which is called Breathless. I just said Which is called Breathless as if you've never heard of it but it's like the most famous French movie ever but anyway I've never seen it and Bob says she thinks that she is a lot like the main girl in it so I want to watch it because it would be nice to watch a movie that sort of has a Bob in it because the director is probably in love with the main actress and the movie must be sort of a little worship of her. I think to myself that one day maybe I would like to do something nice like that for Bob to do a little worship of her. And also it will be nice to just watch a movie containing someone like Bob and not have to worry about if she sees me looking at her and loving her.

The movie starts and I like the start and I guess the girl is a little like Bob but not as much as the dragon girl from Game of Thrones at least looks wise I mean this girl in Breathless is cute but she's not very believable I think. And her character is super dumb and makes sloppy bad decisions which Bob is not at all dumb to me although her decision to not be with me is dumb and sloppy I think. I am too tired to read

127

subtitles now and old movies have a very soothing sound and so
I fall asleep again on my couch for who knows how long but when
I wake up the movie is back to the DVD menu so at least 2
hours. I remember I have had this movie at home for like a
month and I'm over it and I do worry about the people at
Netflix thinking I am a sucker for keeping movies at home for a
long time without watching them and so I just keep paying them
and not getting a good value for my money and so I just put the
movie in the sleeve and I plan to send it back to Netflix.

I enjoy ripping the little paper from the envelope even
though I am very afraid of tearing the envelope part as well
but I don't rip that part and I just seal it which is
satisfying when I run the seal between my fingers to close it.

I go into my room because I don't know why and I see
that apparently I have written something in sharpie on the wall
that says

Just stop doing it NOW

And that makes me feel angry because for one I was
supposed to write smart and genius phrases by other people on
the wall and not something dumb written by me when I was
hammered. And for two when did I write this and for three now I
remember a dream I had where Bob found out everything about my
lying and she cried and this made me cry too finally which is
how I knew it was a dream because I cannot cry anymore in real
life and then I had to move again. In the dream. But because I
cannot cry in real life but I was crying I knew it was a dream
and so then I lucid dreamed for a while and turned the dream
around into a sex dream and as soon as Bob's top was off my
alarm went off and so I was in a bad mood for the rest of that
month.

I have dreamed or thought about Bob finding out I lie a lot of times and I know that one day I really do want Bob to find out actually but it has to be in a careful way I plan out and write the whole scene beforehand so she feels surprised but also happy because she knows I had the whole story all figured out and under control from the beginning and that this was all for her. When this happens she will be very angry that she was lied to of course but she will know I had the bigger picture in mind and it was all a great piece of work all for Bob and it will be OK.

You know like those engagement proposals you see on youtube that are also partly pranks as well. Like there is one where the woman gets fake arrested or something and she is crying and then the last cop who interrogates her is her boyfriend in disguise who says like It's OK you're not really arrested because I love you. And then he takes off his mustache and disguise and he says It is me not a cop and Will you marry me and that always works for some reason and the woman says Yes although I would be so livid if someone did that to me and would definitely say No. But I will write it better than that though so Bob will not become arrested.

Honestly (ha) I sometimes just want to tell Bob everything like right now just rip the band-aid. I am afraid that maybe confessing would just be the equivalent of an Alcoholic pouring a bottle down the drain knowing full well he's going out to the Liquor store the next day. But who cares it could only be a step in the right direction. I want to just tell her it all and say I'm so sorry I've done all these awful things and especially to you dear dear Bob but I didn't know I loved you until I had already done all the bad things and it

was too late and I am so sorry. But if you can find it in you
to be better than anyone should ever be expected to be can I
please just start from scratch right now today with you just
start all over again and I swear I won't tell a single even
tiny lie to you or anyone ever again not even a dumb little one
like yes that movie was good when I didn't like it or yes that
dress looks great on you even if I think it doesn't suit you.
And if I do ever say one day something dishonest or just a half
truth or I leave something out or skip a detail then you are
free to walk away and never talk to me again OK I'm just out at
strike one. I know I have no rights because I am awful but the
only thing I know that is definitely true and that is free from
all this awfulness and darkness is that I like you a lot Bob
and so please I have to ask.

If a lifelong liar asked you for forgiveness and
promised he would never ever do it again what would you say
Bob.

TWELVE

So it is now another day. It is a Wednesday and I am doing a
lecture in front of a college writing class but it's not just a
small class like a seminar which I thought it would be. It's a
lecture in the big huge main auditorium and lots of other
people are here not just college students but also teachers and
I think other normal grownups are allowed as well and some book
world people and cameras which I did not expect and I do not
like this ambush at all.

   I am talking about the importance of authenticity in
writing. Like how it's not bad and clichéd to write what you
know even though most people think that means that if you are a
janitor all you can write about is janiting. But no what it
really means is to confront your feelings and observations
authentically and in a real way and it's OK to write about
them. My point in the speech is that it is better to start from
that place of honesty than to start with a lie and then try to
talk your way back to truth. You can never ever do that and
please college students just trust me on that subject.

   What you write the first time might end up being shitty
still and it more than likely will not be your best but you
have to start with truth and I mean real truth which is not
just transcribing of literal events but emotional truth and
integrity. Anyway that's what this speech is about.

   I wrote the speech I am giving about two weeks ago and
so I am just reading it aloud now basically while thinking
about Bob which I realize is ironic since I'm not being
authentic in giving this speech because I'm not thinking about
the speech as much as I am thinking about Bob's breasts. Plus I
mean I'm a big giant pathological liar so that perhaps means I

131

should not be giving this speech about authenticity in the first place. Or maybe it means I definitely should give this speech actually. Like it's not hypocritical for a drug addict to tell people not to do drugs because he knows better than anyone how fucked up things can get.

But it is a good speech and I was very honest when I wrote it and I do not fall back on gags or easy ego massaging very much I think although for some reason I am sort of afraid of the end of this speech even though I don't remember what is in it. But even still for some reason I am now remembering my message to the sad tumblr girl saying Do you want to meet up and be sad together and for some reason this speech feels like that. It is good and well intentioned and pretty honest but also kind of skeevy and not all the way honest.

I do not like giving speeches because even though I have written this already and polished it I do not like performing in any way shape or form and I prefer to write on my own and then polish it and then submit my work to someone else who will get back to me later preferably via email. Or never. Feedback right now is scary.

I do not like people who are performers in general because the skill they have is really more of a variety show kind of freakish talent and it's not real ability or something of any value. Like performers get all this credit for doing a dance or a song or an acting performance or whatever but they only get credit not because the dance is actually inherently valuable. But they get credit because they did it correctly on the spot in a high stakes situation with everyone watching but who even cares about that if the dance is only good if people are watching like that is totally backwards.

It is also the same reason I think that I think like in college taking tests is not any indication of anything compared with writing papers because so what if you can remember some dates and facts for one hour and then forget them forever after the test is done. I think it means more if you can show you know about the real meaning of a subject and why it matters and then if you are really great and smart then you can take the idea one step further or like disprove it.

I mean progress never comes from someone who remembered all the dates right one day. It comes from someone who knows the meaning or sees another meaning and insists on it until either they die being wrong or one time in a million they change everything because they are right but too soon. Like unless you're a doctor or someone who really needs to remember loads of information fast on the spot in real life then I think it just means more to understand why things happen than when.

Yeah yeah I understand why somebody like me would think that understanding the big picture is more important than sticking to the facts as they are. But who knows chicken and the egg I think. I told all this to Bob once and she said

If college classes were graded on understanding and engagement with the material then like one person only would graduate from any school any year.

I think that was Bob telling an easy lie because it is easy to be a cynic I think and people aren't so bad as all that. I mean I am but most people aren't.

And I am kind of saying exactly that in this speech now namely the part about understanding and engaging and really thinking about things and not just regurgitating numbers and saying what your teacher wants to hear so you'll get a good grade because you will not remember your GPA two years out of school but you might remember books and mentors that changed your thinking and your attitude and your life.

These are things I believe but I feel like I am also a little bit ashamed about this speech now because well I am always ashamed of myself every day but specifically now I am ashamed because I am getting a cheap kick out of saying like Hey kids don't go to grad school it's bullshit just read a lot of good books and talk about them with your friends and even online and don't be in debt forever because do you know what teachers aren't automatically smarter than your friends that is just what they want you to think so they feel good about themselves while they're shooting your ideas and dreams down. And I am saying this in front of those very teachers who in a way are the people paying me two thousand dollars to give this speech so that is sort of rude of me and I'm getting a petulant kick out of it which makes me feel like I am lying or at least being disingenuous.

So I feel kind of dishonest about that but it is not the darkness in me that is lying it's not a good powerful deliberate lie with a goal in mind. It's the lazy kind of meh lie like the graffiti lie I told and so that makes me feel ashamed especially since this is a talk to kids about authenticity but I do mean what I am saying though so I don't even know and this is making my head hurt but I know something is not sitting well with me and I want to run away from here.

I do also know that I am a performer as much as anyone else because of all my lies but it is different because I do not want applause for my performance at all which desire for applause is like the main driving force in the lives of performer types because they live for applause and they don't want to actually do something amazing but just to get applause all day long for being their beautiful selves and the same thing is true for people who are very funny people as like their main thing I think they just want to be told they are the funniest ever all the time and keep getting little pills of validation instead of actually making the world better and so please shut the fuck up.

My performance is not supposed to have any applause. Like if I do my performance well and if I am really good at my art then I will get away with it all and I will never have any applause or judgment ever which is the way I want it to be except I would accept a review from Bob at the end of all of this if she wanted to give me one. That is if she ever would speak to me again. I would like to know Bob's evaluation even if it was that I am just the worst. I mean I already think that so how bad can Bob's telling me off even be.

I sometimes think right before you die you should get a list of fun or interesting statistics about yourself just fun numbers and facts which can be as stupid as like how many grains of rice you have eaten total or how many words you have read or how many beers you have drunk. Or it can be more poetic things like fun comparisons like how many laughs you have had versus how many tears you have cried or how many orgasms you have gotten versus how many you have given to someone else.

You also should get a single fact that is the thing you have done the most or best of out of everyone or like one fact that is something ultimate about just you because I think almost all people would have something they have done the most or least or are number one at not like eating rice or whatever but something even serious or profound I don't really know like what though.

And obviously I would want to know my total number of lies. I do not think my number is very different from the average number of lies it is only that mine are just heavier and better thought through. And just basically better.

So that is what I am thinking about as I finish my speech to the students and I get to the end of the speech and I remember what i was feeling afraid of just now and it is this little joke at the end which is not a piece of like funny insight or honesty it is just a cute and easy bit of pandering so that makes me ashamed to say it so today is really a bad day already and it is only the early afternoon and so I am thinking about calling Bob as soon as I am done here even though I am afraid to learn what her plans last night were in case they involved a hipster guy date or something else great.

They all laugh at the lazy joke and applaud me which I hate even more than if they booed because I didn't come here to be applauded or even to get the two thousand dollars though I will accept that money because who knows when I will get money next since I am not writing much any more. The reason I said Yes when they asked me like a few months ago is because they asked me to talk to some smart writing students and even though I am not a genius at all and I really mean that and I really hate it when people call me that which has happened sometimes after the second book and it makes me uncomfortable because they are lying so much and it is not false modesty on my part I just think they're rabidly supporting me because they need a team to play for or like a cause to get fanatical over and make part of their identity as someone who is on the cutting edge of books. Seriously it wasn't much of a book it was a rant I wrote in like a month but they like it a scary amount. I've read books that have changed me but I've only ever just said Wow that book was great. I didn't go like screaming all these superlatives and making fandom of the author like my reason for living you know.

But anyway I said I would do the talk because if they didn't bring me in they would just bring in someone even worse so I think I would probably do less harm to them than someone else random who would tell casual non-deliberate lies about writing or ideas and those are seriously dangerous lies because people trust experts and just say OK he is right without thinking about it. And also it was kind of a dare to myself to do this lecture like that guy who climbed a mountain Everest I think and someone said why did you do it and he said that he did it because it was there. So this talk is kind of like that except I think climbing mountains is also a dumb thing to do like performance because again yeah good for you for climbing it and you get lots of applause but what did that really accomplish and how is anyone in the world other than you any better off because just you walked up a mountain that is hard to walk up. Who cares about any of that except for just you and your pedestrian little ego.

So the people are done applauding which I wish I could just be somewhere else while they do that it is so embarrassing and scary and reminds me of the graffiti when everyone was crying and saying Yes it is so good even though it was really shit. And now the dean or important teacher or some kind of boss anyway comes out and thanks me and I should have seen this coming but I did not and he says that I will answer questions now which I am not ready for that but I can't say no because then I look like I am afraid which is exactly what I am and that's precisely the case but I still can't say no now.

The auditorium is quiet and I think for a minute no one has anything to ask me which is both good and bad. Good because I don't have to answer anything but bad because what if no one was listening to me or doesn't care what I said. If that is true I should not take that personally at all because I never asked even one question probably to lecturers when I was in college and I liked some of those lecturers well enough. But then hands go up all over the auditorium which is so big that a little woman has to run around with a microphone to give to the people who have questions and she reminds me of the crying usher from the movie theater maybe she is her mom.

The first girl with a question asks half her question and then stops and looks at her microphone and says Wait can you hear me. And I think that she is stupid for asking that because I would have said or done something if I saw her talking but couldn't hear her. And even if I didn't do that myself the whole auditorium would have like laughingly yelled and screamed at her that the microphone isn't on and it would have all been this nice big old fucking joke for everyone to laugh at just like the joke about LA native which I am glad that didn't happen because it would have scared me but she is still dumb for asking me it because I can hear her obviously.

I suddenly am picturing everyone screaming at her YOUR MIC ISNT WORKING HA HA HA and cackling and uproar and whooping and I am very afraid of this image right now and I really wish I was drunker than I am right now which is only extremely drunk. Then she finishes her question and it's a total slowball question and I am about to answer it but the dean or boss interrupts me and starts to repeat it for everyone and now I think he is dumb too because you only have to repeat the question if the asker didn't have a microphone and no one in the crowd heard her question because of that. But the girl did have a microphone and so everyone heard it and so I figure there are about fifteen hundred people in this auditorium OK and repeating the question takes like ten seconds so he just wasted fifteen thousand seconds which is like four hours of human life. I can see about forty hands up now and so I am trying to work out in my head how many hours of human life that will be wasted today and it is one hundred sixty six hours which is almost a week of human potential wasted today just by repeating the question and

Oh shit I realize it is time for me to answer her question and I do I answer it and it is a pretty good answer but I could have done better if I had been paying attention.

Now the microphone gets handed to an ancient man who has a question and I think Oh No.

THIRTEEN

I'm driving home or at least way the hell away from this college and I think I have been spending too much time Downtown which is OK because that is where Bob lives but also too much time on the Westside which no one good lives there and I should be spending more time either alone or at least just in my own neighborhood. I am afraid of being outside of my house for too long because the more I am out with people the more damage I do or might do and so a day quarantined at home not talking to anyone is a day I did not make the world worse by lying so I should go home now as fast as possible. For damage control.

When I get home I look again at the writing I wrote on my wall that just says

Just stop doing it NOW

And I am angrier at it than before because I think it's the wrong answer. Not just because I'm ashamed of the thing it's telling me to stop doing although I am but mainly because I don't think I should stop lying any time soon. It is too soon I'm not ready.

And so I look around for white paint to cover what I wrote but why on earth would I have white paint just on hand and Home Depot is a weird place that I am sort of afraid of but I do not know why and it is pretty late out right now but oh yeah they are open very late or even 24 hours maybe so never mind that but I am still afraid of Home Depot even imagining its logo is scary right now and so I just take the sharpie and draw a square around the words I wrote and then I start to fill in the square so there will be just this little black square there now and no words. I will have to think up something to say if someone asks What is that there for that little black thing.

I wonder if I can buy the right color paint on Amazon and not have to go to Home Depot.

This is taking too long of a time and it is hurting my arm and so I get Wine and I pour the Wine and drink about most of that bottle of Wine by the time the stupid box is filled in now.

I sit there resting my arm and smelling the sharpie fumes for a second not like huffing it on purpose but just enjoying the smell of what came off of it naturally just from my writing with it and I remember a joke that goes

I'm not addicted to cocaine I just like the way it smells. And I like that joke and laugh out loud remembering it. Now I am thinking that the fact that I am laughing out loud just staring at my wall makes me think maybe I have had enough sharpie for tonight so I put it away and open all the windows and kind of wonder what to do with the rest of tonight other than drink obviously.

I look out my window and I hear coyotes barking at each other and whimpering which means they are probably fighting over someone's unattended pet that they got. I think to myself that it is dumb of animal rights people to be like Don't kill coyotes. Coyotes are very dangerous and are absolutely worth being afraid of and worth killing if they are in your yard because they are animals with the darkness. And even more dangerous than that for me at least coyotes can smell the darkness in other people they are like sentries or stealth detector radar or something.

Creatures that have the darkness really are best just to be put down I think. Right away and before they hurt the poodles and stuff I mean even if poodles are stupid and weak it's not their fault and they do nothing wrong to anyone else and there are worse things to be than stupid and weak for instance being bad.

Suddenly I do not want to see Bob tonight because I would just tell her about today being horrible and what if her last night was amazing or she let someone fuck her and I don't want to hear it but I don't know exactly why my today was horrible other than that all the grinning and stupid faces at the college that made me sort of afraid.

After my talk when I was leaving one very cute college girl who was really hot like seriously model hot did come up to me and said my talk was good and she wants to be a writer too and did I want to go with her to a party and I said maybe but I knew I wouldn't go even though I mean sex was clearly likely. But then I felt sad because I felt like she wasn't asking me like she would ask a friend or a normal guy she was interested in but instead she was asking like it would be a novelty to have me the freak writer at her party. Like if this was a scene in a movie I see myself being played not by like Ryan Gosling but by like Philip Seymour Hoffman or Paul Giamatti and like the joke of the scene is how gross it is that a hot young college girl is all hot over the gross ugly writer.

But then I think should I take what I can get in terms of sex or whatever but still this feels dumb and not real and instead it feels like it's from Californication or like Squid and the Whale and like I'm sorry there's no way the girls who look like this girl get turned on by English professors and

142

novelists. I mean Anna Paquin's character in Squid and the Whale was pretty much just a total weirdo but still I think it is unlikely as hell. I think that sort of thing only happens in movies because movie writers want to make people believe that hot chicks bang nerdy movie writers all the time so that then in real life they can bang hot chicks because people think that is something that happens.

Because if something happens enough in movies then real hot chicks think that is a real thing that happens in real life too and then it does happen in real life because it happened in the book or the movies. And so that is a pretty dangerous and big lie and I think that is not a good lie to tell even if it leads to me having sex with some hotter girls than I should be allowed to.

So yeah I think this girl only is talking to me because she saw a scene like that in a movie one time. But I don't like think it is mean of her really I know she probably would want to talk about books and maybe even about my books and her books and I know she would listen to what I had to say for a while at least. And we would probably smoke her terrible weed and for some reason I imagine her going down on me and definitely not sleeping with me all the way because she wants to say she hooked up with a big novelist especially in case I get even more famous later she will have a story to tell but she doesn't actually want to actually sleep with me because she is attracted to me. I don't know why I imagine that particular thing and I think maybe it's just a bad thought I should not think it any more and so I don't think about it any more but yeah so I ran away from that girl.

So I drink some more Wine and put on the TV so that if I am secretly being filmed in my apartment for a reality TV show then tonight's episode is not just me sitting there drinking red Wine and staring off into space although really that is what I am doing because I have no idea what I am watching I think it is a show about people losing weight. But it is not like a competition it is one of the sad kind of ones with like crying skinny family members having an intervention for their one obese family member saying you need to lose weight because it is hurting our feelings to see you be different than we would be so you must now stop because we are offended. It's that sort of show. Just in case I am being filmed and recorded for a reality TV show I also say out loud

I know you are there by the way.

Which I think is a sort of psychotic thing to do but better safe than sorry and if there is no one there then no one laughs at me for doing that and if the people really are there then that will teach them and I will have been smarter than them after all. Also I know that that movie The Truman Show about where they film Jim Carrey's life without him knowing and everyone else who is a person in his life is just an actor, I know that that whole situation is exactly what is really happening to me right now. And I know they only made the movie The Truman Show so that I would watch it and think to myself Wow if that was happening about my life right now they would never dare to make a movie about that exact same thing and so it is a really good double bluff. But it's not that good because I know.

I suppose watching me tell more and more stories and just continue to be the worst person ever would be a pretty interesting show to watch though because how long could I keep it up and wow what a total sicko the world would think I am or I guess what a sicko the world would know I am but I don't really care because I have a speech prepared already and I will give that speech if that turns out to be the case and the speech is about how they are the really dishonest ones for doing this to me and torturing me with this instead of helping me and why do they think they are they better than me.

I hope Bob is not an actor though. That is the only thing that would make me feel foolish and then sad is if Bob is reciting a script that is being told to her through an earpiece in her ear or something and the reason Bob won't let me fuck her is because the actress really doesn't want to fuck a total crazy person because what if I am violent in bed or something or hurt her and she doesn't love me at all she is just a very good actress reading a script and basically doing her job. She does sometimes feel too good to be true or like an actress in a quirky romantic comedy or something.

I wonder if that would mean that I am actually in love with whoever writes her script for her and tells her it into her ear piece and I think it might mean that I am in love with that person or that I am just really stupid and fall in love for bad reasons and that I fell for a script. It would be a good piece of irony if I'm a huge liar but am also the biggest sucker for lies ever and totally fell for someone else's lie like that would be totally fitting.

I start to think more about that but there are too many awful endings to that story and thinking about those awful endings is where I always wind up when I think about The Truman Show for too long and so I decide not to think about this any

more and just pretend to pay more attention to what is on the
TV but it is so dumb and fake sad that I can't even do that and
besides it is a reality TV show which only makes me think about
The Truman Show again and so I change the channel to some
comedy show with a laugh track that appears to be about a
yuppie who has to live in the ghetto for a while and hilarity
is supposed to ensue but I doubt it ever will and I just zone
out and sit and drink my Wine and stare into space while the TV
chatters and tells me I should be laughing and asks meanly why
aren't you laughing. Then a commercial tries to make me buy a
sandwich for five dollars.

        After the show ends like twenty minutes later it is
officially night time and the sandwich commercial comes on
again and it is about to say this one part of the commercial
that I hate and am a little bit afraid of and I have memorized
that part and so now I sort of look forward to hating that part
of the commercial and to being afraid of it and so I try not to
listen to that part of the commercial and just think about what
I should do tonight instead but of course when that part of the
commercial comes on I say the part along with it in my head and
hate it more and also memorize it more than before and have it
stuck in my head more so I have to turn off the TV so I do I
turn it off.

        I am almost done with this second bottle of Wine and
only have Whiskey left but I do not want to just sit home or go
online and I think what should I do since I don't want to see
Bob either and she is my only friend and I think of course I
should take one more of this new medicine that is called an ECA
Stack and then I should use that focus I will have to write.

And now I feel bad for having it be that it only occurred to me to write when I had pretty much run out of all other options of things to do but oh well that's how I wrote the other books too and it turned out OK so.

I take one of this medicine and think seriously there is no reason to keep doing this to myself I will feel so awful in like ten hours and I heard it can be dangerous.

I sit at my desk and wait for it to start kicking in and as soon as I start to get nauseous then I start to write the beginning of the book about the guy who has to decide between the perfect girl that he invented and the great book he writes and I realize I am sick of writing about writers and so mustn't everyone be even more super sick of reading about them too.

I start to write the main character and he is like me but happier and he is not really tortured at all and then I realize I have to change that because a person without a darkness would never be able write the great sad novel he has to write but I still hate the character because he's just generic and not real at all and I can't stop thinking about Joseph Gordon-Levitt while I am trying to write him and that would be a lot of danger later if they make a movie of it because the girl is going to be written to be just like Bob and then Bob would want Zooey Deschanel to play her and I love Bob so I would like make a fuss with the director to make sure she got who she wants to play her and then it would be 500 Days of Summer all over again with Zooey Deschanel and Joseph Gordon-Levitt so I wonder if I could convince Bob that she would like to be played by the dragon girl from Game of Thrones but then that girl is English and that would be very different and wouldn't work and so instead I try to think about someone different instead of Joseph Gordon-Levitt but I keep seeing him because he sort of looks like me and this makes me not want to write this book any more.

Then I think Wait it could be interesting if the writer isn't even the main character instead it's the girl who is the main character and we meet her first and she is cute because she is Bob and we all love her but then some guy comes up to her on the metro and says Excuse me no offense but you are not a real person because I invented you and I wrote you in this book and we are going to fall in love and then you will die. And she will believe him because he will tell her things about her life he couldn't possibly know unless he did invent her. Oh and also we will have established that she doesn't remember any of her childhood which we now know is because she really was just invented by the guy and she is only actually two years old even though she is a grownup but like she really was invented by him and I am thinking this is cool and could be a very good and very sad and also original book. It's kind of more sci-fi but in a good way like it would be a very sad love story with a sci-fi setting.

But no wait he can't not be the protagonist because her being written by him has to be his secret that he can't admit out loud. so he has to decide which ending he wants without her knowing that she might die because obviously she would just say Uh yeah no I prefer to live and so go away from me so that I don't fall in love with you and die. And besides I could never fall in love with someone who would choose to be with me while lying the whole time about the fact that being with me would kill me in the end. I think if Bob found out about me she would say that exact sentence to me.

Or that could be a good story in another way like she finds out there's this book that will kill her if it is published so she has to get it from the guy and change it fast before she dies or something but then no that is just like Stranger Than Fiction then exactly.

Actually I do not know about Bob's childhood at all but that is because I talk and talk and talk so much and never let her talk. I will ask Bob about her childhood next time we meet up which will not be tonight.

Maybe both the guy and the girl are the main character and that is what is cool about this book is that it's not just one point of view it is two. But then I think it has to be one point of view really especially if it is going to be a movie later and then I realize that this is all too complicated for right now and I will write it another day.

I check my bank online and I still have plenty of money and I know the movie of my first book is Coming Soon to DVD and Blu-Ray so I will get some more money from that and also more people will buy my books for a while after that comes out too so that will help. They brought out a new version of the first book with like pictures of all the actors from the movie of it on the cover even that guy who is probably still yelling in the bathroom.

I hate that version of the book so much it is not even possible to say how much I hate it and I even asked the publishers to keep printing the normal version as well for the people who want it but they said no because everyone would buy the non-movie version instead and therefore the movie would not get advertised and so it is better money wise to just have the movie one as the only one you can buy and so now you cannot buy the normal version which I am very angry about. And also because Bob painted the picture that is the cover of it even though she wouldn't accept any money for it which I actually think it would have been nicer of her to accept normal payment for her work rather than make me feel like I owe her.

But anyway I don't need to worry about this new book right now in terms of money so I guess I should go out to drink and yes because it is Wednesday which means cheap but good Whiskey because Whiskey Wednesday is a thing they do at a bar near me where you can have any Whiskey within reason for Well Whiskey prices. I could have Maker's Mark for instance which is my favorite but I never get that so I will probably have Booker's or Bulleit. So that is what I will do and besides the coyotes are howling now and I am afraid of them so I want to move. I sort of like the coyotes though because even though I am afraid of them they are something that it is reasonable to be afraid of not like Home Depot or parts of commercials or the area behind and under my toilet in my bathroom that I am also afraid of that because maybe spiders.

So I'm leaving my house and it is about eight o clock or nine already and it's cooler out than I was expecting and I should have worn more clothes like a jacket. I will go to the bar with the Whiskey but I hope whoever I talk to does not ask me to go dancing later because I'm bad at dancing and at talking and at flirting and at being fun and I wish there were bars where it's known that it's a bar for sad and smart people and maybe there are books to peruse and talk to people about and there is very dim light so you have to share lamp light with a stranger and that is your ice breaker. Or a bar that plays black metal from Norway so loud that it is impossible to talk to anyone you have to order Drinks by pointing at the menu or maybe by touch screen or maybe they only have one kind of Drink anyway and you just sit or stand and brood and if you want to meet someone who is sad you just go up to them and since it's too loud to talk you don't have to talk about like sports or the weather or anything stupid like that. You just either be sad together and later you fuck or she says no thanks.

I turn the corner onto the main street and light a cigarette that is old and gross and not even worth it so I throw it out and stamp it and give the rest of the pack to a group of those like twenty something punk rocker homeless people and these ones have two puppies.

I wonder to myself who those homeless twenty something punk rockers are. Like they always have just puppies and never full grown dogs and they never really look like they've been homeless long like they don't look filthy or sick but I always see them on the streets begging even late at night and all day so I wonder who those people really are. Like what is their lives.

Their tattoos are not terrible I mean the designs are dumb like just skulls and flames and words and hot rods and pinup girls but they are not done like by the guys themselves with a bic pen and a safety pin you know so these homeless people must have paid for them to be done professionally and they do not look like hungry people to me. Like how are you barely twenty and covered in so many tattoos and also broke. They look hungry I guess but like hungry like if you were really busy or on a bender and so you forgot to eat for a couple days. Not hungry like you have not been able to eat regularly for like a month even though you have wanted to so badly and so I wonder who these people are and I even think the one girl punk rocker is actually pretty hot and she has a half shaved head and big breasts in a black bra under a wifebeater which I always like that look and I wonder which of the guys' girlfriend she is and I think the answer is probably all of them.

And sometimes I see these punk people with Alcoholic Drinks like Tallboys of Budweiser or these pints of Mad Dog in brown paper bags and that is why I do not give them money even though if I become homeless I will definitely buy Alcohol before food unless I was literally starved because I mean obviously. Also I feel bad for these homeless people's puppies so I give them money sometimes I mean I give the people the money and hope they feed the puppies food that is good for puppies and not like Flamin' Hot Cheetos but I never see the same puppies twice and so now I am thinking that maybe this is a scam after all but I don't really want to think about them or that or what happens to the puppies so I just stop thinking about them which I should anyway because now they are a few blocks behind me and gone so who cares.

So I go back to thinking about why I find easy things so hard I mean things like dancing and talking and smiling and being fun because those things are easy things and they are things everyone else can do and they even look forward to doing them but I am afraid of them and also driving a car I know such stupid people who are much better drivers than I am but I just find it all very hard and a little bit scary to drive a car if I am going to be honest.

But then again there are things I find very easy that lots of people would find hard like having good ideas for books that become respected or successful and having the motivation to write entire books like that and just do it with no boss or mentor or anything I just get it done.

And I don't think other people would have the strength I need to live with this awful thing of the darkness and the lying all the time every single day and moving all the time and always being on the run that is the hardest thing I do but I do it every day and even though it takes up a huge amount of energy to keep it going it really isn't all that hard to me anymore I am used to it.

Mostly.

Most people I think would not be able to handle this thing living in them and they would probably kill themselves or just go totally off the deep end if they had this dark thing I have where there is another evil person inside of me. And then I wonder if all those homeless insane people you see are just like me and have this dark other person too except they were not born to rich and proper parents who could buy them like all the best mood stabilizers and send them to expensive shrinks who made sure to teach them how to pretend to the world like they didn't have this dark thing. It would have been better for me to admit a long time ago that I had this dark thing and then work on that than to just pretend otherwise. Because I mean look where pretending has gotten me.

I wonder if these homeless people if their parents threw them out of the house for having the darkness or for lying even and they just struggled with the darkness until one day they couldn't any more and the darkness took them over and then next

thing you know they are the man with a big beard running up the
street with no pants or underwear on peeing while running and
yelling about Jew Niggers did 9/11. Whatever that is supposed
to even mean.

That is a real person I saw him last week.

Even though I am so super lucky overall because of like
I do not have any diseases or anything unless you count this
darkness as a disease which I do not and I never want to call
it a disease because every stupid thing is a disease nowadays
or a syndrome and it is not true for me. Like I know exactly
what I am and that is I am an awful person who does awful
things that is all. Like OK maybe there is some chemical fuckup
that makes me more likely to do bad things and lie but come on
I make a decision every time I lie just like an addict makes a
decision to drink or do a drug. And if I do get exposed I will
not say

Don't blame me I have a syndrome! I will just be like
Yeah I'm an awful person that is true you got me. Then I will
probably just run away again unless someone loved me enough to
forgive me but no one could be like that. Sucks because anyone
who would do that is someone I know is automatically a sucker
and I wouldn't like them anymore so yeah basically fucked.

Like OK maybe being insane is a disease in a way but I
don't think I'm insane I'm just an asshole. Like OK so maybe I
feel like there are more than one person living inside of me
most of the time and that is clearly not exactly an optimal
scenario mental health wise but that doesn't mean insane it's
just like a weird thing I have. Like Walt Whitman once said Do
I contradict myself? Very well then I contradict myself. I
contain multitudes.

And I do not contain multitudes just two people. And lots of normal people are fans of Walt Whitman and think he is cool so I am not insane I just have a big issue I am working on at the moment and the unfortunate symptom is that I am making things up a lot and living with darkness. OK I mean I'm not really working on it or doing anything about it but I'm worrying a lot about it so that's something it is a start.

I am also lucky I never had to worry about money or food I mean my parents are pretty well off just like Bob's. Although now I start to worry about that because I cannot talk to my family any more obviously and so if I ran out of money here I would really be in trouble like everyone else in the world. That is suddenly frightening to me because money has never been a big deal like I said I never freaked out that I might end up like the homeless people. And also like I live cheaper than most people I know most of the time but now I am worried about money.

So I think I should make sure to work on that book tomorrow and I should spend money on less stupid stuff like books which I buy so many books when I should be downloading them illegally for free for my Kindle instead and then I buy new bookshelves to hold all the more new books which instead of all that I should also be selling old books because I never will re-read a book ever because I already am very afraid of dying without having read enough books so why would I re-read a book. But I keep books because for some reason I think if I have a library of books I have known and loved that maybe that will be one way I can keep parts of my past around that I don't have to be ashamed of. If I can read enough books then maybe I can bury myself in enough stories told by other people and then maybe they will pile up higher than the stories told by me and I can just die forgotten if not forgiven because I am unforgivable but forgotten will be OK.

So yeah even though I am basically very lucky and I do know that but it doesn't change the fact that I am still so very tired by this evil darkness and exhausted all the time and just so tired. If I could ever be OK with this thing I am and this other person in me like if I could just accept him for five minutes or he went away I think I would sleep for so long I would starve to death before I wake up.

The normal me and the darkness that is also me are bitter old enemies but they also are almost friends sometimes. Like they are old rivals who respect each other's role in the fight over who gets to be in charge of me or something. But at the same time they both know only of them is walking away and I am scared because the darkness is looking more powerful every day.

Enemy is not the exact word for what the darkness is and what is the right word I think. Yes I know what the word is and it is

FOURTEEN

Nemesis.

Even though it's definitely scary to have a darkness inside me fighting it out with the good person I still can't help but feel like being split in two is just as essential a part of me as being normal is essential to normal people. Like you're probably thinking Oh how weird it must be to be like this guy but it's not weird to me it is normal even though I know it is bad. If I woke up without Nemesis I don't know if I would feel relieved or alone.

For the record the various characters I play when I lie aren't so much like other people inside me like Nemesis. They are just like symptoms and like actions that this other person this Nemesis makes me do. Inside there is just me and him.

As for what he looks like sometimes I see Nemesis as a grinning but handsome and sexy man who's a lot like me but way more aggressive and attractive. And then other times he is just a purple and black kind of liquid sphere of like anti-matter or something and sometimes he is this purple and black wolf with like facial markings and other times he looks exactly like me but a really sexy girl instead and sometimes he talks to me and pretends to be Bob but I know it is not Bob and it is Nemesis.

And Nemesis makes me pretend to be all of those other characters like lawyer guy and band guy and backpacker guy because Nemesis shows me how weak and pathetic and ugly and fat and stupid I am and he says But you don't have to be like that you could be like me instead and I am sexy and confident and I get what I want and I would have fucked Bob like a million times by now if you were me and so you should choose to be me instead.

But I say No Nemesis I know what you really are and so I will not be you I will be anyone but you but also I can't be the real stupid normal me who I really am obviously because I am the worst. And so I decide to be other characters and make up stories to escape Nemesis and his name calling. But then I wonder What if he is really winning if I do that and what if that is what he wanted all along is for me to be afraid of him and do bad things as a result.

By the way the word Nemesis doesn't exactly mean sworn enemy or opponent like people think it does because it means not so much enemy as it means like counterpart or counterpoint even like complementary more than opposite.

Like the actual Greek word nemesis means to settle a deal or to cancel a debt or to restore balance. Like the word economy comes from nemesis and you can kind of see the word nemesis in the word economy. So I think even if Nemesis went away which I want so badly because I am just so exhausted from dealing with him and being afraid of him and his laughing at me but even if he did finally go away I do not know what would be left because the guy who was left wouldn't be the same without him and there would be a big imbalance. I mean the main guy would have no idea who he is without Nemesis that's for sure and even if I'd be free from Nemesis I would have to actually start over and think Who is it I want to be for real in my new life as a good person and I would have no idea and would probably just sit in my room staring at the wall being nobody forever.

But the main guy the nice guy is better than Nemesis and he is more like other normal people. OK so maybe he's a big wimp but at least he doesn't hurt anyone else and so what if maybe he doesn't get all the things he wants like girls and happiness and Bob but at least he doesn't make up lies that hurt his family and wife and Minnesota girl.

Meanwhile the normal me thinks that Nemesis is like a brute and a beast and basically a rapist honestly on a moral level. And then Nemesis thinks the smart and civilized and social and fun guy is a giant pussy and also most of all a big fat fraud and a fake nice-guy who uses guilt to get girls to fuck him which Nemesis thinks is more evil than just preying on women but not pretending anything.

Sorry that was all a lie I do not actually have a Nemesis I just get a little bit sad sometimes and it makes it easier if I invent a bad second character who makes me feel sad rather than just being sad for basically no reason.

No that was the lie actually I definitely do have Nemesis but that is the one lie I want to tell the most and have it be true and god I wish it was that easy to just say I don't have him and he would go away and I would stop making an enemy of myself for no real reason.

This is not Fight Club by the way I know that book and movie is kind of about this same thing but while Nemesis is kind of like Tyler Durden because he is like tough and aggressive and like physical and sexy I do not imagine him outside my body as like another real person I mean I would have to be totally Koo Koo for Coco Puffs to do that so yeah this is not Fight Club.

And plus that idea has already been done obviously.

OK so Nemesis sort of is my Tyler Durden I guess but he stays inside my head to taunt me and does not exist outside of my head and so I am not as insane as the guy in Fight Club OK.

Also this is not Fight Club because we are talking about this openly now and not waiting for the end like some kind of twist ending to talk about Nemesis for what he is OK.

I wonder if Chuck Palahniuk who wrote Fight Club has a Nemesis too and then I think well you don't necessarily have to just wonder because he is still alive obviously he's not even old and I mean I have published some books so I wonder if I could get John my agent to arrange for me to get in touch with Chuck Palahniuk and ask him one day because Nemesis and I do fight each other that is for sure and I sort of feel exactly like that one scene from Fight Club sometimes like I am just hitting myself in the face over and over.

So while it is nice to at least have a name for it now and that name is called Nemesis it still makes me feel sad because it is when I let Nemesis take over that I end up being sexy and able to seduce women or perform well in like high pressured pitch meetings or even just going out and getting things I want to get or do but that I felt guilty about getting while I was the other guy the normal me. I end up feeling guilty about them the next day when I am the normal guy and Nemesis is sleeping but at least I got them when I maybe wanted them or something.

For some reason I am remembering now I had this sex dream once about this one sort of cute girl who works at the coffee shop I go to the most and in the dream she was awful in bed like she just lay there and I woke up and wondered why I would fantasize about having bad sex I mean it's my dream why wouldn't I have awesome sex with her and then that made me feel sad because I guess even on like the most subconscious level I do not think I deserve to be happy and have awesome sex so I make sex fantasies for myself where I'm not even happy and that is a pretty sad state of affairs I guess because I know if Nemesis dreamed that dream he would have had really awesome sex with her in the dream and then probably in real life too.

I know I need to stop living in my head so much and like live in the present moment more so I stop thinking and just look around and so I do I look around and take stock of my surroundings now. I am walking past another bar I sometimes go to and it is too full of people who are just happy and laughing and cheersing steins of German Beer and being happy and I do not have the strength to be happy tonight.

Because of Nemesis I really honestly do not feel lonely ever and I do not know what that might feel like because I always have this other presence with me and he is more than enough he is too much actually and I just wish I could be alone for real without him. When I am alone though I do not get lonely like other people say they do I just get afraid because then it is just me and Nemesis and he is obviously stronger.

Whenever someone leaves my house like especially when Bob leaves from visiting me and she closes the door I sort of picture it in my head like that scene in lots of movies where you know we have all seen this kind of scene before. Like there is an abusive husband and his wife is there and there is a friend who has dropped by to borrow something right when the husband is in the middle of hitting the wife and like you know the wife is there with a face that will be puffed up soon so the husband wants the neighbor to leave right away but the wife wants to tell the friend so badly she wants to say Help.

But she doesn't because she knows if she tells on her husband then the consequences will be worse but she wants to say Help. Anyway but she doesn't and then the friend leaves clueless and the door closes and you know the situation is about to get even worse inside the house behind the door yeah well that is what it feels like when Bob leaves me and Nemesis just looks at me and knows it's just him and me now and I'm about to get hurt.

It's dumb in the movies that the wife doesn't say Help. Or just run away to the cops because the husband would go to jail and she would be safe from him. Like the wife could just say she is going out for something else and go to the police or even just text her friend Help me call the cops he is abusive and then the husband would not be able to hit her any more because he would be in jail.

But I cannot do that because no one can take Nemesis away from me and even though I sort of want to say Bob help. I mean what would that even mean like how could she help me anyway and she would stop being my friend if she knew all this stuff too and then at night it would just be me and Nemesis again and he would make fun of me for being a big baby and asking for help from a girl and not just any girl but a girl who I should be acting tough around and seducing and not asking her to help me.

What is weird though is that I think Nemesis thinks if I let him win and take me over completely that things will actually get much better for me and sometimes I wonder if he is right. Like I will get more things that I want probably but I am afraid to do that I am afraid because it is like the vampire thing I talked about all I have to do is say OK Nemesis we will try it your way this time you can come in completely. And then there is no going back and I don't want to become a bad creature like that but he is still rapping on the window and grinning and saying Come on let me in I'll be good for you.

I also think that Jekyll and Hyde is a metaphor for this thing also and then I wonder if maybe Robert Louis Stephenson had a Nemesis of his own. Or even the very same Nemesis who is inside of me now that is kind of a cool idea actually. Like what if there is only set number of Nemeses throughout time like an evil version of a muse who is eternal and hops from person to person that could be an interesting story. Like the story would be from the point of view of the Nemesis obviously.

Thinking about other people having Nemesis makes me a little happier. But then not really because who cares if I am not the only one who has a Nemesis because it's still my life that is terrible for having him and I do not feel better from knowing other people are doing worse.

Lots of people do feel that way though like they feel better if other people do worse and I am proud that I am not like that because at least that is one thing I do that is brave and not weak and I know Nemesis loves it when other people fail and so that is another reason I do not want to let him in.

Actually no that is a lie. Well it's not a lie but it's not true I was wrong and that's different from being a real lie but anyway it was not true. I actually think it might be the other way around actually I do not know because the rational and mild mannered me is more the jealous type actually because like when Bob tells me she got laid the civilized person in me gets very jealous and angry but Nemesis doesn't even care he's just like Whatever the only sex life that should affect your mood is your own sex life so the only time Bob's sex life should matter to you is if you are fucking Bob and so her sex

life is your sex life too and otherwise who cares. And I know
Nemesis is right about that and in a way he is braver than me
for saying that.

That is what is hard is sometimes I think Nemesis is
more moral and braver than the other me so what do I do with
that.

Ugh I am so tired of thinking about this it is all I
ever think about and it almost doesn't matter who is right or
wrong they're both here and fighting and no one is leaving any
time soon. Or maybe it does matter to think about it maybe it
matters more than anything else.

I don't know and I am a little bit afraid to think about
this any more right now and I wish the Whiskey Wednesdays bar
was closer with its loud music.

The other thing I think about now since there is like
three more blocks and I have to think about something and I do
not believe people who say they can just think about nothing or
just stop thinking I think that is a lie because there is no
way you can turn off the voice and narrative in your head. That
is just stupid and some dumb yuppie yoga B-S.

So the thing I think about is that I think that maybe
this feeling is also what people talked about in the old days
when they talked about people being possessed by the devil or
even a minor demon or whatever. OK wait hold on I don't mean
like I am going to turn my head all the way around and speak in
tongues or anything or start burning black candles in my room
and like shave my head and have just a goatee or burn a church
down or something ha-ha. Nothing like that but I do feel kind
of invaded that is for sure and I think possession by devils is
just a good metaphor for having a dark visitor really.

It's insane though that loads of people nowadays actually believe in like literal devils and stuff though and are like so afraid of actual literal demons they won't let their kids read like Harry Potter or play World of Warcraft because it contains demons that might get into the kids.

I'm no example of goodness obviously but I know plenty of people who have read Harry Potter and who play World of Warcraft who are not invaded by a Nemesis and I highly doubt that the reason Nemesis came into me is because I played the wrong video game as a kid. Although that is also an interesting idea for a book or a movie but there must already be a movie about a haunted video game but just in case I make a note of that idea on my iPhone anyway to check later and to write it if not. What was the other idea I just had that was good. Shit but oh well. I'm glad I have loads of ideas.

Jesus fucking whatever who cares about any of this.

Anyway thank god I am at the bar now and I know the bouncer and he claps me on the shoulder and I nod and do not shake his hand because that would take some seconds to talk to him and the music and Whiskey has to happen right now and the voices have to stop right now I get into the bar and the music is something loud it is Guns N' Roses and that is a stupid phony band for white trash but right now anything loud is just fine. I'm not white trash though.

FIFTEEN

Guns N' Roses is not really sexy to me because it's just so
over the top talking about sex explicitly and like I said I
need to be able to see a sadness in something for it to turn me
on and Guns N' Roses is just happy sexy happy all the time.
Like when I hear Guns N' Roses I feel like I am being sold sex
as a product and so I feel about as sexy after listening to
Guns N' Roses as I feel like I want a hamburger after I watch a
Burger King commercial. Which is not at all. Because I feel
shifty that someone is trying to rip me off. But right now in
this rock bar the Guns N' Roses is very loud and that is good.

The bartender knows me here which I both like and sort
of am also afraid of because I sometimes think the bartender
thinks about me when he goes home and maybe he thinks I drink
too much on my own and so I am lame and I also think maybe he
sort of thinks I am a chump because I tip him pretty well even
though he secretly has this really low opinion of me. But then
again he has seen me here with Bob a lot and he has also seen
me take a few girls home from here so maybe he thinks Bob is my
beautiful and great girlfriend and then I am also a big player
on the side and so maybe he thinks I am cool I do not know.

Anyway he is pouring me a Whiskey Diet before I even sit
down even though my favorite Drink is actually Maker's Mark on
The Rocks but how is he supposed to know that if I have never
ordered it. And so I think to myself that I like him for
pouring me a Drink right away as I sit myself on the bar stool.
Just like always I sit funny on it so I do not fall off of it
ever and I miss Bob a little bit now.

I think to myself and I am remembering my idea for the
movie about Katy Perry and Zooey Deschanel sisters and now I am

thinking that another way to go with that movie would be that they are the same person and like Katy Perry is the Tyler Durden and Zooey Deschanel is the whatever Edward Norton's character's name was but that would be another movie entirely and I do not want to think about movies or writing but that is better than thinking about Nemesis so I will think about that movie idea until the Whiskey Diet makes me stop thinking about anything at all and so I ask for another one before I have even sipped the first one but that is not Alcoholic of me it is normal because they are 2 for the price of 1 that is what Whiskey Wednesdays means.

I am kind of closing my eyes and focusing everything I have on drinking this Whiskey and thinking about the guitar solo which I always hate this guitar solo in Sweet Child O' Mine even though everyone loves it I think it is lame.

Someone punches me very hard on my arm and I think that this must either be Bob by random coincidence she is here or maybe it's this one guy I sort of know who would punch someone hello because he's like a bro in that way. But if it is not Bob or this guy then I am about to become in a real fight I suppose and why did I have to come here to a bar where there is a fight and this was all a mistake.

I look and it is not Bob or a fight but a short and sexy girl who cannot be much taller than five feet tall and she has an amazing little compact body and tan skin and like a girl version of a pompadour haircut and lots of black eyeliner and torn black jeans and she is Latin or something like she has one of those amazing faces like an Aztec princess kind of but whatever race she is I definitely want to have sex with her because she is very hot and who says hello with a punch anyway but I sort of like it I think it is cute.

I remember that I used to punch Bob on the shoulder in a friendly way but she never punched me back so I am guessing she did not like that or she did not think it was cute. Or maybe punching me back is just another one of the many little physical things Bob could do with me that wouldn't cost her anything but it would make me so very happy but she refuses to do them because she hated me.

So I look at this punching girl and I have a face on like OK so what was that all about just then but I also have a little bit of a flirty face on at least I hope that is what it looks like anyway and she looks up and is kind of looking through me so she is a little bit very drunk already which I also like and so now I am liking this girl a whole lot.

I think that I hope I get a chance look at her breasts soon because they look big definitely bigger than Bob's 34C and her tank top is low cut but I know I can't look not yet I am just meeting her. So she looks up at me and she says to me

Isn't it all just better… drunk?

And I say to myself Yes I like this girl very much now and I tell her that. I say Can we fall in love please because this was the best intro I've heard in a long time and it would be a great story to tell our friends and grandchildren and yes it is all better drunk and what can I get you in terms of to drink.

I am feeling a little bit smooth and sexy for saying this now but not really because of the words themselves which were clumsy. But more my sudden attitude and confidence like I am feeling Nemesis rising up in me and taking charge of this situation and I am OK with this because I know Nemesis sees this punching girl and recognizes her as one of his kind and so I decide to let Nemesis call the shots because he will know what is best to do with this one.

The first thing Nemesis says to me is This one's good because she's a drunkard like you and so she'll look at your drinking and think that it is your only darkness because if people know you have one major darkness they won't think you could have another darkness that is much worse so I will be safe from her but she will not be safe from me and neither will you.

Then this girl says to me Sorry I only date women but we can be drinking friends tonight. And suddenly I feel angry again and wish I had never even come out of the house tonight at all and now Nemesis is like What the fuck man I just woke up for nothing. And I am a little bit afraid of what he will do now because I had told him he could take care of this situation and now there is no situation for him to take care of so what if he creates a situation. A bad one.

But then I switch from Nemesis back to the wimpy character which takes a lot of effort and Nemesis does not care for this decision and wimpy me is not happy either because he was kind of ready for like a rest or a nap or something and I also am not entirely happy about this because this girl would respond much better to Nemesis either way so no one is happy and everything is ruined but I have to pretend to be happy and not ruined now. Or should I be sad for this girl actually maybe she would like that and Oh No what do I do now and how do I be.

I just say Oh.

And the girl says Cool so you don't have to buy me a
Drink now I will get my own. And I say No I still will. And I
wonder why I said that but it felt like the most proper thing
to do which means mild-mannered wimpy me must be up to bat
again. Because Nemesis would have been like OK yeah buy your
own Drink lesbian. She says No don't worry about it seriously.

She looks at the bartender to order a Drink and now I
have the chance to look at her breasts and I do and they are
great and possibly they are fake because they look really round
which I still do not know if I have an opinion on that whole
important question of fake breasts but it doesn't matter anyway
because she is a lesbian so I will never find out.

It would not be the first time I fell in love with a
lesbian because I usually do like girls who are a little
tomboyish and spunky like Bob and my wife and also for instance
I was on the set when they were making the movie of my first
book and I kind of fell in love with the sound girl who was
really cute and little and wore this cute toolbelt and I like a
girl with a toolbelt for some reason and I asked her out and
she was a lesbian.

But now I do not even know if I can handle this scenario
but hey I am talking to her apparently about the song that is
being played and I do not know what it is but it is some kind
of really poppy hair metal like maybe Poison or Ratt or Warrant
or Whitesnake and it is obviously awful but at least it is safe
music because it is so obviously posturing as a sexy commercial
that it has no chance of actually turning anyone on or having
any effect on anyone who is not stupid white trash.

So I say to her Have you seen the music video for this
song. Which is a bit of a risky lie because what if this is not

a big single and so it never had a music video and she knows all of that. But she says Of course I have seen it I had MTV in the nineties.

And I say to her OK seriously so how were these spandex wearing poofy hair men ever supposed to be like super manly and sexy and she says I know you are right and that's why I never got into boys as a teenager was because yeah I love rock music so much but the men who were making rock music when I was a teenager were all such gigantic faggots how am I supposed to want to fuck them.

I do not know how I feel about the fact that she just used that word faggots because at first I am shocked because it came out of nowhere and then I think Oh wait it is OK for her to say that word because she is a lesbian. But then I think Wait are lesbians actually allowed to say faggot or not I don't know. And then I kind of find it sexy that she used that bad word and called Poison or Ratt or Warrant or Whitesnake faggots and then I feel very very bad about all of this because I know hate speech is very bad and I have nothing against gay people and I sympathize with them a little bit because I suspect that being gay and closeted might feel sort of like having this darkness because it's this big secret that it feels like if everyone knew about it then everything would be ruined but it's doing more damage not dealing with it than if you just came out. Sometimes I look at openly gay people and I am happy for them but then sad for me because they look so comfortable with themselves and proud and I wish I could have that instead of always being ashamed and afraid.

But then I feel worse than ever though because there is a major difference which is that being gay isn't bad but this

Nemesis and lying is very bad like I should truly be ashamed of
it like that is the right response is to be ashamed but gay
people shouldn't be ashamed so then I feel bad about myself for
even thinking that.

So yeah I should not be OK with this punching girl using
that word or actually I shouldn't be OK with liking that she
used it. But then I also think Hey I should not feel bad
because it is not my fault that those bands actually kind of
are faggots. I mean they are the ones that got together one day
and were like

You know what. Those bands that are around now like
Venom and Annihilator and Testament and Dark Angel and Napalm
Death and Overkill all those bands yeah well they are not real
heavy metal but you know what we could do that would be way
more heavy metal than all those bands would be if we all wear
spandex and lipstick and glitter and poof our hair out and sing
power ballads about flowers and rain and friends we had who
died. And yeah then that will get fat white trash housewives
all wet in their jorts that don't fit. Yeah that sounds much
better than being in some dumb band like Slayer or Celtic
Frost.

And so I think to myself it is their fault for totally
pussifying heavy metal and so that is what I tell this punching
girl. I tell her Why did rock and roll have to get pussified in
the early nineties anyway and she says I know right. And then I
take a huge risk and say something honest but unpopular and I
say OK so everyone says grunge was the antidote to all that
hair metal crap because it was real and not theatrical and it
was honest but I think grunge as a movement and a scene is
bullshit and wearing a cardigan and moping around all day is

just as much of a costume as looking like Van Halen. Thankfully the girl says Yes I do agree in general but Pearl Jam are actually a very good band from the grunge time. I say I will check them out more I have not given them a fair chance. And I add Nirvana has some good songs and she says Meh and I say Yes actually meh is right about Nirvana.

So now I am thinking this is a pretty good conversation to be having and Bob does not know about heavy metal so this is nice and now I am not as angry this girl here for being a lesbian any more because the feeling of horniness has passed even though she is still very sexy but I can deal with it and just enjoy the fact hat I am talking to a hot girl about metal. Like we might flirt a bit but it's just for fun and not with all the drama that comes from trying to seduce someone. I realize now Bob stresses me out so much because every little talk we have is like dripping with my wondering if this is part of a seduction conversation. Seduction conversations should last like a half hour and not several years like I've been having with Bob without her even having it back. That is too tiring.

So we are talking about heavy metal for a long time now and I like that we share some opinions on heavy metal bands that no one else has that opinion or at least that they lie about like for instance that Motorhead only ever wrote one song and they are not all that great of a band they are more of a soundtrack to drinking and smoking cigarettes. Which is fine it's not a bad thing but you can't really talk about them like seriously. Although Lemmy is obviously a total badass.

And we say that Dio is a very overrated singer and even if maybe he is technically a better singer than Ozzy who cares because Sabbath totally sucks without Ozzy and also guess who's still alive and who's not alive and she says Oh that's too soon but who cares it's true. Then even the bartender says It is both too soon and also true and he puts on Children of the Grave by Black Sabbath with Ozzy on the bar's iPod just for us and all three of us take a Shot of Jack Daniel's.

And we say You know what some of these awful Hot Topic kind of Mallcore bands that usually have emo hair and a girl playing on keyboards and too-long names are actually fun to listen to. Like everyone hates those bands because they are such easy targets but do you know what well some of those bands are really just fun to listen to and to rock out to and isn't being fun to listen to enough of a thing for heavy metal to be and when did people start taking metal so seriously and academically like not every band needs to be all serious. And I say It's because everyone has a blog and so they think their dumb little opinion matters so they feel obliged to be super serious all the time in case like in ten years someone laughs at them for once saying a fun little rock album was good and not sellout. And the punching girl says Yes that might be true and that rocking out and having fun is good but Poison are still a bunch of fags and I say Yup.

Painkiller by Judas Priest comes on at the bar music and I think Hooray and then Oh No because I love the drums at the start and the guitar riffs and solo are really really awesome but then I think Oh No because I hate Rob Halford's squealy voice a lot.

Then this punching girl is like reading my mind and she says Rob Halford has a really annoying high voice and the band would be better with a more normal singer. And I say Yes and

high five her and then I think of a joke to make and I make it
and this is the joke I say

You know what. And I slap my hand on the table like I am
about to make a big declaration and I say Even though Rob
Halford is actually a gay man. Which by the way he really is he
is actually literally gay. I say Even though Rob Halford is
actually a gay man who literally likes dick he is still less of
a faggot than Poison.

And this girl laughs a very big loud laugh from her
belly and it is a really definitely real laugh not a fake one
and I realize how long it has been since I heard a real big
laugh and I am pleased that I made her laugh that big laugh and
she is laughing and she puts her hand on my upper leg like to
say Oh you are too funny but where she puts her hand is
accidentally where my penis is which apparently I am half hard
which I did not notice that and she feels it and says Hello.

I am obviously instantly super horny again now because
this hot girl just talked to me about heavy metal and then
touched my penis even accidentally and now Nemesis comes out
and he is like Hey dude I know she said she is a lesbian and
everything but I know what I am seeing here and I'm going after
her anyway so stand back. And I say to Nemesis No we will not
be able to get her she is a lesbian. But even I have to admit
to myself that if this was any other girl I would think I could
probably ask her to get out of here right now and does she want
to hear my own music and we would be having sex within like a
half hour and so I am confused about this punching girl.

She has not taken her hand off me though but isn't like
doing anything about it either it's just kind of there and then
she says Do you want to get out of here. And now I am so

confused I can't even deal with it and I start to say something like Wait but I thought you said.

But then she interrupts me and says Let's go to another bar because you need to walk that off. And by THAT she means my being basically having an erection right now right in the middle of this bar and so I say OK good call.

I go to the bathroom to pee away the erection real quick and also just to pee because by now we have had four Tall Boys of Budweiser each which is what eighty eight ounces which is like what about two thirds of a gallon of Budweiser which seems like a lot of Beer and I am now remembering my idea of getting interesting facts about your life right before you die like I would be very curious how many gallons of Beer I have drunk total because I bet it is a whole lot of gallons of Beer.

We also drank three *Jäger* Shots which I am happy we did because Bob hates *Jäger* so we never drink that together and I do not love *Jäger* exactly because if I loved it I would drink it myself whether or not Bob likes it but *Jäger* is kind of a weird Drink to drink just by yourself. Anyway I do not love it but I do like it from time to time and it is an excellent Shot to take with someone when you are talking about heavy metal.

I am peeing and my pee is highlighter green from all the vitamins and pills I take and so I don't want to look at that and I am reading the graffiti on the walls above the urinal and I am thinking that this bar is very new and that there is no way that is like real graffiti that someone really wrote and probably some really well paid like skinny gay interior designer who probably goes on interior design reality TV shows on like HGTV it is probably him who put that graffiti there and pasted the band flyers there and I wonder if they are even of real bands.

And I realize that the idea that this is all fake and manicured would make me angry most of the time but right now I just think it's kind of goofy and dumb and funny that's all. Like seriously what difference does it make to me if a bar is kind of fakey. I feel glad to not be angry about something for once.

So I realize I'm having a pretty nice night after all I guess even though I know I will end up being angry later at the end of the night because I will not have sex with this hot girl and by then I will really really want to especially if we drink more at another bar but overall I am not feeling very angry about that and so we will deal with that when we come to it.

And while I am peeing I

OK stop you know what I am really talking way too much now about breasts and peeing and erections and stuff like that I mean that is obviously not a good enough of a subject to talk about. Everyone pees and everyone has either breasts or a penis and nothing is interesting about those things unless you are like fifteen years old. But actually who cares because even though the thoughts I have about those things are not like the most profound thoughts that I ever have they are still thoughts that I have pretty often and not every piece of writing has to be like fucking Dostoevsky. I am sort of lying to make that reference because I have actually never read anything by him even though Bob always tells me to read him and you cannot be a real writer or even just a real grownup and not have ever read any Dostoevsky. But yeah who knows maybe Dostoevsky does write about breasts and pee and erections I don't even know.

177

I leave the bathroom thinking Yes I really am in a pretty good mood after all and I wonder if it is Nemesis or wimpy me who is happy right now and I can not tell but overall I'm not feeling very angry or sad and so that is fine to not be able to tell if it is normal me or Nemesis.

I get to the punching girl again and she is sitting down on a stool and I put my hand on her bare shoulder which is showing because she is wearing a black tank top for some black metal band with an illegible logo and a red bra and I put my hand on her shoulder but firmly and I kind of rub it a little bit and lean in to her like I am flirting which then I think Why am I flirting with her she is a lesbian but I still want to and so I do and I think this girl's shoulders are very nice but not quite as nice as Bob's shoulders because I just think nice shoulders look the very nicest when they are very white and Bob is very pale and has no freckles I have ever seen and this girl is tan or Latina and that is not racist her shoulders are nice too I just like very pale shoulders that is all and then I realize Oh stupid I should have punched this girl on her arm that would have been a fun flirty thing to do but her shoulder feels nice now so whatever. Also what if it was the wrong girl I punched then I would become in a fight after all.

This girl turns and she looks me in the eye which she can do because me standing up and her sitting way up on this stool makes us the same height and she does this really sexy grin that is totally a Let's have sex grin and I think What the hell is going on and she says to me Has the popsicle melted.

And I think to myself That is a kind of lame joke but then I also think that I sort of like when hot girls make lame jokes and I do not think I would want my lovers to be better at

178

jokes or being smart than me other than Bob and then I remember this girl is not my lover anyway so who cares. Why do I have to decide what my ultimate opinion is on everything why can't I just enjoy the joke and not have to wonder what I think about it on like an existential level and let's just move on OK.

Anyway I say Yes. And I try to think of another way of saying it that is better than Has the popsicle melted but I can't think of it and then I'm thinking if there is a joke to make about like comparing sticky melted popsicle to like pre-cum or something and then I think This is all so very dumb and you do not talk about pre-cum to a girl you just met even if she made a popsicle joke and What is wrong with me and lets just go and so I say Let's go and we do we go.

She hops off the stool and I realize now she really is tiny like five foot zero which then I think very short girls really are just so cute especially if they have great bodies and full breasts and are kind of spunky and I think Bob is pretty short too and spunky but not as short as this girl because Bob is five feet four and this girl can not be more than five foot one inch at the most.

We get outside and I offer this girl a cigarette and she says I don't smoke cigarettes they are gross. And I am surprised she does not smoke cigarettes but I agree to myself that Actually yeah they are definitely gross but also great. And then I am sort of angry because I only took the cigarette out to offer her one and also to light it for her like I light cigarettes for Bob but now I have to smoke a cigarette I do not entirely want all on my own but oh well what does it cost like twenty five cents.

SIXTEEN

So I am outside the bar with this punching girl and I say Where
do you want to go and she says This way. And she points to the
left and I say OK where are we going to go and she says What I
just told you this way.

I say Right but what bar are we going to or club and she
says It doesn't matter because we are taking this road in this
direction and that is all that matters.

And I say What is that from is it from Kerouac or is it
from Bret Easton Ellis or what is it from and she says No it is
from George and I say It is from George who and she says It is
from George me and I say Wait really your name is George and
she says Yes it is short for Georgiana but I go by George
because Georgiana sounds too much like vagina.

I laugh out loud and it is a real laugh that's for sure
but not as big as her laugh inside was. And laughing honestly
feels very weird to me and it sounds unnatural and a little
scary so I am instantly sad about my laughing feeling so weird
and alien but anyway I am laughing because I am thinking Yes of
course her name is George because all I need in my life is
another beautiful short woman who has a boy's name who I want
to have sex with and have be my girlfriend and who that will
never ever happen.

But I say What do you do George like for work and she
says Shut up that is a dumb question and we already talked
about way better and more important stuff than what do you do
for work and where are you from originally and what is your
star sign and I say OK I guess.

But who knows what to talk about next because now I have
to come up with something really good and again I think Where

are we going and I do not feel in control of the situation now because there are really no good bars any further this way just offices and sketchiness but she goes right ahead and we are now walking down into The Metro apparently and I am thinking Why are we going to the metro because I was not planning on leaving Hollywood tonight it is already kind of late and I am tired and I want to write tomorrow in the morning which I realize is a lie I do not want to write I just do not feel comfortable going somewhere unknown with this punching girl right now.

So I ask again Sorry but just where are we going and she says Chill out it's not the destination it's the journey and I think to myself What is this the nineteen sixties that's so cheesy. This is how horror movies start and not how porno movies or buddy movies start.

But I say Yeah OK cool let's do it. But not because I am excited for an adventure which I am never excited for an adventure I always just want to go home but because I just don't have it in me to argue with anyone right now or be in charge of the whole world's every decision or whatever.

George buys a one way metro ticket because she does not have a metro month pass like I do.

We go down to the platform where there is a white homeless woman shitting over the edge of the platform onto the tracks and I cannot help laughing again really hard and loud this time and like honestly laughing so hard because it is so stupid and weird of a scene and it is so unexpected to see it and it was exactly at the same second as I figured out what this woman is doing being squatted over the edge of the platform that the shit came out so I am laughing at that and other people on the platform are laughing and running away.

George is not laughing she is just standing there with her jaw hanging open and I look at her and say You see George sometimes having a destination in mind is better if the sights along the way are just shitting homeless. And she says Yeah let's just take a taxi directly somewhere instead now and we go back up to the street level but now I am laughing again even harder because I am thinking about the train coming and either cutting off the woman's butt or just splashing shit from the tracks onto people who came later once the woman had gone away and did not expect shit to come up from the train tracks because why would you ever expect that and then them realizing slowly Wait is this actually shit right now oh my god it is it's shit oh my god and now I am laughing even harder and feeling like You know what maybe I really am fifteen years old after all because all I can think about apparently tonight is breasts and shit and erections and pre-cum and stupid stuff like that. But to be honest with you it is sort of nice that those things are all that I have thought about tonight because they are not difficult or scary things like Nemesis or worrying about Nemesis or being sad or afraid or just stressing out and so that is nice for once.

So we get a cab and she says an address that means nothing to me but it sounds like Silverlake or Echo Park or something and I say I could go for a Beer but like a Good Beer not like more Budweiser but something stronger and kind of hoppy and she doesn't say anything to that so I ask Did you eat dinner George and she says No I did not I only had some chips but there is food where we are going. And I am thinking to myself What the fuck does that mean Where we are going. That's like the sketchiest phrasing I've ever heard. But I decide I am being afraid for no reason like usual and so I say I didn't eat dinner either but I am not really hungry but I could have a snack maybe sweet potato fries even though I got kind of maxed out on sweet potato fries when they first came around and every restaurant had them all the time but it has been long enough now that I would have them again and she says OK whatever we don't have to get food and I say Whatever. And then I feel a little bit weird and dumb because I can't tell if we decided anything about food one way or the other but I don't want to be awkward and say Wait so what did we decide actually about getting food or not. Because that is another version of asking where we are going and I am not allowed to know any information about tonight apparently.

I am thinking now that even though I am a little unsure about what's happening later but tonight has already been a lot of fun and I am wondering Do I need to tell Bob about it next time we are together or should I just have this be a nice little secret night for myself just between me and this girl George. I roll down the window all the way because the taxi smells like the driver's B-O and I like the feeling of wind on my face and a few seconds later George does the same on her side and we just look out the window like that and don't talk for a few minutes but it is nice not weird.

I think to myself You know what sometimes it is the best thing to do to just go out even though you don't want to because if I had stayed home the best thing that would have happened is I would have maybe written something but I would have probably just drunk some Whiskey Diets while pretending to try and write something and I would have just ended up doing not much other than trolling people online and then getting desperately hungry at like four in the morning when nothing is open that will deliver to me and I am too drunk to drive somewhere.

But I did go out tonight and now I have had a little adventure and who cares if I do not fuck this girl named George it was just a nice little night and I saw a funny thing and talked about heavy metal and got drunk with someone other than Bob and maybe I have a new friend.

I do not know if it is because of this weird new medication I am taking for weight loss and concentration which is called an ECA Stack and is very bad for your heart I read even if you are healthy which I am not. And so I wonder why do I even take it because how dumb would that be if I died from a weight loss and concentration pill heart attack I was taking for no reason at twenty nine years old but I just do take it all the same. Anyway I wonder if it is because of that drug or just because of something else unrelated to drugs but I am feeling very peaceful like Nemesis is sleeping and the real me or whatever the Edward Norton wimp me is also sleeping too. Not real Edward Norton I mean his character in Fight Club.

Now suddenly I am remembering this one character I used to play who I have not played in a long time and he is like this sort of spiritual zen yoga person who just meditates and is at peace with the whole world all the time and has no connection to identity or ego and thinks time is an illusion of the mind and all that stuff like that and he is who I am being while I look out the window just doing that and nothing else.

I dated someone for a very little while who was very into those spiritual things like The world will end at 2012 and crystals and smoking salvia and shopping at a co-op and eating only raw vegetables not even honey was OK. I do not know why I dated her or even more I do not know why she liked me so much but she did and I liked her until I was bored of pretending to like eating only raw vegetables and dirt like actually I am not even lying or exaggerating this time she would eat this special expensive dirt you can buy online and I could not drink Alcoholic Drinks in front of her because she thought like Alcohol was poison for your soul and I was like No I'm pretty sure that being sober and miserable is poison for your soul and anyway you are a girl who eats dirt so what do you know.

And I was also bad at pretending to like salvia which seriously is like the worst drug I have ever taken it is so dumb and it is over so fast like sixty seconds literally and the whole time you are on it you are just afraid like Wait is something even happening then Oh my god is that a snake and then Wait you mean it's over now what the fuck was that I'm never doing it again.

I remember that girl now and wonder what I was thinking dating her and her name was what was it I think it was Rain or something or Willow or Mmmmaude yeah that sounds right and wow that is so awful of me I cannot remember the name of someone I dated even though it was only for like three weeks but still yeah that is really awful. I think Wait do I not remember details about her because I made her up but then I remember No she was real I dated her.

But even though she was overall pretty dumb I did find comfort in some of her ideas she showed me about like time being an illusion and who cares about the past or the future because the past only has control over you now if you allow it to. Kind of just like the vampire.

And then the future is just a now that hasn't happened yet and so that doesn't exist either until it is actually now and then it's not the future any more and so that means there is no such thing as the future and so if you spend your whole life worrying about the future then you will never have had a good now. I know that's cheesy and I think it's a bit of a copout but right now I'm looking out the window and feeling the air and not worrying and so now feels good enough to me.

And it's kind of true because Nemesis is really only scary because of what he is threatening to do in the future that's for sure. He has never really hurt me in any present it's just what I'm afraid he will do later that makes me be bad and lie and run.

But that hippie girl was wrong about the past. Because trust me all I ever do is try to make the past never have happened and just be who I want to be right now and start fresh over every day and every new city and that is like exactly why I make stuff up so much is so that finally I can just exist right now and be who I want and who is best for this moment but it is not easy like she says because Nemesis also knows the truth and he knows all the different people I have pretended to be and he knows that really I am not as cool as any of those people I pretend to be and I never will be.

And then also the real wimpy more civilized version of me scolds me and says I am bad and that I can not forget the past because I have hurt some good people so very badly before by lying and it is not OK to forget that because they probably have not forgotten it even though I hope for their sake they have forgotten it and moved on.

Our taxi goes past a strip club I have been to once when my friend had a bachelor party and George sees me sort of look at it while we go by it and she says Do you like that place and I say Actually I don't like strip clubs all that much and she says Bullshit I caught you looking at my tits like five times. And I like that she called them her tits but I am still embarrassed to be caught having looked at them and I say OK well I like tits just fine but not strip clubs because they are really sad and the women are too aggressive and mean when they are trying to get you to buy a dance and it makes me feel like I am being hassled by a salesman at Best Buy not like I am at somewhere sexy. I think to myself it is like Guns N' Roses selling me sex like a burger commercial it just doesn't make me want sex or a burger on their terms.

Then I say to George And who even wants to get turned on a lot and then not get to come and then you pay lots of money for that and why would you do that but no I have no objection at all to tits in general though.

But I kind of pause before I say Tits because it's not a word I normally say it is a more dirty word than I would usually say I would normally say Breasts. And George catches me being nervous to say Tits and just laughs and says You can look at my tits if you want. And she faces me and pulls her tank top down a lot and pushes her bre I mean her tits up and together.

I know this is some sort of a trap but I don't care and I look at them and I do not think her breasts are fake any more no definitely not and it is great to look at them but now I am getting frustrated because this is like my third separate erection tonight over someone who the second thing she told me is she is a lesbian and off limits and my body is like What are

187

you doing and Nemesis is like What are you doing and the yoga guy is like Ohmmmmm and the normal civilized me is like You should feel ashamed of wanting to have sex with her or anyone or ever be happy in any way so stop that now and start feeling bad that is what you deserve. And this all makes me feel very angry and a little bit afraid so I just look out the window again and I kind of say in a huff You have beautiful breasts. I say Breasts not Tits and she looks kind of disappointed in me as if I was supposed to make a move on her and her pushed together tits but like what the hell and I am very confused about all of this like what was I supposed to do make a move on a lesbian in the back of a cab and I am not in as good a mood as I was any more.

We get to the address and it is apparently just her house and I do not want to go in there really I am sort of afraid of her house for some reason even though it is nice enough. Like it is weird right now because for instance if she was not a lesbian I would not be afraid because we would be going in to have sex but she is a lesbian so it's like why am I here it's like I followed some dude home to his place and I have no idea why and no one knows I am here and I wonder should I text Bob my address just in case George is a murderer or something. I am wondering all of this but wondering too slow because she has already paid the cab driver and not tipped him enough I notice so I feel embarrassed by that but anyway she's out of the cab now so I think OK so I don't want to go in there but what am I going to do now we are in the middle of what looks like Silverlake at like two in the morning and I don't care what anyone says Silverlake is really sketchy at night.

And who knows she might have more to drink inside and chances are she is not a murderer I mean come on.

And then I think there is not even any metro near here so how will I get home. I guess I will find a bus in the morning which will suck because buses are awful in LA and never come on time or they just take days off for no reason and without telling anyone so you just stand there like a jackass forever waiting for a bus that will never come and now that sort of reminds me of me and Bob for a minute.

And so maybe I will just call a cab in the morning I mean I keep doing these cheap things that are so inconvenient even though I have some money now. And time is more valuable of a resource than money because money will probably grow back but maybe later I will want back that hour I spent waiting on a bus that never was going to come but too bad. Then I think about me and Bob again and wonder if that means I should just ditch Bob even as a friend forever but anyway it doesn't matter because now George.

Then I wonder where George thought we were going to go on the metro because there is no metro here but who cares anyway and she says Well come on. So I get out of the cab and close the door and it drives away and for a second I just pause and the air seems unnaturally still to me. It feels like artificially frozen. It feels like the difference between a video of people standing still versus a photo of the same scene. Does that make any sense probably not. Now I am thinking about the tides and waves and I think OK so there has to be one split second right in between a wave coming in and going out where it is not moving at all right. Where the wave is perfectly still. Just a tiny fraction of a second where yeah there are forces acting in both directions but the wave is not moving at all in either direction. This feels like that. Or like a pause in between breathing out and breathing in.

This feels eerie but also peaceful and so I do I go into her house which has lots of punk and metal stuff in it like posters for old bands and a signed guitar by someone and there are empty 40s and full ashtrays which I think is interesting since she said she does not smoke but maybe she has a roommate or they are joints but I don't think so. Secretly I think she was lying about not smoking and she just wanted to mess with me outside the bar.

I say Hello to a black cat she has who seems pretty cool to me and she says Don't mind him his name is Cliff which is short for Cliff Purrton. Of course I realize that is a pun on Cliff Burton who was Metallica's first bassist who was good at the bass although not as good as people say he was now in hindsight I think. But anyway he died in between Master of Puppets and ...And Justice For All when Metallica's tour bus crashed and what is both really funny and also really sucks and you should not laugh but you will is that he was only pinned underneath the bus and he was alive and not even that badly hurt and would have been OK or at least lived but then they lifted the bus off him with a crane but the crane broke or it dropped the bus on him or something and then he died from that like something from a cartoon. Like seriously it sounds like Wile E Coyote or Itchy and Scratchy.

So anyway that is who her cat is named after and I think it is pretty cool but would be cooler if he was just named Cliff Burton The Cat I think and she did not make a cat pun out of his name even though I usually like puns but not for names of cats really because their whole name then is just a joke. Your name is important and you do not want a name that makes people laugh at you and I swear animals know when you are laughing at them and I hate being laughed at myself.

And we sit on her old couch and she turns on the TV and it is some Adam Sandler movie where he plays a retard so that could be like one of seven movies right and she packs a bong that has a dragon or something on it and she says I need to mellow out tonight I am stressing so I should smoke this and she packs it and hands it to me and I think I really do need to mellow out and so I light the bowl and start pulling and my mind wanders and I am thinking what Bob would make of all of this story and that the things that have happened tonight are a lot weirder than a lot of stories I have made up actually even though it is true. So I wonder Would I be putting myself in unnecessary danger by telling it to Bob and that is totally what would happen to me that something true would be the thing that has her say Wait a second I don't believe you and wait nothing about you adds up makes sense and you are a liar.

I wonder again if I should tell her about it or not and I think there is no harm because she is my friend right and this is just a fun story. And a true one so why should I be afraid of it right. I mean if Bob was my girlfriend or even my ex girlfriend it would be weird to talk about this girl George. But I have talked to Bob about women I have had sex with or dated before and it has been OK even though I sort of don't want to talk about dating with Bob because I just want to date Bob. And besides George is a lesbian so I will not even hook up with her but all the sudden this feels like a date kind of or even not a date but something significant and real. Even though

191

it would be nice to hear what Bob has to say about all of this because I bet she would have a good insight or something awesome to say I cannot help feeling like part of me would be telling Bob about George with a mean intention like I am saying Look Bob I am having a sex life and loads of adventures without you and I do not need you Bob so if you want to be with me you better get on with being with me because I am in demand and a sailing ship.

Which like I shouldn't feel that way towards Bob because she's not a bitch she is nice she just isn't in love with me. And so it should be OK to talk to Bob about this because it's Bob who does not want to be romantic with me not the other way around and so it's not me being mean because she could care less about me romantically I am a joke to her and so she should only just be purely happy for me right if I have an adventure or make a new friend or even get a girlfriend.

So if it makes Bob jealous or upset to hear these things about me then that is dumb because she already knows I've always wanted her to be my girlfriend and that I still do and so that is just her being lame if she feels jealous but then maybe making her feel jealous will make her think Wait why am I jealous oh yeah because I actually do like him. And then she will realize that I am who she should love all along and who she should be the girlfriend to and she will snap out of being dumb and then yes Bob finally at last. But this doesn't seem like a very good thought process to be having because it's basically being mean to Bob even though I like her and it's not her fault she doesn't feel

Wait

Oh no I have been pulling on this bong for that whole entire time and the pipe is completely cloudy with white smoke and George looks impressed and says You better clear all of that bitch. Which I do not know if she means clear that and the bong is the bitch or if she is calling me bitch like just for fun and emphasis but it does not matter and then I do I inhale it all and holy shit I realize I am about to be so fucked in about four seconds. I hold it as long as I can which is not long enough because I have not smoked weed in a long time let alone like this so it burns and I am about to breathe it out when George quickly straddles me and kisses me very hard and I breathe the smoke into her mouth and she keeps inhaling hard even after all the smoke is out of me and that feels very sexy and good and I grab her breast I mean tit and it is definitely real and she exhales the smoke but through her nose now and it smells very good mixed with her perfume and a little bit of beer taste which is very pleasant even though I know that sounds kind of gross but it is not it's nice.

My sex drive is like Yeah right I am not going anywhere buddy because fool me twice shame on me. But Nemesis has woken up and starts things moving anyway and my pants are off and she takes me in her mouth which I think to myself is basically the least lesbian thing you can possibly do but then I realize that that is my meek wimpy personality that is thinking about that sort of thing and like analyzing and Nemesis tells him Shut up and go to bed for the night with like a cup of cocoa and a sleeping cap or something because this is obviously awesome so let the big guys take care of this.

We go to her room and I'm inside her right away but don't worry wearing a condom that I apparently brought and I am

realizing I am not nervous at all for once and I do not close
my eyes or get caught up in my own head and thoughts because I
am only here right now being present and truly with George and
nothing else is important now and nothing else is real right
now especially not Bob she is not even real to me right now.

Like for just one second I do start to fantasize about
Bob just because I am so used to doing that but that idea of
Bob is just not as interesting to me right now as George and I
do not need to think about Bob just to stay turned on because I
am very attracted to George and this thing she is doing with
her hips and how she is sighing softly and nicely which is a
surprise I thought she would be loud and rough but she is
intense and slow and romantic about sex like me.

We try some different positions and stick with the ones
that make us closest to each other and touching as much of our
bodies together as possible and I hold her in my arms and kiss
her a peck on the lips and we both kind of laugh a little bit
then go back to being intense but in a friendly way.

I look at our reflection in her full wall mirror which
usually I do not do because most girls get angry because they
think it is like tacky and that it is like disrespectful to
them to look in a mirror. And I realize now that I have been
telling girls even Bob that I don't like looking in mirrors
during sex because that sounds like the right thing to say but
now I realize that I really do like looking in the mirror just
a little because it's hot and and what is so wrong with that
anyway.

Like Not in an American Psycho muscle flex kind of gross
way but to me it is like saying that what we are doing is sexy
enough to watch as well as to do and to kind of celebrate each

other both in person and in the abstract a little bit or something. I don't know what the words are for it but I know it is nice and not mean. So this time I do look in the mirror and George does too and she likes that and so I position her so I am behind her and we are both looking at the mirror and we are smiling at each other's reflections and we are only moaning and saying Oh or Yes when it feels so good that we have to and we are not making sounds just to put on a show.

After a while I say I am about to come and she says Yes anywhere you want and I think I have not really ever heard that before and I do not even know what Anywhere I want even would be. Which is weird and probably a little sad.

I now remember that my wife had like strict rules about when and where I could come and I would get in trouble for days if I messed up and so it ended up being that even with other women than her years later I still get stressed out right before coming which I know is when you should be the least nervous of all is when you are right about to come but now I am not nervous at all about coming for George.

I suddenly remember my favorite Drink is not the Drink that I drink the most often and that is dumb because you should have all the pleasures that make you the happiest if you can get them in life and so I pull out and take it off and throw George onto her back and straddle her and she grabs me with one hand and she says Oh yes come on my tits. But she does not say it to be dirty and slutty and degraded like at the end of a porno. She says it with kindness and happiness and joy and I know what she really means is You have permission. Forgive yourself for once and be happy here with me. You may.

I collapse onto George and I don't care that now the
come is getting on me too because I think what is the big deal
it's just come and it's just my come and her come and it's just
proof we both made each other feel amazing so who cares what is
the big deal. I kiss her neck and she runs her hand through my
hair humming a little to herself. I am glad she is not like
most women who are OK with one night stands who throw you off
of them as soon as you are done like they are saying What is
wrong with you this was just sex why do you want to like be
close to me and cuddle now ew I am not looking for like a
relationship get off me you freak. That really makes me feel
angry and sad.

A few minutes later or maybe more I don't know if we
fell asleep like that or not but honestly it doesn't matter.
Some time later we are lying there and then I sit up and I ask
Do you want a shower and she looks down and laughs a little and
says Yes I better have a shower and I watch her go into her
bathroom and I hear the shower running and am reminded of the
girl from the poetry reading and how her shower was running but
then I am more interested in George than in any other girl even
Bob so the poetry girl goes out of my mind.

Nemesis and wimpy guy are all somewhere else and I am no
character not even myself I am just no one in this nice moment.
George hums something that might be a song or it might just be
nonsense humming but it is nice to hear it. After a minute I
join her in the shower and we have sex again there and then we
go back to her bed. Apparently it is dawn already and we take a
naked nap together spooning in the sunlight while we are still
wet from the shower.

SEVENTEEN

So we are walking into this tea place now George and me and it
is a weird place and very like vegan organic local overpriced
and sustainable white guilt hipster place and all that jazz and
I am surprised that I am being brought here by the same girl
who was taking Jäger Shots last night talking about heavy metal
and taking bong hits and saying Oh yes come on my tits and now
here we are looking at a menu of like eight dollar teas from
like Sudan and Kuala Lumpur and places with Js and Qs and
apostrophes in their names that I think are probably made up.

This seems like a different George and she is even
wearing this like nice white kind of Mexican dress with flowers
on it and her hair is just kind of loose and not straightened
like last night's pompadour and I am wondering if last night
what if the George I met and had sex with was George's version
of Nemesis and she just happened to collide with my Nemesis at
the right time and now this is the more normal George and more
normal me.

I wonder which version I like better and I do not know
because right now I am being the normal me like the civilized
version of me because Nemesis is definitely asleep and normal
me likes things like fancy tea. This version of me is liking
this version of George a lot even though Nemesis liked the
Nemesis version of George a lot last night too. Then I think
does it even matter and no it doesn't so shut up.

I think for a second that Wow I have not lied to George
at all oh except that one sort of lie when I asked if she had
seen the music video which isn't even that big of a lie or at
least it's not important and we actually talked about music
which is a very tempting and easy place to lie about stuff so

197

that you look knowledgeable or trendy or elitist or whatever and I didn't do that I was very honest actually and it feels good that I have not lied to George in any major way yet. I hate that I just said Yet.

And so for a second I think about running away with George and just leaving Bob and LA with no word of goodbye at all and just forgetting about Bob and here and just having sex like last night all the time with George and just being normal in the day like now and just going somewhere else right this afternoon after the tea.

We are in line and I sort of don't want to ask but I am too curious not to and I say OK so I have to ask I thought you were a lesbian. And she says I said I only date women but I sleep with guys sometimes.

I think that is a dumb line to be honest and it sounds like a bad line from Entourage or Californication or something and not from real life and I do not think it is the first time she has given that line to a dude which I do not like that. Like she set up the whole night based on maybe not a literal lie but also not a whole truth and all so she would have the upper hand and keep me really confused. But then I think who am I to complain about that.

She says It was fun though and I don't think it should be the last time we do that even though we're not going to date for serious. And I say OK whatever because what am I going to say No to more sex like that. No way.

We are going to be in line for a long time and I ask her What tea is good here and she names a few she likes and I say That Vietnamese one with lemongrass sounds pretty good and she says Yes it is good and it is also good for a hangover and I

say Good so we agree I will have that and she will have some
lavender situation.

Now we are the second people in line there is this
skinny hipster couple in front of us who were making out the
whole time they were in line and so they never looked at the
menu and they get up and it is their turn and the hipster guy
says What kind of tea do you have here. Like seriously he says
that. The woman behind the counter who looks very sleepy or
stoned or maybe both just starts saying them all one by one and
the guy asks Oh what does that one taste like. After every
single one. And I am now remembering the dean or professor
repeating every question and wasting so much time after my
lecture and so now I look at all the teas and I imagine there
must be probably forty kinds of tea and if he asks about all of
them at about ten seconds each that will be four hundred
seconds wasted and double that because George is here which is
like thirteen minutes or something wasted of just George and my
life because this chump couldn't get his act together.

I look at George and we smile and I realize that
normally this dumb guy would make me very angry because he is
both stupid and rude and wasting everyone's time which I hate
and also because he is the total kind of guy who Bob would let
fuck her with his tiny dick but that does not matter to me
right now and that surprises me that I am not mad. I do not
know how to feel now because it is a nice surprise that I am
not angry but at the same time I hate all surprises in general.

Right now I don't really care and I am happy enough to
have my time wasted because whatever I'm just hanging out with
George and what better things am I going to do. Nothing. That's
for sure.

We get our teas and it's like fifteen dollars for the two of them which is ridiculous you could get two really good beers on happy hour for that much and we sit down at the one table there is.

Like so OK at this tea shop there is only this one really long table with benches so everyone has to sit together at it which is so not my sort of thing because yuck strangers and also because the tea shop totally thinks it is being super cute for being difficult this way.

I always think it is gross when couples sit next to each other and not across from each other so I go around to sit across from George even though we are not a couple but still we're together so. That means I need to go all the way around the whole table and push past sitting people and it's a pain in the ass and I spill some of my tea and burn my hand. The tea is in this little strainer kind of French press thing but it is shittily made and so it is also leaking.

Anyway I sit down and George says to me OK so since we've established that I guess I'm a bit of a slut already don't make any jokes or judgments OK but what is your name.

I realize I haven't told her my name which is actually pretty slutty of her I guess because a good rule of thumb I think is you should say What is your name before you say Oh yes come on my tits but whatever and so I tell her my name and then suddenly I am very surprised and afraid because I realize I just told her my real name and not my LA name.

Like I told her the name that is my actual name that my parents know and that is on my birth certificate and I guess marriage license and the name that my wife called out in bed on our honeymoon and that is on my college diploma and I do not know why I did that but already I am thinking of all the ways this could spell trouble like oh for instance if she ever meets anyone I know here in LA at all really and so this is very bad and why did I tell her my real name.

She says Cool. And we drink our tea and I can tell she is being weird like after one night stand weird and acting like we should talk about something that is not sex like she is guilty and I am not feeling weird I'm just like Chill out we can be quiet together for a minute even though I am freaking out about the name thing but George is being weird and so then this is all making me feel angry and therefore also weird.

I sip my tea quickly because if I am sipping tea then I cannot be talking and so then that is something I am doing in that second and I am not just sitting there not talking and I sip it too quickly and it burns my tongue and makes it feel leathery and I am pretty angry at this whole tea place overall right now but it does taste like lemongrass and it is kind of good tea if it was cooler but it's still too hot and it's not seven dollars good that's for sure like you could get two Forties and some chips for that instead of bullshit mouth burning tea.

I am sort of freaking out now because this place is totally the sort of place that the kinds of hipster guys that Bob lets fuck her with their tiny dicks would come to in the morning and Silverlake is hipster central and so what if Bob let someone fuck her last night and now he is taking her to this place and she will meet George which on the one hand will be good because Bob will see that I can seduce hot women just like that even though George was totally in control of everything last night but Bob does not need to know that and then what if Bob comes up and she says Hi and calls me by my LA name and George calls me by my real name and then oh god. I guess all that would happen is that George will never talk to me again which I mean that is a shame because that probably was the best sex I've ever had since my wife but whatever.

Except then what if the fact that I used another name gets Bob thinking about me and my stories and that is how everything starts falling apart until I am exposed and that is totally how it would happen too is some stupid little sloppy encounter like this and so no this is a bad place and I want to go away and why did I tell her my real name. I could lie to Bob and say I am not into George that seriously and I planned to ditch her so I gave her a fake name which is the one that's really my real name. That is the best plan I have so far so if something goes down that is what I decide to do it is not perfect but it will do for now.

George perks up and I can tell she has thought of something to say and she says Hey and I say Sup and she says What were you thinking about right before I punched you. I say What and she says You were like super deep in thought and like all intense when I first saw you and I said hey to you a couple of times but you didn't hear me so I punched you and what were you thinking about I bet it was really interesting.

I know I was thinking about Nemesis but obviously I don't want to say that so I say Um. Like I am trying to remember but really I am saying Um. Because I am trying to think of something harmless and not Nemesis to say that that was what I was thinking about but nothing is really coming to mind and so I just say

I can't remember but nothing special I was just very
tired.

Then I realize I just told the lie you used to tell in
college where for no real reason you would just say Oh wow I'm
tired. Just to say something. And I am really angry that I told
that dumb college tired lie just now like eight years later
than college and I feel like George knows everything about me
now for some reason and I should go home right away.

This is a new feeling for me I am feeling and I feel bad
that I lied to George now even though I don't really love
George at the moment because even though last night was fun I
am now angry that she does this all the time but it was like a
big deal once in a lifetime event for me to have good normal
awesome honest sex with a real woman who is cool and really hot
and all of the sudden I am missing someone very badly and I do
not know who I am missing but it is someone from very long ago.

I look at my phone and say Shit I forgot I have to meet
with my agent and George says That's a lie why are you freaking
out now because last night was just fun that's all like it can
be just sex. And I say Yeah it's not that and she says Well
what then do you regret doing it now and I say No. But I'm not
sure if that is a lie or not and why is she like confronting me
now and I really want a shower now but not with George where we
have sex. I want one where I can just go shower by myself and
scrub myself very clean and then lie on my bed in a spooning
position but by myself obviously in the light of the sun and
still wet from the shower and I want to imagine Bob is here and
she's the little spoon and I am holding her 34C breasts.

I feel pathetic about that thought now because I mean I
am in front of a hot girl who I fucked last night who I could

probably fuck again right now but instead I am fantasizing about being sad about not having Bob what the hell is that all about I am a freaking mess and I kind of snort at myself because yeah massive contempt for myself.

George asks Are you laughing at me now. And I say No I wasn't laughing at you and I don't really laugh at all ever anyway. And George says You laughed last night and I remember that I was laughing about the shitting woman and I am now very angry that I laughed about that because it was so childish and dumb and immature and everything that I hate and I wish I had strong coffee and some Alcohol in front of me and not this bullshit hipster lemongrass burning small dicked tea. And I say I'm sorry I really have to go and she says Whatever.

I know she knows I'm full of shit but I don't care I just need to be somewhere else now and as I am getting up I remember that Oh yeah and besides Bob's dead friend has a funeral tomorrow I need to go to with Bob as like her date or whatever but not date obviously but like to support her and be her company and so I will need to gather all my strength today and drink a lot in order to go to that tomorrow and why didn't I just tell George about that funeral I could have gotten away from George and it would have been true.

I hate going to funerals because I have to pretend to be happy and then also pretend to be sad as well. Honestly I am never actually sad in truth at funerals because people die and everyone will die one day and so yeah it's kind of sad especially when it's a surprise or they were young but it really is nowhere near as hard as living sometimes I think. But so yeah I have to pretend to be generally happy in life which is a lie and then on top of that lie I have to pretend to be specifically sad about the funeral and that is also a lie.

But I can't just be the real kind of sad that I really am every day and just be that way about the funeral because that is a very different kind of sad entirely and it looks a hundred percent different.

I go around the table and sit next to George for some reason and this surprises me because I got up thinking I was running away and I look at her and she gives me the wrong look. It is a kind and friendly sort of look and a sad sort of look even though she should be angry with me not kind and sad. And I feel like the look kind of says

It's just me. Just breathe and don't be weird. I can tell you're working through some major shit right now but that doesn't mean you don't deserve a little happiness and payoff every once in a while so why don't we just keep doing this until one of us doesn't want to any more. I don't have all my shit together either so why are you fucking this up by being weird now.

I don't know why but I love George immensely all of the sudden all from just her look and I hate myself for being the way I always am and for being so awful a person and for only falling for girls who are total lost causes from day 1.

I kiss George and she kisses me back that's for sure and I hold her breast over the dress right here in the coffee shop and I am guessing her breast is like a 32 D or even DD because when you have a very small frame and even just medium big breasts the letter goes up.

I say Let's go back to your house again and she takes my hand away from her chest but nods kind of sadly and so we go back to her house. Without saying a word or making any sex sounds I take her dress off and pull her underwear to one side and we have sex again on her bed but it is different this time.

I get behind her again and point her at the mirror and she looks into my eyes again and does not look away but I am not saying like Aren't we so sexy and beautiful like how I was last night. I'm saying

Just look at yourself. Look you slut.

And I'm talking to myself when I say that.

Even though this sex is too rough right now we're both enjoying how angry it is because we are not really angry at each other. We're angry at the world for putting the two of us together at this awful time right now when people like us shouldn't even meet anyone or be allowed to interact with anyone let alone with each other.

I don't know if George comes or not but after a while I realize I'm not going to so I pull out and put my clothes on and leave without saying anything.

I'm dialing Bob before I am even out the front door and I am still hard when I hear her pick up and say Where have you been.

EIGHTEEN

I'm walking from the metro to the bar to meet Bob and Bob
arrives at the same time as I do and she looks sad. I go to hug
Bob but she is not interested in a hug and she pushes past me
into the bar and I follow her thinking Uh Oh. I wonder if this
is it and she knows all about me but then I think Why should
she have figured it out now all of the sudden but then I also
think Why wouldn't she figure it out all of the sudden just one
day on her own and so now I am back to thinking Uh oh.

I am very very sad most of the time and very happy every
once in a while and Bob is very very happy most of the time and
very sad every once in a while. I have never seen Bob angry
like this though. Not so sad or angry she won't even say Hi or
hug me that's for sure.

Like always the bartender says
Whiskey Diet and a Rusty Nail?
And I say Yeah two of each and he says That kinda day
huh and say Yeah I guess so. I wish he would shut up. I sit
next to Bob who has her face in her hands right now and I
cannot tell if she is crying or not I think she is more angry
than sad so I am obviously worried about this. She is wearing
this medium length jeans skirt and a white kind of puffy blouse
that I think looks really nice on her even though I know this
is her emergency outfit for when she has not quite gotten
around to doing laundry.

I know ordering two rounds of Drinks at once is really
bad but then I remember it is OK because drinking is my cover-
up darkness and if people know you have one major darkness they
won't think you could have another darkness that is much worse
than that like lying.

We get our Drinks and I hand over my credit card and say Keep it open. I sip mine a little just looking at Bob but not trying to stare and I don't know what my face is doing exactly but I am trying to make it look concerned but not like I am forcing a story out of her but just letting her know she can tell it to me if she wants. Who knows what that face actually looks like but it doesn't matter Bob's face is in her hands.

She breathes in deeply in her hands and I can tell she is not crying. She takes her hands away and her face is puffy like she has been crying recently though and has not slept much. She still looks beautiful to me. She looks down at her Drinks and she is not interested. She looks at them like a picture of an old boyfriend who she is now disgusted that she let fuck her. She looks at me sipping mine and looks at the Drink then at my eyes with an expression of contempt and inside I'm like What the hell don't tell me you're going to be all judgy about drinking now. I go

Bob what's up.

Nothing.

You can talk to me.

Forget it I said.

I think to myself that I never know how to act in this kind of situation. There's another stupid safe joke people like to tell and especially married men tell it and it goes like

Oh if a woman says Nothing is the matter then you should run away because everything is the matter right HA-HA. Or something. Whatever. Women are weird that's for sure but there is nothing wrong with telling a woman who you like that she can talk to you about what is making her sad if she wants and you are there for her. If that is bad and makes me a pussy or something then fine I'll be a pussy. Everyone else's faults are always forgiven and mine are evil so fuck it just this once I will be oh so terrible and be a friend to Bob even though I should be being alpha at her while she is sad so I can seduce her later. Fuck off I'm so over even thinking like that. I don't get sad about my being sad but right now I'm sad that Bob is sad.

Her eyes move left and right and left and right in that way that means she is looking at my left eye then my right eye. Back and forth. Furious. She has definitely been crying I can tell now and for some reason her blue eyes look like the moon reflected on the sea at night to me right now. We breathe in at the same time and there is a pause just like the split second when a wave is neither coming in or going out. It's just still.

I have seen this look. I know what comes after this look. Even Nemesis is hiding from this look. We hate this look.

I ask if she is upset about the funeral tomorrow. Her face relaxes a little bit and she looks down at her Drinks again and she says

Fuck it.

And she picks one Drink up and drinks her Rusty Nail quickly through her wide red straw. She puts it down and then through a kind of a long tired sigh slash groan because of how strong the Drink is Bob says

Yes. I'm sad about that.

But her tone says that that is not the whole story.

I say OK well what's up. Bob says

Forget it.

And she starts on her second Rusty Nail. She says

What did you do last night it sounds like you had... *an adventure*.

Again I am wondering if I should tell Bob about George and like how much detail to go into. Bob is my best friend so I should be OK telling her I had a really nice encounter and I had good sex that was really honest and nice or at least the first sex was nice and I mean I wouldn't go into details about positions or where I came or whatever but she is my friend she should be happy I was more comfortable with myself and my body than I ever have been before right.

But then I think No do not say that because then she will think I am not interested in a sex life with her if I am talking about fucking other people so cavalierly and almost boasting to her and besides something in me says just not to go there especially if Bob is feeling sad or angry about something.

I decide something. I'm kind of angry at myself for deciding this because it feels like a mean sexist strategy that I am about to perform but I decide that Bob really does want to talk about whatever is going on with her but not quite yet and so I will just talk about some not important stuff until she decides she is ready and then she will probably interrupt me to talk about what is upsetting her and I will not mind being interrupted by her more important news or feelings.

I think that is the nicer thing to do for Bob even though that makes me sad then because I want to be doing these nice things for Bob because she is my girlfriend and it also makes me feel sad because I am about to tell Bob that everything will be OK and I wish that I could also say I love you. That little I love you might help her feel a little happier but then no I remember Bob hates the fact that I love her and I don't want to make her remember that terrible fact now it will only make her angrier.

So I say Well so last night I met this lesbian at the rock bar OK and she said Hi just by punching my arm. Then she said the weirdest thing to me. She said Isn't it all better… drunk?

And that's how I start the story. I mention lesbian so Bob doesn't think I'm about to brag about sex. And I continue and say We had this good conversation about heavy metal and then you won't guess what we went into the subway and then on the platform there was this woman who was

And I don't even want to say this story right now but I have to say something and what is wrong with Bob and I think to myself Why should I have to tiptoe around Bob she's the one being emo right now and maybe she should either talk to me about what's wrong or just go and be alone for a while so I say Hey come on Bob what's going

Bob interrupts me and says

I've been such an idiot about you.

I think Ah shit.

It's been staring me in the face and I haven't wanted to see what's been going on so I haven't. Jesus.

I think Fuck. Fuck. No.

But I see it now and I feel like a total fucking fool.

I think Fuck again.

Nemesis is hiding. He hates this part. It's the only thing in the world that he is afraid of is the scolding after being exposed. The mild mannered wimpy me comes up to the front and he cannot wait to get punished. There is nothing he wants

more than a telling off. A reckoning. Fair Justice and
Damnation. All he wants is what is deserved. What's coming to
us. He tries to drag Nemesis out so that Nemesis will see this
too and he wants to rub his nose in it to say

Now you see what comes of all of this bad behavior. But
Nemesis is full of the strength of a beast in terror and cannot
be dragged out by anyone. I don't know what I want to happen
right now. Bob says

I m only going to ask you this once.

I think Don't Bob. She says

You only get one try to answer honestly.

I think Don't make me answer this now like this. Bob
says

When and why did you decide that I'm so fucking perfect
anyway.

I am so confused. I say Bob you're amazing what do you
mean.

Bob says

Look I let this drag on too long. I know how you've felt
and I pretended not to see that because it's hard to know what
to do. But still I just let it get worse by not doing anything.

I say No Bob you haven't. Bob says

But I'm not what you think. You've got this like huge
opinion of me like I'm some sort of perfect goddess woman and
I'm not. I'm just normal and stupid and sometimes I'm weird and
shitty and mean.

I say Bob you're wrong you are great. Bob says

It's like as if you invented this kind of dream girl
character in your head and then you met me and just decided I
was that person you invented. But I'm not. Like you think I'm

some sort of Zooey Deschanel little cute dream girl but I'm not. You give me too much credit and it's stressful to live up to that all while wondering how I can do the decent thing by you.

I wonder if Bob has to die in order for me to have the right ending that is honest or can I have Bob as well as the right ending. Bob is crying now and says

And besides what the hell am I supposed to do on a pedestal that I never asked to be on. Like how can you expect me to be able to engage with you in any real way if your only relationship with me is like this fucking one way adoration and worship all the time. It's a total monologue and there's no way I can participate in that. But there you are pining away all the time making me feel like the asshole. But you're the asshole too. I mean what good does your pining do me other than making me feel like a bitch for liking you but not knowing how to figure out if I can be with you or not. And I'm not saying I do want to be with you OK. Right now it feels a lot more like no than yes OK fair warning but I should still be given half an honest chance at the beginning to figure that out. Although maybe not who knows how fucking twisted you'd be over this now if I'd just said Why not and given Us a shot.

She's never said Us before and it kills me. I didn't even think Us was a word she knew. I say Bob you've got it wrong I mean I do like you a hell of a lot and yeah I want to be with you romantically but that is mostly because I like you as friends too and yeah OK so I am interested in trying to see if we could make something more but

And Bob interrupts me and says

I'm never going to be the fixer you decided I am. I'm sorry I let you think that. But you shouldn't have carried a torch this long either though. No one made you do that. Maybe I should just go.

Nemesis is laughing his ass off now howling like a hyena laughing that we're not all caught and that Bob was mad at herself and a little bit at me because I'm basically a pussy but she is not mad at us for the real awful thing. Mild mannered guy feels completely blue balled on the justice he has been aching for. I want to hold Bob and just say No no no no.

Bob wipes her face and says

Jesus I must look like total shit.

I say You look really nice tonight.

And I'm not lying. Bob says

I've taken advantage and feel like shit.

I say You haven't taken advantage of me for a second.

And I'm not lying.

I say You're very dear to me and I don't care what we call it Bob.

And I'm not lying.

I say I'll treat you more like a person and less like a goddess and I'll listen to you more and let's start over right now I promise I will do my best to do that every day.

And I'm not lying.

I say Bob I love you.

And I'm

Well I'm

Bob says

You expect too much. This girl you fell in love with? I'm not her. She never existed. You made her up one day and I was handy.

Bob sighs and pushes her Drink away. The bartender has been pretending not to have been listening to us but I mean who is he fooling. Bob says

I'm going outside to smoke. Get me a Gin and Tonic. I fucking hate Rusty Nails and I never want to have another one for the rest of my stupid life. I don't know why I let you keep ordering those fucking awful things for me.

Bob walks outside with her alchemist's bag.

I say One Gin and Tonic please. And I'll have a

I start to say Maker's Mark on the Rocks. But I don't. I say Whiskey Diet.

And I've never been more ashamed of myself in my life.

NINETEEN

I really hate funerals. I mean everyone hates them because they are sad but I hate them because they are just big circle jerks of fake sadness and lies. Like my whole life is nothing but real sadness and lies and so funerals are just a bunch of normal people playing like they are tourists into my world.

Like why can't they see how awesome and beautiful a thing truthful crying is because it is such amazing catharsis and it is like an orgasm and these people are wrong for calling crying such a terrible thing. It is worse being like me which is sad and not being able to cry than it is to be like other people which means not needing to cry most of the time but you can when you want to. At things like funerals. Active sadness is so much better than vague misery.

All I want in the world besides Bob is to be able to cry. It would mean I could let go finally. But I can't cry and I haven't been able to cry about anything since I had to leave home because of my lies even though I am sadder every day than I was yesterday but still it is impossible for me to cry. These normal people have no idea how lucky they are.

It's lack of catharsis that is what death is really all about. No punchline. I never know what to say to normal people who are grieving. Like actually permanently sad people like me I have plenty to talk to them about and relate with them about. I am a little bit disappointed that the sad tumblr girl took exception to me because I think we could have been sad together without trying to fakely make each other feel better and that would have been nice.

So I feel bad about Bob being sad today because I will not be able to say anything to help her other than to say I am sorry. I hope this is over soon and Bob and I are back to normal and can just go to the bar and be together. Sad or happy I don't care I just hope so much that this is a chance to start over and do it right now and sitting in this funeral I look up and I promise

I promise I won't lie ever again about anything if I have not lost Bob.

I don't know if we can be normal after our last talk because it was so honest and that is totally new territory for me. I don't know what to make of any of this.

This guy whose funeral we are at died from a cocaine overdose and I remember my old worst lie about my friend dying from a cocaine overdose and I hope I didn't somehow cause this guy's death by my lying about my imaginary friend. But no this guy caused his own death.

I hate thinking this way but if this guy had been more of the worrying and cautious type like I am then this would not have happened. And all these people would not all be sad today. Even if it is a different kind of sad to mine they definitely are sad today.

If someone thinks they are sad I guess that automatically means that they are sad doesn't it. Even if someone on the outside like me thinks that these other people don't know the first thing about what being sad is really all about that doesn't change the fact that the other person is just as sad as they know how to be.

Like you can talk to like a 16 year old girl whose first boyfriend dumped her and she will be like

I have lost the one love of my life I am heartbroken and he was the only one for me I will never love again.

And on the one hand you know she's wrong and being a melodramatic little brat and she will get over it sooner than she thinks and that this is not actually the end of her life but you can't just flat out say

Yeah yeah we've all been dumped and we all lived so get over it. That doesn't help her. Because if she thinks she was in love with him then maybe that means she was in love with him. If she thinks she is heartbroken then maybe she really is. It's weird. Like I say she is not in love and she says she is in love and neither of us is wrong and neither of us is lying even though we're saying opposite things.

Every time I've been heartbroken some part of me knows it's partly a performance and me acting all Boo hoo for me because feeling sorry for yourself and being drama feels good sometimes.

Everyone here at the funeral thinks they are very sad. I think they're not really sad they are not truly sad they are just crying. But no one is wrong and no one is be lying.

This is tricky.

Weddings can be scarier than funerals sometimes because what if this is the wrong person I am marrying. I don't know if I hate weddings or funerals more because with funerals at least you know what you're getting into. Weddings are question marks disguised as exclamation points. Funerals are periods in no disguise.

I feel like my entire life has an asterisk.

I honestly don't remember my own wedding very much. It was over so fast and not really memorable to me. Like I said the words and all and my wife definitely looked ridiculously beautiful and sexy and it was all moving and it felt like a good day at the time and it was a good party and everyone was happy for us. Maybe I should have been more drunk or less drunk I don't know. Maybe drinking had nothing to do with it.

I wonder what will happen at my funeral and if anyone will come. I don't know if anyone would come anyway but even more so if all this stuff about my lying comes out when I die then no one will want to come see me because I've been so bad and lied to them my whole life. They would not be wrong to feel that way and abandon me. Dying alone is a total like emo existential song lyric cliché but it's a deserved fate for some people. I can think of one person it is deserved for but I can't say who it is out loud. Not even out loud on the inside.

I check in with Nemesis and the mild mannered guy and it does not feel like Nemesis is doing much right now I think he got scared yesterday and is still hiding.

I reach into Bob's alchemist bag and sip Whiskey from her flask I think it is Jameson and I don't put it back in the bag I just keep a hold of it because I will be having more any second now that's for sure.

I put my arm around Bob and hold her nice white shoulder and pull her so she leans her head on my shoulder and I smell her hair which she has not washed super recently but I like just the smell of her head. It's nice. I look at the tops of her breasts in her black dress which in my opinion is a little too sexy of a dress for a funeral and I kiss the top of her forehead and pretend for a second that she is my girlfriend and we are not at some guy's wedding or I mean funeral. Instead I make believe that we are on my couch watching a movie after coming home from a lame party which we would rather be at home together just cuddled up than at that lame party but she hasn't changed out of her sexy dress yet because she is saving that for when we have sex later.

I sip more of the maybe Jameson which burns pretty bad and I think to myself that considering how much I drink I am very bad at drinking warm Alcohol of any form. I mean not deliberately hot Alcohol like Mulled Wine or Irish Coffee but like just room temperature straight Liquor. And then I think in a way that is actually good that I cannot drink like that because maybe I have a hope of not being an actual Alcoholic then because no one except a real Alcoholic should be able to drink warm Alcohol just like that.

The reason I worry if I am an Alcoholic or not isn't because it would be unhealthy for me if I was. I worry because I just do not want to have a bad label attached to myself that is this bad bad name and proof that I am weak and even some kind of victim. I hate the idea of being accused of Alcoholism because if I am an actual Alcoholic or even worse if I am not but I am forced to admit that I am an Alcoholic that then I will be forced to also admit about Nemesis. And I wonder what a rehab clinic for people with darkness like Nemesis would be like and then I realize Oh right that is the fucking loony bin that's what it is called so I'd better not admit Nemesis or allow people to call me Alcoholic or look at me in any way.

I should run away from Bob.

Of course now I remember the Mitch Hedberg line where he says Alcoholism is the only disease you can get yelled at for having and I always loved that joke especially the next part where he says You do not get yelled at for having lupus and then he says You can say dammit Otto stop being an Alcoholic but you can't say dammit Otto stop having lupus. And I like

that joke because Otto is just the perfect name to choose for
that joke for some reason but anyway I struggle not to laugh
about that joke now because I am at a funeral and a lady is
talking about how the dead guy was just swell. I bet he was
too. I'm not sad about this guy not really honestly but I'm not
a total grinch OK. I can tell that this is very awful.

Otto is also the perfect name for that joke because I
partly imagine Otto the school bus driver from the Simpsons his
name was Otto and I imagine him both having lupus and being
drunk and driving the bus anyway and getting yelled at by
Superintendant Chalmers.

I like Otto on the Simpsons but not because he's a giant
stoner. I like him because he functions in the main normal
world of the Simpsons but in truth he is totally lost in his
own little crazy person world. And his brushes with normal
people are the rare part and not the common part of his life.
Like his little visits into normal land are big efforts and
then whenever he's off camera it's like insanity but he is at
home there.

He has a dark secret which for him is being a total
burner and if anyone found out that secret they would say

How dare you be a bad person this whole time who lives
in crazy land most of the time but you have been driving kids
to school you do not deserve to be allowed to be close to
normal people so now you are banished.

Or something. And I am afraid of being found out and
banished again too so I like scenes where Otto is particularly
belligerent and reckless with the kids' lives because he is
tempting fate and daring the grownups to catch him.

But of course The Simpsons is a comedy show so no one ever finds out that Otto is a total burner and catches him.

THAT'S THE JOKE.

I look around the church which is more of a theater or like generic space you can rent. It's not like an actual church with a denomination and this makes me feel sort of angry too. Not that I am religious at all no way I am actually very angry at religions because they tell enormous lies and make no effort to make them even close to plausible and yet billions of people go to churches every week and say they believe the most insane things and that's like totally OK.

And yet atheists have the reputation of being like basement dwelling neckbeards and Aspergers kids who rant about Richard Dawkins and 9/11 Truth and Ron Paul on 4chan all day or something.

But yeah then I get busted because I tell my wife one lie about how the reason I graduated college a year late is because I studied abroad for a year when the real reason is because I had a major meltdown between junior and senior year and just kind of ran away and just drove around for a while until I got caught like I guess there was a missing persons thing out on me but so I got caught and was returned to my folks and then had to go to a like spoiled version of a crazy person's home for a while for like time out and that was the real reason I was a year late to graduate.

Like I just told that one little lie saying I studied abroad which the lie is so much more believable and less complicated than the truth and most of all it makes me look less insane and better. But still eyebrows are raised research gets done and everything gets unraveled and so I get busted.

But like a priest saying Here is your communion of
zombie meat and magic blood and God is a man in the sky who has
a plan and all the badness in the world is really OK it's His
plan and you are just dumb or not enlightened enough if you
think anything in the world is maybe not good. And then
millions of people are like Yeah that all sounds good to me
good deal here is my dollars and life.

So I do not love religion but I am hating this secular
non-denominational event space even more because like all the
funeral people are lying now and not even blaming religion for
the lie. Like right now the guy's brother is saying he knows
the dead guy is looking down on us from heaven now and I am
thinking No you do not know that at all. If so how.

But everyone is nodding and saying they know it too and
crying and letting this guy have a free pass to tell any amount
of lies because he is sad today. And why is that just fine for
him but not for me. No one says it is OK for me to lie when I
am sad which is always.

Why can't this dude just say

You know what I am not going to say any nonsense that is
just a safe cliché lie to tell and so all I am going to say the
truth and that is that I miss the fuck out of my brother and I
am heartbroken and completely devastated that I never get to
hang out with him again and I'm mad as hell at him for being
such an asshole about stupid drugs and for leaving the rest of
us and making it harder for us to feel like it's a good idea to
love people. I'll be sad later but right now I'm just mad and
crushed. God dammit.

Like would the world really end if someone said that.
But I guess basically yeah it would. And who am I to talk shit

on people telling stories to feel better about themselves. I really should just stop thinking forever and maybe I should leave LA before I get caught or something even worse happens.

To do with Bob.

Bob is crying now but a different crying to last night. It is a less honest crying I think but I hold her closer and hold her hand which her knuckles are white.

The wedding I mean funeral is wrapping up and apparently the plan is to go back to Bob's place and have everyone basically drink themselves into oblivion and cry together and crash for the night. Bob's apartment was chosen because she has lots of floor space but I'm like Huh floor space isn't comfortable and why can't all other people just go away from me and Bob. But whatever. Who knows why anyone does anything.

So now I am driving Bob and a guy and a girl who are a couple I have met one time I think or who knows. But I am driving them to Bob's place which I do not want to do because I do not feel comfortable driving other people and it is hard to drive Downtown if you ask me because of all the one way streets and you make one wrong turn and you find yourself accidentally on the freeway halfway to like Vegas. And Bob sometimes criticizes my scared kind of driving which she is right to do that because I do drive like a bitch but I still don't want to hear it today.

I can't decide whether to put the radio on or not so I don't but then I feel like I have to say something because I am the only one who never met the guy who died and so I feel responsible to be the one person who is in control of himself enough to be able to talk without crying and I have to be responsible for the entire situation and make everything OK so it is my obligation to say just the right thing but I cannot think of what is the right perfect thing to say and I wonder where Nemesis is in all of this.

I am feeling angry at myself that I cannot think of a good lie to tell that will make things better.

I park in Bob's parking spot in her building's garage and I ask where her car is and she says

Somewhere else.

And I think that is very suspiciously vague so I will ask her about that but not now another time because the couple are looking at me really weird now for some reason.

We get out of the car and go up to her apartment which is most of the way up her tall building and it has a good view. The elevator has a man in it which I think is really unnecessary and just a superficial hallmark of luxury that is totally sad and pathetic. Like really are people so insecure in themselves that they need to know there is a man whose whole life in their opinion consists of nothing but pushing elevator buttons and remaining silent. Does that kind of thing really make normal people happier. Does it. I mean does it.

I think to myself I wonder if the elevator man thinks Bob and I are together and I think there must be a lot of things that the elevator man must think.

We get into Bob's apartment which smells like pot and I think that is weird because I did not know Bob was in a smoking pot phase at the moment. She picks up the cat she keeps who I am friends with and she throws it into her room and closes the bedroom door because so that she can leave her apartment front door open so people can just come in whenever they arrive and the cat will not run away. The cat yowls from in there and sounds like it is asking Why have you done this.

Bob's living room is one enormous room with floor to ceiling windows on the west wall and a square of four couches all facing each other in the middle of the room around a coffee table that is just an enormous real tree stump from like Bolivia or something like that and there are white walls with nothing on them except a few of Bob's self-portraits and there is a projector system that comes out of a hidden panel in the wall if you want to watch TV but it is totally invisible the rest of the time. Bob and I have never watched anything on it together here though and I think that is weird.

Bob goes to take a shower which is kind of weird of her and not a good hostess of her but I do not blame her for taking a shower that sounds nice to me actually and frankly who cares life is so short you should take a shower when you want. Now I want to take a shower and might ask her if I may take one later if she is not super angry at me or just angry in general.

I've showered in Bob's shower before it's super nice and has amazing water pressure and it stays hot forever like even scalding if you want and you feel so clean afterwards because it basically blasts all your dead skin off which I love and I am kind of obsessed with being clean so I love showering at Bob's house even if she calls me a dork for wanting to do that. She only calls me that because she doesn't understand that some people she is friends with do not have every single nice thing like she does.

I know I should not think about what Bob thinks of me right now but I can't help it. I usually take three or four showers every day because I never really feel clean enough.

But then sometimes I don't shower for like four days if I'm just home and not seeing anyone which is plenty of the time too so I don't know if I'm gross or OCD or both or nothing at all. I suspect the only answer is that I'm nothing at all.

The guy who is the guy in the couple says Nice place and I say Yeah it's pretty great huh as I go to the kitchen.

Bob's kitchen is just a long counter along one wall of the living room and a fridge is there too and the kitchen is not separated from the rest of the room by anything it is just that one wall of the room is her kitchen. I like Bob's place.

I go to her bar which is really just the section of countertops that she keeps lots of bottles on and I ask what the guy and the girl want to drink.

The girl says I don't know. She's making a scene and lying like she's too frazzled to even ask for a Drink. The guy is making a scene like he's heartbroken too but being stoic for his girlfriend and so he says Whatever just something strong.

I think he is right and a Strong Drink will help everyone today.

I say OK how about Scotch. I think Scotch sounds like a good stiff Drink for mourning people and the guy says Perfect thank you and I sort of like this guy now for being both low maintenance but also knowing what he wants in general and having a bit of a spine. I think he is pretty OK actually.

But the girl kind of whimpers and says Mm-mm meaning no and so I say OK how about Bourbon and she shakes her head no and I say OK what like Vodka on the Rocks maybe with a little tonic and she says No and starts crying to her boyfriend as if I am bullying her and she wants him to make me stop.

I am thinking I sure as hell am not mixing this girl a
cocktail with more than like three things in it like if I have
to break out the muddler or a shaker or like fucking Angostura
Bitters then this girl is a total bitch in my mind and so I'm
now feeling angry that I have to magically guess what this girl
wants and it's not even my apartment it's not even my
girlfriend and so what the fuck.

I say OK well you just think about that. And I go and
get two tumblers which I know where they are and I am thinking
Scotch sounds really good right now because it is also kind of
cold out for LA and I look out the giant window which faces
west and the sky is gray and the clouds are not moving at all
just sitting there like on pause.

The stretch of Wilshire Boulevard going all the way to
the coast looks distorted by the smog combined with the grimy
window and it almost looks super pixilated like a new video
game you're trying to play on an old computer. I think to live
in LA you have to turn the resolution way down or it gets too
choppy to even move around in.

The guy says Hey nice picture. And he points at this one
painting that is about one third finished and he says Is that
of you. And I say I don't know probably not.

I look back at the guy and I say Is an Islay Scotch OK
and he says Yeah and just get one as well for Crystal which
apparently his girl is named Crystal and I think of course that
is her name but I like that the guy made a decision and that he
knows about Islay Scotch.

And then I feel a little bit angry at myself because I
was sort of being a Whiskey snob to these people by choosing

228

Islay Scotch and who cares about out-snobbing mourning people at a funeral.

The guy says An Islay is perfect and she'll feel better after she has something strong. I put ice in a third tumbler and find Bob's bottle of Caol Ila 25 year old Scotch which I know is like two hundred fifty bucks a bottle and it's one of the best Drinks ever and I think The hell with it I mean this is an occasion right and what does Bob care about money anyway. So I open it and smell it and I think I am in heaven but then I realize this girl is going to like take one smell of it and say

Ew no this is gross make me a Pina Colada. Whatever. If she says that then I will just drink her Scotch and tell her where the nearest Mexican bar is. Why am I incapable of feeling bad for these people honestly it worries me.

A little bit of the ice has melted into the glasses so just a little bit of water is at the bottom now just like I wanted and so I take the ice cubes out and toss them into the sink which makes a louder noise than I wanted. I pour the Scotch like two Shots' worth in each glass and swirl them and I hold up the Scotch I have decided will be mine and I watch the water twist around in the Scotch and then I give the other glasses to the guy and girl and I am surprised and kind of angry when the girl likes it after all.

I think to myself how fucked up it is that this Scotch is older than the guy who died and this bottle is only worth two hundred and fifty bucks so if this guy was a Scotch he would only be worth like two hundred bucks which seems like not a lot of money at all for a whole person to be worth but then again I think to myself I know a lot of people who are worth a lot less than that in my mind. I used to be a good Scotch I think. My wife ordered a bottle of good Scotch but it turned out to be a bottle of Laphroaig filled with like plastic-bottle Scotch. What fucking happened.

More people are coming in now and saying Hi and asking for a Drink and I say What do you want. I do not really feel like being the bartender here but then again if I am the bartender then that is one way I know I can provide people with some support and comfort and make a gesture like I am trying to help the bad situation so I decide I will be the permanent bartender for the night just so I can contribute something even if it's all Bob's Liquor anyway.

I ask what people want and they say Oh just whatever we're having. So now I regret opening this very good Scotch because you should never get this Scotch for saying Oh just whatever we're having. Because it should be ordered specifically and with respect but whatever. Enjoy it or don't I don't give a shit honestly I will drink whatever of it you don't want and who cares about this endless snobbery on my part like when has being such an elitist ever made me feel better about myself in any real way.

There are like twenty people in the apartment now and the bottle is almost empty and I tell them it is actually empty so that there is some left for Bob and then I think wow Bob has been in the shower for an awfully long time and I am very afraid for just a second but then the shower sound turns off and I hear Bob cough a little bit then I hear her electric toothbrush so I know she is OK.

Most of the people are sitting on the couches around the stump just facing each other and not knowing what to talk about. Everyone has pretty much cried as much as they can cry for the moment and so they are just drinking and thinking which I like because that is a very good pair of things to do in my opinion. And I am glad people are not just talking just for the sake of hearing their own voices or filling silence.

I think to myself this is a nice honest little moment. I should take note of what this feels like for the future. Although I still am sad that everyone has had a great old cathartic cry and I still cannot cry no matter how hard I try.

I see Bob walk from the bathroom to her room holding a towel around herself with one hand and dragging her black dress behind her with the other hand and she has a lit cigarette in her mouth and I admire her shoulders and the white tops of her breasts again.

I'm very startled by the pop of a champagne bottle opening. Some drunk girl opened it clumsily and the cork ricochets off the ceiling and bounces loudly into the dish filled sink but she doesn't even flinch or notice because she is so fried. She is making a point of not wiping away her running mascara so everyone can tell she's sad. I think that's a selfish lie of her to do that and make it all about her.

I think champagne is a weird choice considering you know DEATH but whatever drunk is drunk right. And besides. The Drink you like the best should be the Drink you drink the most and I wonder if Bob has any Makers Mark which is my favorite Drink even though I haven't had it in years and Bob must have some Maker's Mark right.

The air feels really stale so I get up to turn the AC on just to get some fresh air into the room and move the pot smell around even if it will make the apartment colder when it is already pretty cold. I get back to the couch and my spot is now

taken and some girl is also sitting on the stump in the middle
and I am suddenly afraid that this girl is going to make it all
about her with some little performance or maybe she'll say

Let's all go around the circle and say something you
remember about the dead guy. Kind of thing but she does neither
and she just sits there and I think OK whatever. But I still
think she is making it all about her by sitting in the middle.
But then again there is not really anywhere else to sit so
maybe I should stop analyzing and criticizing everyone else.

Someone starts passing around a baggie of coke and a key
and I am really amazed that no one gets offended by this
considering the guy died of too much coke and it seems way too
soon to me and I did not even know him and I am like Whoa are
you serious that's too soon. But no one else minds so whatever.

I think if I had been the one who started passing coke
around everyone would be like how dare you it is too soon. But
whatever who cares about me right now. Or ever. I do not take
any coke and I just pass it along but I sort of regret that
once I do and think if it comes around again I might have some
but then Bob comes out of her bedroom wearing her black dress
again and I wonder why she put that dress on again after a
shower she should have put on something comfy like pants and a
hoodie but she is in the dress and it is the first time I have
ever seen Bob truly look like hell. Bob says

Sorry everyone but get out.

And she throws all the people out of her place and says
she will pay for their taxi or whatever if they are too drunk
to drive she is just overwhelmed and has to be alone after all.

I am sort of proud of Bob for that because it would be
much easier for her to lie and to think to herself

You know what I do want to be alone but it would be rude to these other sad people to say Get out of my place as soon as they got here and so I will just sit here stewing and being miserable instead. For the greater good.

But Bob did not say that and so I am proud of her because I think it was brave.

It's weird that saying you're proud of one of your friends is like not an OK thing to say these days. Like the implication is that like only parents can be proud of their kids or like that only people who are more advanced can be proud of someone less advanced because the less advanced person did something surprisingly advanced or something. Like it's patronizing to be proud of your friends or something.

Or is it that people are only proud of other people when the other person does something that reminds the first person of themself. I don't know. But these days it is bad or like arrogant to say I'm proud of you.

And I don't know why because it should be the opposite you are just saying Hey I admire what you just did and I don't know if I would have been as brave as you just were if it had been me in your position.

Like I told my wife once I was proud of her when she did this one brave thing and we were all out with her friends and we were newly married and she told this guy she is old friends with to shut the fuck up because he was really drunk and running his mouth about how he used to hook up with her and he was saying it because he is basically in love with my wife but he did not get her in the end and so he got drunk and basically tried to rub it in my face the fact that they used to hook up which I didn't even get mad about at all because Nemesis was in charge at that moment and he knew they used to hook up already and who cares everyone has hooked up with someone else before so big whoop and besides I'm the one who's going to go home and have sex with my wife tonight and forever and not this guy and so this guy was the only one who looked like a fool.

But yeah anyway I was just deciding to be mature and let it slide because he was drunk and everyone else even his friends were just basically laughing at him for being a dumbass and the only person looking like a chump here was this dude but my wife laid the smack down and told him to get the fuck out of the bar go home and sober up and that she and I would both accept an apology tomorrow.

He left angry and even stole the pint glass he was drinking from which made me afraid he was going to like break it and do something bad with the broken glass but he didn't he just kept it. Actually he makes a point if I am at his place of always serving me in that pint glass like some sort of passive aggressive move but I never mind because whatever he's the one still upset.

And then all of her friends we were with told her and me like Yeah that guy gets too drunk sometimes sorry. And his roommate apologized to me on his behalf and I said No worries we have all hooked up with someone and we have all gotten too drunk before and I don't care so much about the past as the present and my present and my future is with this girl right here. And I kind of softly shoulder checked my wife affectionately and that was the total right thing to do I think even though she didn't really react to that. And then later at home I said I was proud she told him to take a hike but then she got mad at me and said

Who are you to be proud of me I'm a grownup too and older than you actually. And I said Well yeah I know that but I am still proud that my wife is strong and awesome and didn't take any shit from this drunk dude. But no that was the wrong thing to say apparently so big fight there even though I thought I was good.

But whatever I am proud of Bob for throwing everyone out right now but I do not know if I will tell her that because she is really super emotional right now. Plus between the funeral and whatever the hell our blowout was last night I don't want to risk anything. I'm getting ready to leave with everyone else and I'm wondering again where Bob's car really is and she says

Hey not you.

And she says it almost laughing a little bit like she's saying Obviously you're not leaving you big dummy you live here. And now I'm truly sad for the first time all day because I'm wishing so much that I did live here with Bob in this empty apartment that just has four couches and me and Bob in it and when everyone else goes home it is me and Bob still. A unit.

Bob looks up at me and her eyes are wet but more than sad she just looks totally completely exhausted and not even just by the funeral or whatever last night was but just exhausted by life. Like she is long term wiped out. And I know that look because it is the look of someone who has been dealing with darkness for a long time and just could use a goddamn day off.

Bob looks up at me and says

Listen.

And then Bob looks away and she looks ashamed. Bob says

You are totally allowed to say no, OK?

I say OK even though I already know whatever she's about to say I am going to say Yes I Will. Bob says

And I really mean that literally you can say no. And if you say no I will totally understand and not be pissed. But I have to ask. I really need to be close to someone I trust right now and. I mean. I just.

And then Bob pauses for a second and takes a breath and looks me in the eye as if to say Who are we kidding. Bob says

Look I know you're really into me so if it would make things awful for you to be close to me and just hold me then that is more than fair and it's totally shitty of me to even ask this but I guess I'm asking anyway. So say no if that's what you need to do for yourself but I had to ask if you'd just make it so I'm not totally alone right now.

I think to myself that it actually is kind of very mean of Bob to ask me that because she knows I am going to say Sure no problem whether or not it would be total agony for me because of how much I do want to be comforting Bob and holding her but for being her boyfriend and partner and not some chump buddy of hers. Like if I just asked her in the exact same way if she'd sleep with me because I'm just really horny tonight that would be awful of me. But whatever all that's my problem and not hers and again she was just giving me enough credit that I would say No I'm not OK with that if I'm not. But she gives me too much credit by doing that. See who's giving whom too much credit now huh Bob.

I say Sure no problem. But I say it too fast like I haven't thought enough about it which is true I haven't really.

She says

I overreacted yesterday.

I say You didn't say anything that wasn't true. She says Yeah but still.

I say It's OK Bob.

I pause because I kind of don't know what the best thing to do is and Nemesis and mild-mannered guy are fighting it out hard over what to do.

Nemesis says I can definitely turn this into making out and the other guy says That is taking huge advantage of her being sad and anyway if I make a move and get turned down I could easily lose Bob forever and even if I don't get turned down and we go all the way that then this could make things even more impossibly awkward and I could lose Bob forever that way. Nemesis says So what she's a grownup she's sober and she started this so stop trying to take responsibility for everyone in the world and just go after the girl you love and see what happens. Besides she fucking owes you one after all this shit.

Mild mannered guy says No girl ever owes a guy sex like that. And I agree with that but still don't know if I would turn it down if it happened. So mild-mannered guy says I should either say OK we can cuddle and then I should just resolve to not make a move or I should just say Bob I'm sorry but I just can't trust myself around you and it would be agony for me and then I would go home alone instead and leave Bob on her own too. Both miserable and wishing we were not alone.

Nemesis says I should just say OK let's cuddle. And then kind of see what happens once we're cuddling and I just cannot take these god damned voices one second more.

I close my eyes and push on my sinuses and ears hard as if I am trying to blow my nose or ears and I go cross eyed as my ears pop and I see stars. A splitting headache I didn't even

237

know I had just goes away and after the stars I see that kind of moving crocodile skin pattern you get from pressing on your closed eyeballs.

Suddenly everything is quiet even though I didn't know it had been loud in the first place. Like as if someone turned off an air conditioner in the room and the baseline level of white noise is a lot quieter. I open my eyes and look at Bob and I know I am neither Nemesis or the mild mannered guy. I am no one. I just am. Jesus Christ Bob looks like hell.

I kiss Bob on the lips and realize this is the first time we've kissed sober. Her lips are dry from crying but her tongue is tiny and wet.

Bob looks at me then nods and walks away. She changes out of her dress in private into blue Seersucker PJ bottoms I have never seen before but they are so cute and a gray tank top.

I take my shoes and socks off and my belt so it doesn't scratch Bob when we cuddle but I leave on my pants they stay on. We get under the covers together and also under her bamboo sheets in her platform bed. She faces away from me like she is the little spoon and I put my arm over her not really knowing where to put my hand on someone I am being close with but not being sexy with. I just reach my arm around her further and kind of put my hand flat palm down on the bed which is awkward and I feel like the worst and lamest loser.

She shifts so my arm is under her arm around her tummy and I am holding her hand which yes that was the right way to arrange ourselves and I should have known that because I have seen this position in romantic movies before.

I am not really feeling horny over Bob but I am feeling myself loving her a whole lot right now and I hold her close and sort of put my forehead on the base of her neck and I think to myself You know what this really isn't all that agonizing like I thought it was going to be and I look over at Bob's cat who I am friends with who is napping on its cat tree and it looks cozy too. Bob is already asleep and sort of snoring in a cute way.

After about ten minutes I guess Bob stirs and is half asleep and kind of relaxes her back and shoulders which have been tense all day and I hear her back crack. As she moves positions my hand falls on her breast over her shirt. I move my hand right away and onto the bed again and Bob takes my hand in hers and puts it under her shirt and back on her breast which is fuller and softer than I imagined it would be. I squeeze more firmly and she gives a deep sigh and reaches behind her butt and puts her hand down my jeans. I smell Scotch and cigarettes and her apple shampoo as I feel her pull her PJ bottoms down just enough.

I slide inside Bob and I look past her and see her bra lying on the floor. I feel very confused because the tag says 32D.

TWENTY

Bob and I are sitting on the roof of her building which is one floor above the twenty seventh floor. We are facing west and waiting for the sunrise. The sky is pink.

It is pretty chilly out no actually it is actually honestly cold I have goosebumps and it is about to rain which is rare in LA. But rain is not as rare as LA people act like it is when it happens that's for sure.

Whenever it rains in LA it's always like it's the first time it has ever rained in LA and the way people get so panicked and offended is a huge communal lie that is exactly like the Oh wow you never meet an actual LA native lie. People drive at 10 miles an hour and call in sick at work and that is totally allowed because this is LA and everyone gets super butthurt when it rains and it's like supposed to be all cute and Aren't we all great that LA people are so inexperienced when it comes to rain because it's always such awesome weather here all the time and so they all act outraged and betrayed like they DESERVE perfection and for nothing to be bad or even different ever. They think it's cute to be like

This is LA we can handle 7.0 earthquakes like no big deal LOL but rain is just too crazy for us tee-hee aren't we cute.

And I call bullshit on that too because guess what everyone shits their pants over earthquakes too. And we should always shit our pants at earthquakes. The earth opening up and swallowing us is something that it is not unreasonable to be afraid of.

But no when it rains everyone acts as if it's raining indoors. They act all disenchanted and betrayed like as if they are kids who have been waiting all year to go to Disney and then they finally make it there and it up and rains on them at Disney on THEIR BIG SPECIAL DAY. It's like how dare the universe mess with them now that they've decided to go to the land of dreams and showbiz and lattes and TMZ and colonics and You will be famous one day just keep at it and keep paying us with your money and time and life in exchange for staying here.

Everyone comes here to escape real things and sad things like rain and lies and families and histories and Nemesis and accountability for our actions and we thought we had escaped a hard life by coming here. But the rain is the reminder of the life we thought we had escaped and left behind and doesn't exist any more but it does because here it is look it's rain. And everyone gets reminded that it's all just a big theme park and it will have to close one day and we will all have to face the real world then and go back home to chores and school.

Back to that awful mean grownup place where people who care about us say No I love you but you have to engage with the world you have to grow up and take responsibility for your life. And the children say No I don't you're not the boss of me now I am moving to LA where there's no adults allowed and so nah-nah. And they almost always slam the door on the way out.

And so people come here and just stay that stupid little brat forever with like Mickey Mouse ears on except instead of Mickey Mouse ears it is a permanent invisible hat that says I Heart Hollywood and they never take it off and they get their picture taken with Goofy or Dane Cook or Donald Duck or Kim Kardashian or Chip and Dale or Luke and Owen Wilson and that makes them think they have a shot at being famous like those people themselves one day which they won't ever. It's so sick how people feel like they can't be real people themselves until they are celebrities but celebrities are the biggest non-real people in the whole world. The only thing people are afraid of is anonymity. Being no one. But we're all no one. Even famous people. But people care more about being seen than being substantial.

And yet apparently I'm the asshole because my lies are oh so awful but shit like TMZ is just harmless diversion.

You can't hide here though not for real. It's just the island in Pinocchio where the bad boys run away to to go and smoke cigars and play pool and break chairs and have no parents and then one day they all turn into jackasses and get sold. I wonder how long my nose is at this point and when I will start braying and sprouting ears.

Here's a brainteaser. What happens if Pinocchio says My nose will grow now.

The glow from the sun comes over the horizon. Confident. No. Not confident. Indifferent. Indifferent to the rain. Indifferent to what you think of it. Indifferent to what story you make up about it or yourself.

I am now wondering if Nemesis is my Jiminy Cricket. That's a dark thought. Nemesis hears me thinking this about him now and says And always let your conscience be your guide.

No I think. And then I think

Bob is my Jiminy Cricket. Nemesis is my Tyler Durden. Then I think stop. Why can't I just have Bob and Nemesis be who they are without trying to force them through some pop culture filter. Forget it OK please do just forget all of it.

Bob and I are sitting under this umbrella she has in case it does rain hard later and I am wearing just my underwear and she is wearing a bathing suit and it is a black one-piece and I like that she is modest like that and wears a one-piece swim suit even though her body is like totally great and I am the only one up here with her and I saw her completely naked all night last night but she's still modest. I like that.

We are smoking Marlboro 27's of course and drinking La Fin du Monde Belgian Beer and waiting for the sunrise and we have two of the big 750ml bottles of that Beer and we will definitely drink them both but we are drinking them one at a time and sharing it between us because it is more fun to pass the bottle back and forth. But the mood is not fun right now it is sad and angry.

Bob once said something really smart when I first moved to Hollywood and I had just met her and I was looking for a hardware store near me because I wanted to hang some pictures and needed nails and a hammer and those picture hanger things and I could not find a hardware store anywhere and Bob said

There are no hardware stores in LA because no one who cares about good art stays here long enough to hang a picture.

I think Bob saying that is a little bit of a lie in that it is more of a cute little hating on Hollywood snipe. But then again it is also a little bit true. But then again again why is she still here.

I then wonder why both Bob and I both have apartments with basically no furniture in them and I realize we have never talked about that and maybe that's another thing we should have talked about. On the one hand for me I have no furniture or art because I never know when I might have to up and leave this place.

Keep running.

Why settle in.

I'm only renting my time here month to month anyway. We're all renting life month to month if we're going to be Honest. But it makes us feel safer and secure to sign long leases and contracts and mortgages because we feel like if we are bound to some paper for ten years then that means we can't die tomorrow.

So why buy furniture. So I have an apartment full of fewer things than there should be and a head full of more people than there should be.

I ask Bob if she still wants to have seafood for our birthday dinner which now is tomorrow. She doesn't say anything and she puts in her headphones.

The sun has just begun to crest and the mist has turned into a legit drizzle but it's OK we are under Bob's Spongebob Squarepants beach umbrella. I pass the bottle of La Fin Du Monde Belgian Beer to Bob. She takes it and drinks from it angrily. Deliberately and deeply but not desperately. She drinks again. Longer. Deeper. Gulping.

Getting more so I get less.

She puts it down and stifles a burp softly into her fist. Bob used to love to burp wide out loud. Not any more I guess. She hands the bottle to me absently and says

I so don't give a shit about a birthday right now. Just meet me at the bar at 8.

I say OK and put in my headphones. The song we are listening to is ending and I think it was a Halou song or maybe Sennen. It's sad though and I am glad she has chosen her "Sad Playlist" playlist.

Bob has these cool headphones that go in your ears and are wireless but you can have multiple sets of headphones attached to the same iPod and router so like we are both listening to the same song at the same time but we don't have to be plugged into anything else or each other so that's great.

I wonder about that. I don't think the problem was ever that we were too plugged in to each other. Probably the opposite.

The song changes to Spirit Street (Fade Out) by Radiohead which I love that song a lot because it is so very sad and I think this song is kind of redeeming in how hopeless it is. Like it's saying how the oppressive things in life that feel like one day they will consume you? They will. They'll get you. But even they will one day just fade away into nothing and they'll be eaten by something else. And I think that is kind of comforting because if you admit that you personally are headed the same place as the things you're afraid of, then they're not so scary any more.

And like even if you spend your life trying to defeat other people just so you feel like a big boss and the top of some meaningless lie of a food chain so what.

We will all fade out too and all that will be left is this beautiful end of the world sunrise right in front of me and Bob that couldn't give a shit less about who is Executive Producer of what or who's signed where or who is fucking who or whether or not I end up with the girl I am in love with right now. Shit comes and goes and you can't win. You can only survive. Until you don't. That's what I think the song is about anyway.

I think to myself I know there is a story about Thom
Yorke writing this song and I admire Thom Yorke a lot because I
know he has this dark thing that I have as well and he is not
pretending to be a tortured artist just because it is
fashionable and allegedly sexy. That guy has some real demons
and he can turn that all into amazing music about his Nemesis
and that is honest and beautiful and frankly that's all you can
do if you have Nemesis. You can't fight it so you have to do
something with it or just quit.

Some people I know pretend to love Radiohead because
magazines tell them Radiohead is genius and no one wants to be
the first one of their friends to admit that they don't
understand something that experts say is genius. But I think
honestly like 1% of people can really understand the sadness
and real beauty behind Radiohead on an emotional level but then
again I worry that that's just me trying to be a giant snob and
put myself into some elite category that is better than
everyone else because I'm sad and smart or something.

It's totally possible that I'm wrong, but I'm not lying
about how I think you can't truly know why Radiohead is genius
unless you have a crushing darkness in your life on the scale
of Nemesis really. You don't have to live it every moment but
you have to know what it feels like and be able recall that
sensation at any moment.

But whatever. I mean if millions of happy people want to
support Radiohead then that should be good because Radiohead
should be rewarded in every way for being geniuses and they
sell every ticket for every show instantly now which they
definitely should but I cannot help feeling like maybe that
doesn't mean anything to Thom Yorke and he'd trade all the

money and all the grinning idiots in the audience who are just waiting for him to play Creep and he would trade them all for just a little peace and quiet or someone saying It's OK. I mean it's not OK it's terrible but you're doing the best thing you can do about it and that is amazing.

I should shut up honestly. Who the hell am I to say what Thom Yorke thinks or wants. What have I ever done. I'm just some fuckup liar sitting on a roof with someone I'm in love with who loathes me for all the wrong reasons.

But I think I know there is a story about Thom Yorke and this song and so I reach for my iPhone and type some stuff until I find it and I am reading it while I am listening to the song and I like what I am reading and this is it. OK before I do tell it to you though I want to say two things. Maybe this is someone's copyright and if so I didn't mean to steal it I just wanted to tell you about it. Second I cannot find out where it is from so it is possible that it is not truly from him or he didn't say it just like that. If so I'm sorry and it is a mistake not a lie on my part. But whether it's true or not it affected me deeply so here it is. OK here it is.

It's from an interview I think. It goes:

"Our fans are braver than I to let that song penetrate them, or maybe they don't realize what they're listening to... They don't realize that 'Street Spirit' is about staring the fucking devil right in the eyes... and knowing, no matter what the hell you do, he'll get the last laugh...and it's real...and true. The devil really will get the last laugh in all cases without exception, and if I let myself think about that too long, I'd crack. I can't believe we have fans that can deal emotionally with that song... That's why I'm convinced that they don't know what it's about. It's why we play it towards the end of our sets. It drains me, and it shakes me, and hurts like hell every time I play it, looking out at thousands of people cheering and smiling, oblivious to the tragedy of its meaning, like when you're going to have your dog put down and it's wagging its tail on the way there. That's what they all look like, and it breaks my heart. I wish that song hadn't picked us as its catalysts, and so I don't claim it.

It asks too much.

(very long pause)

I didn't write that song."

I think to myself that is just how Nemesis is. He is not just my sadness but he is also my biggest ambition and my life's project. He chose me and I wish he never did choose me because I would trade happiness for him in a heartbeat or even just solace and some peaceful rest but who cares what I want.

Everyone's stupid lies and my own lies included are just failed attempts to try and put a story and a narrative to this complete nonsense empty vagueness people call their lives. And if I can build a beautiful and satisfying lie that has a beginning and a middle and a proper ending for a few good people like my dear beautiful Bob then I've helped the problem just a tiny bit. Maybe. Even if it's a sad story it's still a story and Bob will feel like someone was in charge and there is meaning to all of this and so her life will feel like there is a little bit of architecture and answers. I know there really isn't any of that. But Bob's life should not have to be as sad as mine is. Because she is too great for that. I think that's better than just admitting it's all chaos and hopeless isn't it. Maybe. I don't know.

This is a perfect song for right now I am thinking because the dawn is up now and this enormous cloud is black with a red center bursting through like a lava flow rolling its way towards us and it looks like the end of the world out there and the rain is pulling the smog down out of the air and way out west over the ocean the sun is a hot pink semicircle on the horizon that looks like the tip of a giant's finger.

And the finger comes up fuller and longer and it is pointing. Accusing us all of being weak. Cowards. Cheats. Big fat fucking liars.

It's a big pink and black and purple Neverending Story cloud coming from the ocean to just steamroll this stupid place and make us all start over and live it better this time.

Telling us, Learn to swim.

The Nothing is coming. Wait that's wrong. The Nothing was here all along. And the Hollywood coyotes are like the wolf Gmork, harbinger of The Nothing. And Nemesis is their leader.

Bob changes the song before it has gotten to the chanting part at the end of the song. I wanted to sing along to that part because I know a nice sad harmony to sing along with that part and I am so angry at Bob for doing that that I could slap her face right now.

In the silence between songs thunder claps over Century City and I see lightning. The whip has cracked and the horsemen are loose.

I snatch the bottle back from Bob and look at my
knuckles which are white. I drink as hard as I can while
looking at my shitty knuckles and weak fingers and I think to
myself

These look like big good strong hands don't they.

TWENTY-ONE

I wake up in my own bed. I look at the square of sharpie blackness that is left on my wall where I had written something. I don't feel anything about it one way or another.

It is early afternoon and it is my birthday and it is also Bob's birthday and I feel rested. I never feel rested.

I sit at my computer and try to write. It's no use. I don't think I will do any more writing.

Like. Ever I mean.

Something's wrong. The pressure or something is wrong in the air. Nemesis' hair is on end. Mild mannered guy keeps looking around to see if someone is behind him.

I go outside planning to walk around thinking about what to get Bob for her birthday which seems like a stupid idea and not important as soon as I see what the world outside my apartment looks like.

The streets are wet from the rain and a lightning scorched palm tree trunk lies sodden across Hollywood Boulevard. The combination of burned and wet scares me a little bit. The tree reminds me of a big wet cigar.

No one has put any emergency tape down or like cones or signs or anything. Everyone just knows to hide inside their houses until an announcement is made saying

It's OK Disneyworld is fine and Jurassic Park is back online and the rides are open.

In the middle of the street in broad daylight outside a lingerie and sex shop, five coyotes fight over what's left of the homeless punk rockers' puppies. I do not feel anything about this. I see furry flesh being eaten. I see areas of bare

251

skin that this dog's owner shaved thinking it would be cute, which the coyotes see as weak spots. Points of entry. Breach.

For some reason the coyotes remind me of the homeless punk rockers themselves. I'm imagining that the homeless punk rockers turned into the coyotes during the storm. They stayed too long on the Pinocchio island of being bad and now they're stuck as beasts forever. They'll never get to go home. They'll never become real boys.

One of the coyotes looks at me.

I look back. We know each other.

Where is Nemesis I think.

I never thought I'd ask this but

Where the hell is Nemesis. The coyotes scatter. I do not know why. They could have attacked me and eaten me and I should have been afraid of them but I was not I felt nothing about them one way or another.

Down the street The Druid stands on the corner of Hollywood and Vine on top of two cars. One foot on the hood of each. The cars crashed into each other head on but across the street not down the street as if the drivers went crazy and arranged this crash in like a suicide pact or something.

The Druid is the only person on the street I can see. I pass him and he is laughing. Not a sick or scary maniacal laugh like I would have expected from him right now. Just a slow deep peaceful wise old laugh like Uncle Remus.

The gourds on his staff shake and he hands me a joint which I take. I light it and it crackles like a fireplace. No, more like the fireplace channel on TV. I take a deep hit and it not the best weed but it will get the job done. I offer it back to him. He shrugs his shoulders and laughs a little harder and it sounds like Hih-hih-hih-hih then he hops off of the cars and walks down Vine street towards Sunset.

I ride the empty subway from one end of the line to another and back again and back again and back again while smoking this joint. I do not see anyone.

I am wishing I can hide here underground alone forever and pretend it's not the end of the world above me. Eventually it is time to meet Bob for our Birthday Drinks which seems ridiculous considering it's the end of the world but hey what else am I going to do. Gotta do something. I wonder if the bar is even open. Or even still there.

I get out of The Metro and Downtown looks like no one has lived here in years that's for sure. I see a homeless man I assume is dead but don't really care one way or the other.

The neon sign outside the bar is broken off and dangling from the wall. I am a little bit afraid of it in case of electrocution but it is not sparking like it would be in a shitty movie it is just hanging there.

I get into the bar and I am looking around and there are some people at the bar but I do not see Bob and then my phone buzzes and I look at it and it is a text from Bob which is weird I think because she has never been late to anything ever she is very punctual. I am the one who is late apparently.

It is three separate texts sent back to back from Bob
and they say

I'm out of your life now. That's for sure.

I hope I found you a good present.

Sorry. Sorry. Sorry.

I look up and the three people at the bar turn around
now and I recognize them and I think

No no no how did Bob get in touch with them she cannot
have their phone number this is impossible.

It is my mom and my dad who both look very very old now
and my wife is wearing a blue low cut tank top which shows off
the tops of her breasts which now I remember are a 34C.

This can not be like Fight Club.

I look at Nemesis and he is being devoured alive by the
coyotes and he is laughing the whole time and he looks at me
and says

If people know you have one major darkness they won't
think you could have another darkness that is much worse than
that.

Whiskey Diet and a Rusty Nail?

I wish that song hadn't picked us as its catalysts.

I can't have a darkness that is much worse than Nemesis.

It asks too much.

(very long pause)

I didn't write that song.

In front of my mom is a glass of White Wine with ice

In front of my dad is a Sierra Nevada.

In front of my wife is a Rusty Nail with a wide red
straw.

Next to that is a glass of Maker's Mark On The Rocks
which is my real favorite Drink even though I hardly ever order
it

but the drink you drink the most should be the drink you
like the best and

and this one is just for me and

and

and why am I crying.

JB Burgess lives in Los Angeles.

www.facebook.com/Jbburgessbooks
www.twitter.com/Jbburgessbooks